Dragon KING

THE BRIDE HUNT BOOK 3

CHARLENE HARTNADY

DEDICATION

To living with horses

CHAPTER 1

The room was large. The air-conditioning unit made a soft whirring noise. Unnatural light from the UV bulbs lit the windowless space.

"Why are you here, Miss Kincaid?"

It was weird that someone not much older than her would address her so formally. Especially since he had such a warm smile. Then again, he wore a stuffy suit and his hair was gelled to perfection. This was an interview. One that could potentially change her life, so maybe it wasn't so strange. The guy across from her clasped his hands in front of him on the table and leaned back in his chair; his eyes were trained on her.

Why had he even asked the question? He knew why she was here.

"I responded to an ad in the paper, you called me."

His smile widened and he licked his lips. "Why do you want to date a vampire, Miss Kincaid?"

Her blood rushed at the thought. Excitement coursed through her. It wasn't because they were super hot and sexy. She'd seen groups of them come into town on occasion. They were tall, built and very attractive. Like *Men's Health* cover models, every last one of them, but that wasn't it. Sure, it was a huge bonus, but that wasn't it. Not the real reason.

Roxy sucked in a deep breath and locked her gaze with the man interviewing her. "I'm looking for love. Real love. It's my understanding that vampires love fiercely, that they believe in forever." She paused. "Well, call me old-fashioned, but so do I. That they happen to be vampires is irrelevant."

"So, you don't specifically want a vampire. It could be a human or say . . ." He looked like he was thinking on it. " . . . a shifter maybe?" His eyes met hers once more.

It was a bit of a strange question considering she had answered an ad that was headlined—*Would you like to date a vampire?* She shrugged, hadn't given it much thought. "I guess, although, I hear the shifters breeze in and out and that it's mostly about hook-ups for them. Don't get me wrong, I like sex as much as the next girl but I want more. I know on occasion, some women do disappear into the mountains with them. So some have to be in it for the forever part, but you don't hear about that happening as often. I guess what I'm trying to say is that I would be okay with a shifter as long as we were dating with the intention of it going somewhere. It would need to be serious."

Shit! It didn't look like he liked her answer. He folded his arms across his chest.

"Um . . ." She needed to get this back on track. She was losing him. This interview was slipping away from her. "I want love. Real love. The species of the man is of no concern. I would prefer a vampire for the reasons already given." He didn't look convinced. "Look, about a year and a half ago, my boyfriend of eight years left me." A dull ache rose up in her. It didn't hurt so much anymore. Not like it had before. "I should've guessed that something was wrong when he wouldn't take the next step. Marriage . . ." she whispered the word. "He kept on saying 'next year, next year' . . . well, next year became a whole lot of years. I'm thirty-one, I'll be thirty-two in a few months. I can't end up wasting my life on someone who won't commit. Not again. I've dated a couple of men, human men . . . no offense." She didn't wait for a response. "They want sex nowadays. Forget marriage, they don't even want a boyfriend/girlfriend relationship. It's all about the sex. I've stopped using the online dating services." She gave a laugh. "Try meeting someone organically in a small town like this." She waved her hands around the interview room. "Forget it, not going to happen." He didn't say anything. He seemed to be mulling it over. "I want a chance at love. These vampires are in need of women, not just for hook-ups but for real relationships and that's what I want. I want marriage, I want forever . . ." She swallowed thickly. "I want love." It wasn't too much to ask, surely?

The guy across from her—Sean, he'd introduced himself as Sean—gave a nod of the head. "We'll be in touch, Miss Kincaid. Either way, we'll be in touch."

'Either way'—did that mean that he wasn't sure? *Relax, it probably didn't mean anything.* Her gut churned.

Had she done enough?

Had she said too much?

Roxy had to bite down on her lip to keep from saying any more. After standing, she reached out her hand and shook his. "Thank you for your time." She forced a smile. Her nerves were getting the best of her. She wanted this. She really did. Roxy had initially applied on a whim but the more she thought about it, the more she wanted this. The more she felt that this was just the thing for her. By this time next year, she could have it all. A man who loved her, a family.

CHAPTER 2

"Would you like something to drink, my lord." The female vampire gave a small curtsey. Her cheeks flushed red, her eyes remained on the ground at his feet.

"Just water." His throat was parched from the flight there.

The female lifted her gaze and stared at him from under her lashes. "Yes, my lord." She smiled at him. Ten seconds later and she was still there, unmoved, her eyes still glued to him.

"That will be all, Charlotte," the vampire king, sitting across from him said. His mouth twitched, even though his words came out sounding harsh.

The female's eyes widened and she chewed on her lower lip before scampering from the room.

"You have had quite the effect on our females," Brant said, his expression deadpan. He huffed out a breath sounding part bored and part irritated. "There will probably be a crowd of them waiting to catch a glimpse of you when you leave. Are you sure you don't want to court one of the vampire females instead? Your offspring would be just like you, a dragon shifter—as evidenced by little Tinder. Although, the baby drinks blood because of her father, she is very much a dragon shifter like her mother." The male smiled. "She burned down Kai and Ruby's bedroom. She keeps wrecking furniture. The little mite leaves piles of ash in her wake."

The second vampire king, Zane, choked out a laugh. "Yeah, we were forced to ban the little one from certain parts of the castle. At least until she can control her flames. One burp or extra loud giggle and *whoosh.*"

Blaze nodded, he couldn't help but smile. "My niece is a strong dragon. The combination has worked well. Unfortunately, we don't know if she will ever be able to shift or if a shifter male with a vampire female will produce similar results. I'm afraid, as the Fire King, it is a risk that I am unwilling to take. Your females are . . . delectable but . . ."

Zane gave him a pat on the back. "Brant wasn't being serious. We are in discussion with the wolf shifters. Our females and their males are highly compatible. We are in the process of conducting a census to check how many of our females would be interested in pursuing such a union. So far, the results have been positive."

Thank fuck! Blaze didn't want to offend either of these males. He hoped that they had made a decision and that it was favorable for the dragons. That things would progress as planned. Then he could visit his sister and niece. Ruby was pissed that he hadn't stopped by when he was here last week.

"Have you had a chance to consider my proposal?" Blaze was done with the small talk.

The taller king, Brant, crossed his arms across his chest. The black pinstripe suit he was wearing pulled tight across his shoulders. Zane's arms remained relaxed at his sides. The male wore tight leather pants and a thick leather vest. Blaze shuddered at the thought of wearing such stifling garb. He wore a pair of loose-fitting cotton pants, as was customary.

"We have." Zane nodded once. "We're torn."

Blaze had to stop himself from rolling his eyes. Of course they were. Two kings with equal power, he wondered how on earth they got anything done. The males were very different. Blaze wasn't surprised in the least.

"I don't like the idea of misleading the females. They are responding to an advertisement to date vampire males, to be a part of The Program. They are not expecting to be hunted and mated by dragon shifters."

Blaze clenched his teeth. "We spoke about this." He worked hard at keeping his voice even. "The females would sign those human papers."

"Non-disclosure agreements," Zane added.

Blaze gave a nod in the male's direction. "Yes. Non-disclosure agreements. They would be fully briefed and able to choose whether they wanted to take part or not."

"Briefed." Brant gave a small shake of the head. His jaw was tense. "They will not be told that you are dragon shifters. They will assume wolf shifters. It's misleading."

"And necessary." Blaze growled, unable to keep the emotion from his voice. "We can't let word get out that dragon shifters exist."

Brant gave a shrug. "It's lying by omission, I'm not sure I want any part of that."

"We are being forced to abduct females." Blaze dug his fingers into his hair. "The current situation is much worse."

"We have no association with your current situation," Brant said.

"The females would know enough prior to coming to dragon territory. They will be told that the destination is remote. They will be briefed fully prior to the hunt. That shifter males will track them and fight over them. As well as the fact that there is more of a chance that they will end up becoming mated than if they were to take part in your program."

"I still don't like it," Brant said.

"There are plenty of females who wish to mate non-humans. We adjusted some of the interview questions in order to probe which females would be—" Zane paused, choosing his words carefully, "—open to mating males who are not vampires and, for the most part, the results were favorable."

Blaze nodded.

"It sounds promising, but it would still be so much better if the human females were willing participants from the start," Brant said, still looking unconvinced.

"That's not an option." Zane looked relaxed. "I think we should allow a trial. Let's see how it goes."

Brant's stance tensed. "This could come back to bite us."

"This would go a long way to strengthening our alliance." Blaze had hoped to avoid the whole 'dragons are stronger than vampires' card.

Brant snorted. "Your sister is mated to one of our elite warriors, we are in an alliance already by default."

Blaze shrugged. "Do this for the dragon shifters and we will be indebted to you. A mere blood alliance will only get you so far."

Brant clenched his jaw so tight for a second or two that it looked as if he might crack his jaw from the sheer force. "Fine," he finally huffed. "But if there are any fuck ups it's over. I will do the preliminary briefing of the females myself. I want a team of five vampire males to observe the hunt and—"

Blaze snarled, the vampire king was going too far. He had clearly forgotten his place. Blaze needed help from these males but he wasn't about to bow down to them to get it.

Brant snapped his mouth shut, his eyes widened. The other king didn't flinch, his arms remained relaxed at his sides.

"There won't be any fuck ups." Blaze could hear the growl in his voice but it couldn't be helped. "We will handle it ourselves. The females will be properly briefed once they arrive. Nothing will go wrong."

"I'm sure it will all work out fine," Zane said. "Blaze will inform us if there are any . . . issues."

"Yes." Brant's eyes went from Zane to Blaze. "We will need to be informed of any problems." His face was red, his hands fisted at his sides. "I am responsible for these females."

"They will no longer be your concern once they are on dragon territory."

"That's where you are wrong." Blaze could see that Brant was working hard to keep his voice even. "I will recruit them and, in my opinion, under false pretenses, so it is important that they are happy and safe."

"Agreed." Zane's eyes narrowed.

"They will be. Females are worth more than gold and jewels to us. These humans would be our future. They will be cherished. I will report back . . . as a courtesy." He quickly added the last.

Brant finally nodded. "Okay then." He held out his hand and they clasped at the wrist. He did the same with Zane.

A weight eased. At least no more females would need to be abducted.

The little girl gurgled and smiled. Such a happy little thing. He shifted her on his lap so that her head was resting between his knees. He had to smile, there was more drool around her mouth than inside it. Her eyes were wide. It was like looking down into his own. They were a bright, emerald green. Tinder gave a little squeal and smoke wafted from her nose.

"Don't get her too rattled," Ruby warned. "Last week she set the curtains alight with a squeal." His sister was smiling broadly. She sat across from him, looking the picture of happiness.

"An accident here or there is perfectly normal."

Ruby looked at him like he'd grown a pair of horns. "Not this many accidents and never this severe. She's burned down half her bedroom several times already. If she screams, she becomes a flame thrower."

Blaze choked out a laugh. "Good to know our blood is so strong. Tinder is a royal after all."

Ruby raised her brows. "Yeah, she is a royal alright."

"She's beautiful." Blaze ran a hand over the baby's soft head, feeling her downy hair beneath his fingers. Something in him blossomed. A deep-seated need. It was a feeling he hadn't felt in a while.

The need to procreate.

It scared him because in order to procreate, he needed a female. A mate. The feeling of unease grew. Blaze wished for the billionth time that he could have heirs without the hassle of a female. Especially a human female. He could do without the aggravation.

It was as if his sister could read his thoughts. "So." He could hear that she was smiling. "When are you going to take a mate?"

The little girl in his arms was sucking and gnawing on her fist. Blaze finally lifted his gaze. "I will take a female in the next hunt."

Ruby's smile widened. "That's exciting."

"It is necessary."

She pulled a face. "The last of the romantics. I suppose you plan on dragging her by the hair to the nearest cave."

"Something like that. My mate will be the queen of all four kingdoms. She will want for nothing and in return, she will give me heirs."

"What about love?"

He shrugged. "What about it? Love is overrated."

"Just because you were hurt once doesn't—"

"Don't." He put up a hand. "I do not wish to discuss it."

"You should though, Blaze. Everyone knows that—"

"Who the fuck is everyone and what do they know?" He growled, a little more harshly than intended. Little Tinder startled and began to cry; smoke billowed from her tiny nostrils.

"Quick!" Ruby reached over. "Give her to me. I like this lounge suite."

Blaze handed the baby over. Tinder quickly settled in her mother's arms.

"I'm sorry." He rubbed a hand over his jaw. "I don't like talking about it. My personal life is nobody's business. It's not up for discussion."

"I'm your sister."

He shook his head. "Drop it."

Ruby gave a nod. "I'm glad you're going to take a mate. I hate seeing you so sad and lonely."

"I'm not sad or lonely. If it weren't for needing

heirs . . ."

"Yeah, yeah. I really pray that she's a special female. That she knocks some sense into you."

Blaze just smiled at his crazy sister.

"That she makes you fall in love with her." Ruby smiled broadly.

Blaze made a choking noise. "Not going to happen. Love complicates things."

"Love is wonderful. Everyone should have someone special in their life. I really wish that for you."

"Speaking of which, where is your mate?"

"He should be here any minute." Ruby's whole face lit up.

"Is he taking good care of you?" He narrowed his eyes.

Ruby nodded, a goofy smile took up residence on her face. "Yeah." She sighed. "I never thought I'd find a male like him."

"Good." Blaze was glad that things had worked out for his sister. To think he'd almost messed things up for her. It was never his intention, but everything he did was for the good of the four kingdoms and his people. He would do anything for them. *Anything*. Even if it meant taking a human mate.

CHAPTER 3

Three weeks later . . .

Roxy clutched her purse tighter to her body. Her mouth felt dry and her heart was just about beating out of her chest.

"Why are we here?" a woman next to her asked, eyes wide. "The Program started last week so we're too late for that. They interview women a second time for each round. I was so sure that I didn't make it."

Roxy shook her head. "No idea. I was shocked when I got the call a few days ago."

"Maybe a couple of the women fell out of the running or something." A sweet-looking blonde sidled closer, joining the conversation. She had shoulder-length hair and a wide mouth.

"Nah," the other woman said. "That can't be it. They always pick way more women than needed. Even if five dropped out there would still be enough to go around."

"Mmmm," Roxy hummed. "That makes sense. They made it clear in the interview that most of the selected women end up going home in the end so there are no guarantees."

"Maybe they're running another dating program right after this one or even concurrently," the blonde spoke under her breath.

"It would be—" the other woman was cut off as the door opened and a huge, really good-looking guy stepped across the threshold.

All the chatter dried up in an instant. Mouths dropped open, while others snapped shut. One of the ladies at the front gave a sigh.

The big guy smoothed the front of his gray pinstripe suit. The garment fit him like a glove. He had broad shoulders, thick biceps and narrow hips. Shit, he was perfection. Even his hair was perfectly cut and styled, not a strand out of place.

A gorgeous woman stepped in next to him, clipboard in hand. She wore one of those high-fitting pencil skirts and a blouse. Who knew that office wear could be so sexy?

"Good morning." His voice was smooth as silk.

One of the women made a whimpering noise and leaned against the wall like she might faint at any moment. Roxy had to bite back a smile. They had to be vampires. The woman was tall and slim, the guy was even taller and so built. Their sheer beauty and magnetism was off the charts.

"Right," the male vampire nodded to the woman. "Let's get this done." He turned his dark eyes back on them. "I'm sure you are all anxious to find out why you are here."

A murmur of agreement passed through the room.

"This is my assistant, Allison, and I am Brant."

"Oh my god!" the blonde shrieked along with a whole lot of others.

"He's one of the kings!" another lady closer to the front yelled.

Brant put both his hands up, his expression didn't change, it was unreadable and serious. "Yes, I'm one of the vampire kings."

There was more shrieking.

"Please," he narrowed his eyes before turning his wrist and glancing at what looked like a gold Rolex. "My time is limited."

This shut them up. Women clasped their chests. Some were breathing heavily. Most had a bewildered look. Roxy was probably with the last group. Why had they been called here? Why was one of the vampire kings addressing them?

The vampire king let his arms fall back to his sides. "You have been selected as potential candidates for a new program."

A collective twitter of excitement sounded as most of the twelve women spoke simultaneously.

"Again, my time is limited so please save the talking for after the briefing." His tone was commanding. He paused for a few beats. "The Program has already started, as I'm sure most of you know. So, just so we're clear, you're not here to date a vampire. I would like a show of hands for those of you who would be interested in entering a program that would involve dating shifters."

"A shifter?" one of the women close by said. "What about the vampires? I thought that this was about dating—"

Brant shook his head. "Shifters. Would you be willing to date a shifter with the purpose of potentially mating them? Not a vampire. The Program has already started and all the places are filled. We are looking for five females for this one. You have ten seconds to decide whether or not this would be of interest to you. It's an opportunity."

"Shifters aren't very wealthy." The blonde said under her breath. "They live in cabins in the middle of nowhere. I don't know . . ."

"Would we be able to apply for a place in The Program again should we choose not to take part in this shifter . . . thing?" a tall girl asked. "I kind of had my heart set on a vampire."

"You can apply as many times as you want." Brant's expression remained deadpan. "An opportunity to be with a shifter may not come around again though. I realize that this is unexpected, but it is what it is." He glanced at his watch. "A show of hands please for those interested?"

Shit! Roxy felt completely unprepared for this. It was the last thing she had expected to happen. It didn't bug her that shifters weren't wealthy, that they didn't live in a big castle. Material things had never really been her thing anyway. She loved the mountains. Roxy had never really considered a shifter before. Did it really matter? A non-human was a non-human right? They all mated for life. This was a program for the shifters to find mates, so it wouldn't be about hook-ups. She could do this.

Brant cleared his throat. "So far only three of you are interested. Is that right? If you are interested in entering this exciting new program put your hand up now."

Should she do it?

Should she?

Or should she hold out for a chance at a vampire? Getting into The Program was no guarantee. Competition was tough. At the end of the day she wanted someone to love, someone who would love her back just as fiercely. It didn't matter to her what species he was. All Roxy knew was that she didn't want her heart broken again. Once was enough.

"Last chance," Brant said.

Roxy thrust up her hand. This felt right. The thought of a new adventure excited her. Most of the women surrounding her had their hands up as well.

Brant quirked an eyebrow, he looked surprised for a second and then schooled his emotions. "Will those who are not interested come to the front?"

"Good luck!" the blonde whispered and moved towards the vampires.

"Your name, please?" The beautiful vampire lady made a mark on her clipboard. She did the same thing when the blonde said her name.

"The two of you can leave," Brant said. "A guard will escort you to your vehicles. Thank you for your time."

Allison followed the women as they left, returning with a stack of documents.

"When your name is called, please come forward. A non-disclosure agreement was sent to all candidates who made it to the final selection. You've had plenty of time to peruse the document and to have your lawyer take a look at it. It is standard. As previously outlined, you are expected to sign this," he gestured towards the stack in his assistant's hands, "—right now if you wish to proceed."

"When your name is called, please come forward and collect your document," Allison said. "Please initial every page and sign on the back. Have two others sign as witnesses."

"And what if we don't sign?" someone to the right asked.

"There's the door," Brant nodded in the direction of the closed door. "Once you sign, you will receive further information."

This sparked another flare of chatter.

"Oh well," the woman next to her said. "I guess we'd better sign the thing." She shook her head.

Brant's assistant began to call names and one by one they all walked to the front to collect their non-disclosure agreements. Roxy had read through hers, tried to understand all the legal terms and had failed. She worked the front counter at the local bakery selling pastries and bread, so getting a lawyer was out of the question. Anyway, why waste money when she pretty much knew what it said in a nutshell? Keep your mouth shut. Whatever she was told or saw could not be repeated to another living soul ever or she would be sued. She figured that as long as she stuck to that she would be fine. There were pens on the table at the back of the room. One or two of the women were reading through the document, most were initialing and signing. Roxy sat down at one of the open chairs, grabbed herself a pen and got to work.

Within fifteen minutes, all of the documents were safely in Brant's assistant's hands.

"Only five of you will be selected. Anyone who leaves here now or at any time during this program may not breathe a word of what was told to you or of what you may have seen. We will not hesitate to come at you with the full extent of the law should you be in breach. Once my legal team is done with you, you'll have nothing left. Not even the clothes on your back." He smiled. It sent shivers down her spine. "I hope that is clear."

Loud and clear.

There were murmurs of acceptance. Roxy nodded, she swallowed hard. It didn't come as a surprise but still, hearing it put that way was a tad scary. That meant that she couldn't even confide in Lauren. Her best friend wouldn't like that.

"The good news is . . ." Brant went on. " . . . that the five who are selected will definitely find shifter mates, if that is what you choose."

Excitement bubbled inside of her. This really was an opportunity.

"Oh wow!" The woman beside her glanced at Roxy. "That's so exciting. Shifters are so hot. Mating one would be awesome." There were plenty of women who saw non-humans as celebrities. They wanted one.

"Yeah, it would," she whispered back. There was a shiver of apprehension that coursed through her. What was she getting herself into?

"Here's the deal though . . ." Brant folded his arms across his broad chest. His eyes were dark and intense. "You will need to agree to leave tomorrow and you will need to be sedated for the trip."

Some women gasped while others muttered in outrage.

"The shifters require strong females, females willing to put themselves out there. Females with a sense of adventure."

"Yeah, but isn't sedating us going a bit far? Anything could happen," one of the women said, her voice filled with irritation.

"All non-humans, that includes shifters, are a species of honor. I give you my word that no harm will come to you. You will be sedated and transported to the shifters territory. The reason for the sedation is to keep the location of their . . ." he paused, seeming to look for the right word, "dwellings a secret. Not even the vampires know their exact location."

"No way! I just couldn't." A pissed looking, dark-haired woman, closer to the front shook her head as she spoke.

"To make myself vulnerable like that," she continued to shake her head. "Not happening!"

Brant nodded. "That's fine, and perfectly understandable. Please take a few moments to decide whether this is something that you would be comfortable with. Unfortunately, it is a deal breaker. If you wish to be a part of this program, then you will need to agree to these terms."

"What if we arrive at the shifters' . . . territory and decide that we don't want to be there? That we would never be comfortable living wherever it is that they live, and that mating one of them isn't for us. Could we come home?" someone behind Roxy asked.

"Once you arrive at the shifters territory, you will be expected to remain for a time. To become acclimatized and to get to know the shifters. Once the timeframe lapses however, you would be free to leave. Please understand that you will be treated well. You will not be forced into anything."

"What kind of timeframe are we talking about?" the same woman asked.

"Two weeks," Brant said.

This seemed to appease the woman, who nodded her head.

There were a couple more questions. How long would they be sedated for? What type of drug would be used? Brant answered the questions one by one.

"Any more concerns?" Brant finally asked.

"What happens once we get there? How is this whole

thing going to work?" one of the ladies asked.

"I'm afraid I can't answer that. You will be briefed once you arrive on shifter territory. Like I said before, no one will be harmed or forced to do anything that they are not comfortable with. You will be expected to remain guests of the shifters for two weeks and if you wish to return home, you will not be stopped. For those who choose to remain, you will be guaranteed a mate."

Roxy noticed that there were a couple of unhappy faces amongst the women.

"No damned way," the lady to her left said. "Sedated my ass. I refuse." She spoke softly.

"Being sedated for the trip to shifter territory is nonnegotiable." Brant raised his brows. "Those of you NOT willing to undergo sedation please come to the front so that Allison can remove you from the list."

Four of the ten moved one by one to the front and gave Brant's assistant their names. Once the women left the room, Brant turned to the remaining six. "That's a pity . . ." He smiled. The vampire king was very good-looking. "I had hoped that by some miracle we would end up with exactly five, as is their tradition. The good news though is that my assistant," he glanced at Allison, "had a really good idea on how to deal with any surplus."

"It's old-fashioned but it works," she smiled. The vampire lady returned to the room holding a cap. Your run-of-the-mill, garden-variety baseball cap. "I'd like each of you to draw a folded paper. Do not open it until I give you the go-ahead."

Allison moved around the room and each of the ladies took a folded, white square. It was up to lady luck at this point. Roxy's hand shook. Surely she hadn't come this far only to draw the wrong piece of paper. What were the odds? She held her bit of paper in a closed fist.

"Written on the papers, are the numbers from one to six. If you have a number from one to five in your hand, then you go. If you are holding the number six, I'm afraid it wasn't meant to be. You may look at the paper in your hand now."

Roxy squeezed the paper even tighter. There were squeals of joy but she ignored them. Finally, she forced her fingers open and unfolded the crumpled bit of paper.

No way.

Really?

Somehow she'd known that she would get the last number. The irony was that six was normally her lucky number. She'd won numerous raffles. It had served her well over the years, until now.

"Will the person holding number six please come to the front?" Allison had her eyes trained on Roxy as she spoke.

Roxy had to force herself to walk. She had to force herself to keep her shoulders square and her chin up. So what if this hadn't worked out liked she'd hoped. There was always next time.

"Bad luck," Allison gave her a genuine smile. "I'll put a note on your file. Try again for The Program. You never know." She made a mark next to Roxy's name.

"Thanks." Just as she was leaving, she heard Brant address the women, telling them to have a bag ready and to be back the following day. She didn't catch the time because the door swung shut.

So close. So close she could almost taste it.

CHAPTER 4

The next day . . .

The lunch rush was going to kill her. Roxy normally loved this time of day when they were so busy that the little bakery felt like it was going to burst its seams. The time flew as she raced to fill everyone's orders. Not so today. When her alarm clock went off this morning, all she'd felt like doing was turning over and going back to sleep. It would do no good to mope though. She needed to get on with her life. So what if she didn't make the shifter program? So what if she didn't get in because of a technicality that had nothing to do with her and everything to do with drawing the wrong piece of paper? She held back a sigh.

Roxy forced herself to smile at her next customer. It wasn't anybody's fault. "What can I get for you today?"

"I'll have two cream buns and a chocolate doughnut, please." The elderly lady smiled back.

Roxy quickly assembled the cardboard box, placing the three treats inside. She sealed the box and was just about to ring up the total when her phone vibrated . . . again. It was for the fourth time in ten minutes. It had to be something serious.

Maybe something had happened? Her mom. Had something happened to her mom? They didn't have a bad relationship or anything, they just didn't always see eye-to-eye. They saw each other once every year or two, which was more than enough. They spoke to each other maybe once a month, which again, was enough. Roxy suddenly felt nervous, they might not get along very well but she was still her mother.

"Just one second, I have to get this," she said as she pulled the vibrating device from her pocket. The call was from a private number. "I'm sorry," she said as she pressed the green button. "Hello."

The elderly lady gave a small nod but she noticed that a couple of the others didn't look too thrilled. She was met with scowls and a few huffs. Well too bad, the call was more than likely something serious. She turned her back on the crowd and took a few steps away. Her coworker Jessica gave her a quizzical look but continued to fill the order she had just taken.

"Hi, yes." The person on the other end sounded breathless. "I'm so glad I managed to reach you, Miss Kincaid. This is Allison."

Who? She didn't recognize the voice. The woman sounded too young to be one of her mother's friends.

"For a second there I thought I wouldn't get a hold of you. Never mind," she spoke quickly. Oh yes! It was the vampire lady, Brant's assistant. Why would Allison be calling her? Her heart sped up. Could it be . . . ?

"One of the five candidates has dropped out. Are you still interested in entering the program?"

What? It felt like a million questions rushed through her brain. After a few beats, she realized that Allison was waiting for her to respond. "Um, yes . . ." she blurted, her voice was high-pitched. "But, I haven't planned anything. I'm at work. I . . ." She remembered Brant saying that they would need to leave the next day. Today was the next day.

"If you're still interested, you need to be here in one and a half hours with a packed bag. You'll be gone for at least two weeks. It can be cold up in the mountains, so pack accordingly."

"Wait! I don't know if I can make it on such short notice." She could hear the panic in her own voice.

"This is a once-in-a-lifetime opportunity. Unfortunately, you need to be at the vampire castle by three o'clock this afternoon or the transport will leave without you."

"That doesn't give me much time." Roxy blocked her other ear. The noise in the bakery seemed to escalate.

"No, it doesn't. If it's something that you want badly enough though, then you'll make it work. I'm really sorry, the other female only just called us to let us know that she won't be joining. I really hope to see you, Roxy."

"Yeah, thank you." Shit! She couldn't do this. Roxy stuffed the phone back in her apron and turned around to face the crowd. If she wanted to make three o'clock, she needed to leave right now. Hell, she still might not make it even if she did move her ass. The only problem was that her coworker, Jessica, would never be able to handle this crowd on her own.

Shit!

"Are you all right, dear?" the elderly lady asked. She glanced down at her box of goodies and then back up at Jessica.

Shit!

"I'll be right back." This elicited several moans and a whole lot of grumbles.

Roxy pushed through a set of swinging doors that led to the bakery itself. Lauren was piping some icing onto a three-tiered cake. Her friend looked up as she approached, a frown appeared on her face. "Is everything okay? Please don't tell me that you've run out of coconut tarts."

Coconut tarts. It was the bakery's signature pastry. People came from far and wide just to taste their famous tarts.

Roxy shook her head. She wiped her hands on her apron. "No, nothing like that."

Lauren breathed out a sigh of relief. "Thank God! We're swamped. I need to get this cake done by three, so there's no time for anything else. Janet is busy with our five o'clock pickups. We barely got the delivery items out on time."

Why was she even back there? They needed her. "Okay. I'll just get back to it." Roxy turned and had only taken one step when Lauren called after her.

"What is it? What did you come back to tell me?"

"Nothing. Don't worry about it." Roxy took another step, not even bothering to look back as she spoke.

"Not so fast." Lauren used her *I'm the boss* tone, which was rare. "It must be something serious for you to leave the lunch rush."

Roxy turned. "Something came up but we're too busy. It's . . . never mind." She walked another step towards the swinging doors.

"Out with it!" Roxy turned back just as Lauren put her hands on her hips.

It seemed her boss and friend wasn't going to let her leave until she knew what was going on. "You know that program I applied for?" Roxy propped a hand on her hip.

Lauren's eyes gleamed and a slow smile began to spread on her face. "Of course, yes." She frowned. "Not even a chocolate fudge sundae could get you out of your funk yesterday. Are you going to give me more details or are you still going to play the non-disclosure card?"

"I can't tell you anything."

"No one would ever know you told me. They would never know you were in breach."

"I would know," Roxy said. "It wouldn't be right."

"What's changed?" Her eyes gleamed.

"Well . . ." Roxy pursed her lips.

"Well . . . ?" Lauren widened her eyes. "Are you going to tell me or what?"

"I've been accepted."

Lauren gave her thigh an open-palmed smack and gave

a yell of excitement. "That's such good news!" Her friend must've seen something cross her face because she quickly added. "What's the problem? I'm sensing a *but* here."

"Um . . . they need me there by three today." Roxy dropped her gaze to Lauren's feet for a moment. She should've told Brant's assistant that she couldn't go. That it was too late. "I'll be gone for at least two weeks, maybe longer, maybe indefinitely."

"Three as in an hour and twenty minutes from now?" Lauren glanced at the clock on the wall.

"Yup," Roxy nodded. "Don't worry though, I'm not going. You guys need me."

Lauren cocked her head. "You're going and that's that. You want this, you need this, you deserve this. You haven't been the same since you and Ben broke up. Since that bastard broke your heart."

"I'm over Ben."

"You've dated once or twice since your break-up. I know how much you love those vamps. I don't blame you by the way." She licked her lips. "Mmmmmmhm. They sure are fine. I wouldn't mind one for myself."

"It's really bad timing though. I can't just leave you during the lunch rush. You guys won't be able to handle it."

"Screw bad timing. You're going." Lauren's *I'm the boss* tone was out in full force.

"You just told me that you guys are just as swamped back here. It's a madhouse out front, Jessica will never cope on her own."

"It's the lunch rush. Its short-lived. I'll handle it. I'll get a hold of the lady coming in at three to collect this cake and tell her to come at four. I'll go out front, help out for the next hour and you can go and snag yourself a vampire," she grinned.

Roxy had to bite her tongue. She so wanted to tell Lauren that she was on her way to meet some shifter hotties but she'd signed a damned non-disclosure agreement. "Are you sure?"

Lauren grinned. "Of course I'm sure. I've never been surer in my life. I'll call the agency and organize a temp. Now, go and get packed. Then get your ass to the vampire castle. Don't forget to pack some lingerie."

Roxy couldn't help but to blush. "I don't know about that." Her answer was stupid; she was going to meet shifter guys with the idea of mating one of them. There was a good chance that sex would be involved. "Yeah, maybe." Roxy was so ready to start having sex again. To jump back into the saddle.

"Definitely," Lauren squealed. "You're one lucky fish! Don't do anything I wouldn't do." Her best friend winked.

Roxy laughed. They both had been single for ages. The thought of dating and possibly having sex again had her feeling terrified and excited. "You're the best!"

"I know I am." Lauren walked over to her and they hugged. "I have a good feeling about this," she said as she hugged Roxy tighter.

"I hope you're right." Roxy couldn't help the sudden fit of nerves that made her heart beat faster and her hands feel clammy.

Lauren finally pulled away. "Of course I'm right. Now, what are you still doing here? Get going or you'll be late."

Roxy nodded. It felt like all of her blood had left her. "Is this really happening?" she said as she unfastened her apron.

"Yes, it is," Lauren smiled.

What the hell was she agreeing to? Maybe she had a serious screw loose. She was about to be drugged and taken to god knows where to meet a bunch of horny guys. Big, strong, horny guys. Shifters were known for their sweet, kind natures though. She was sure to find love, to meet the guy of her dreams.

CHAPTER 5

There were five beds in the middle of a field behind the vampire castle. They were the kind you found in hospitals, complete with crisp white sheets and everything. They looked so out of place on the manicured lawn that Roxy stopped walking for a second or two. It was weird. She didn't really know what she expected but this wasn't it. Now that she thought about it, maybe an SUV, bus or helicopter would transport them. There didn't seem to be any form of transportation in the vicinity. How were they going to be moved from one location to the next?

She was the last one to arrive, so there wasn't any time to ponder on what some of the answers could be. The four other women were already there. As was Brant, his assistant and a short lady in a white medical jacket.

Allison's face lit up when she saw Roxy. She wrote something on her clipboard; it seemed like that thing was permanently attached to her hand. The vampire king, Brant, frowned and glanced at his watch.

Yeah, yeah, I'm five minutes late, so sue me. It's not like she'd had much time to get ready or anything. Roxy joined the rest of the ladies. The huge vampire guard placed her bag at her feet.

"Thank you," she whispered in his direction. All eyes were on her.

"My pleasure." He winked at her before making a hasty retreat.

"Let's get started," said Brant, rubbing his hands together as he spoke.

"Hi, I'm Becky," the short lady said. "I'm a doctor and I'm going to be sedating you today."

There was a table to the right of the line of beds. On it were five syringes and some sealed square sachets. Roxy swallowed thickly. She could see by the looks on the other women's faces that she wasn't the only one who was nervous.

"Once I inject you, you will go into deep sedation and become unconscious. This will happen within ten seconds." The doctor lady walked towards the table and picked up one of the syringes. "You will only be under for a maximum of one hour, so the side-effects will be limited. Having said that, you may feel a little drowsy and possibly a little dizzy when you regain consciousness. The side effects will wear off quickly." She looked at each of them in turn. "It's best to stay calm and motionless. Take it easy for the first half hour after waking up. There are sometimes cases of shivering and headaches reported. And on the very rare occasion patients may feel nauseous. They are equipped on the other side to deal with any possible side effects, so do not be alarmed."

"Once again, I assure you that you are in safe hands."
Brant sort of smiled but Roxy sensed an underlying
tension in the man. It didn't help her nerves.

"Please, can each of you lie down?" the doctor
instructed. "Roll up the sleeve of the arm that you don't
use. If you're right-handed that would be the left sleeve."

They all moved to a bed. Roxy lay down. *Oh god!* She
was really going through with this. She tried to breathe
evenly. *Whatever you do don't panic, Roxy.* This was going to
be a piece of cake. A little nap.

She pushed up the sleeve of her left arm with fumbling
fingers. She was lying on the second bed.

The doctor was busy with the lady on bed number one.
Becky was in the way so Roxy couldn't see what was going
on next to her.

"You'll feel a little prick," she heard the doctor say. The
woman on the bed next to her made a soft whimpering
noise. "Now, that wasn't too bad was it?"

"No, it wasn't. I must say I do feel . . . quite . . .
sleepy . . . I . . . ." Her voice began to slur and then there
was silence.

The doctor lady moved back to the table to collect
another syringe. Within a few seconds, she was next to
Roxy's bed. She looked friendly and seemed to know what
she was doing. She tore open one of the square sachets
and removed a small piece of papery cloth.

The woman, Dr. Becky, clasped her left arm. There was
a squeaking noise as the latex from the rubber glove slid
across her skin. The doctor put a green tourniquet around

Roxy's bicep and pulled it until snug around her arm. She then proceeded to wipe on the inside crease of her elbow with the papery cloth. Her skin became cold. It was obvious that she was using some sort of alcohol-based disinfectant. Next, she removed the lid from the syringe.

This was it.

Perversely, Roxy couldn't take her eyes off the blue veins that protruded from beneath her skin.

"This will only last a second," the doctor gave her a sympathetic smile and turned her attention back to Roxy's arm.

Roxy watched as the needle slid into her vein. There was a sharp pinch and it was over almost as soon as it hit. The liquid from the syringe felt cold going in but within seconds her body began to feel warm. For a second she felt like fighting the sensations. Maybe this wasn't such a good idea. Then she couldn't remember why it wasn't a good idea. She couldn't remember her own name, for that matter, or why she was even there. The sky was a beautiful blue. Blue very quickly turned to black as she lost consciousness.

Dragon shifters.

Wait a minute, she must have heard wrong or something. Roxy stared out of the huge bay window. The view was magnificent. They were high up in a structure that was built into the side of a cliff. And in front of her were rolling hills as far as the eye could see. The sun was still setting. The sky was painted with the most magnificent shades of pinks, blues and even purples. It was enough to take your breath away.

They were in a remote location. Up high in the mountains and they were here with the purpose of being introduced to shifters, but not the kind of shifters she'd had in mind.

Dragons.

"Yes, dragons," a very pretty, dark-haired lady said.

Roxy had spoken out loud. She hadn't meant to.

The lady in question had introduced herself earlier as Julie. She was human and mated to one of the dragon shifters. "I know it's a lot to take in . . ." she continued.

"Dragons don't exist," Roxy blurted. It seemed she was having one of her 'say it as soon as it came into her head' moments.

"Oh yes they do, and you ladies are so lucky to be here. Dragons are the strongest of all the non-humans."

"Why have we never heard about them?" one of the others asked. It was the smallest lady of the bunch. She had strawberry blonde hair and freckles running across her nose. They'd all introduced themselves to one another after waking up in this room. That was at least a half an hour ago and Roxy couldn't remember most of their names. Probably because she'd just woken up after being drugged. Something like that could destroy a person's memory. The strawberry blonde was named after a flower but for the life of her she couldn't remember which one. Rose or Daisy? It didn't matter right now.

"They're a secretive bunch. I'm sure you've read stories

about knights going off to slay dragons? Well, many of the stories are based on facts. Many years ago, humans hunted and killed dragon shifters almost into extinction. Although dragons are infinitely stronger than humans, there are many more humans and when they discovered that silver could kill non-humans they almost wiped out the dragons. As a result, dragon shifters prefer to stick to themselves. That's why you had to be sedated. It's why you were only given a minimal brief. It was out of necessity." Julie smiled. "It is important, should you wish to go home and not take one as your life partner, that you not say a word of their existence to anyone." She paused. "They are wonderful males. Maybe a little rough around the edges, but ultimately caring and loving."

"Why are we here then? Why can't they get women of their own if they are so wonderful?" It was the tallest of the group. Her name was . . . Darcy . . . yeah, Darcy. She was tall and quite strong looking. Her shoulders were broad and her thighs were . . . well-muscled. As her late father would say, she could probably jumpstart a Boeing 747 with legs like that. She'd always found the saying a little rude but it was a good description.

"That's a good question," Julie said. "There have been very few female dragon shifter births and only a handful of those females are fertile. The result is that we are left with a generation of perfectly healthy dragon shifter males with no mates for them. It seems that all of the non-humans are having fertility problems. All except for the elves, if rumors are to be believed. Hence the vampire dating program. Anyway," she smoothed the dress she was wearing. "That's not really relevant. Although the dragon shifters are secretive and prefer to stick to themselves, they realized that it was time for drastic measures. Hence why you guys are here. I, for one, am so happy you're all here. I'm happy for the dragon shifter males but I'm also happy for me too. I could do with some company. There are only three humans, including myself, in the fire kingdom and even less across the other three."

"So how is this going to work? Do we date some of the guys? Is it similar to the program the vampires have running?" Roxy asked.

Julie looked unsure for a moment. She fidgeted with her hands. "Not exactly," was her cryptic answer.

"Please don't tell me that we just end up getting paired up with someone. What if we don't like them?" Lily asked. That was it, her name was Lily.

"Yeah, I don't like the sound of that." It was a dark haired girl with a mocha skin tone. She was beautiful with huge brown eyes and long black lashes.

"Not exactly," Julie smiled. "You see, due to the lack of females over the years they had to devise a system to ensure that the most eligible males procreated. It had to be a system that was fair for all. A way in which the guys could . . . compete for a mate."

"Compete?" one of the others asked, speaking up for the first time since Julie had arrived.

"Yes," Julie smiled. "It's called the hunt. You guys will be dropped in the wilderness and will get a four-hour head-start. The males have to track you and when they find you, they need to fight for you."

"Oh, wow! How caveman is that?" the same lady whispered, almost to herself. "And really hot. Are dragon shifters as good-looking as vampires?"

Julie laughed. "Oh, yes. I do need to warn you though, they are bigger than vampires. Quite a bit bigger."

"What?" Darcy raised her brows. "Bigger? That's fantastic, I'm not exactly a small lady. I outweigh a ton of human men."

"You'll have dinner this evening in the great hall. It's an opportunity to see them for yourselves before the start of the hunt. There won't be any interactions permitted but you'll get to see them."

"So how does this whole hunt work? Do we just head out into the wilderness?"

"Remind me of your name again?" Julie asked, her focus on the last of the group.

"Susan." She was really pretty with big brown eyes and curly chestnut hair. "My friends call me Sue. I work as a hostess at The Wombles restaurant in town."

Roxy thought she had seemed familiar. She and Lauren had gone out to dinner just the other night at The Wombles. It was probably the fanciest restaurant in town. Neither of them had been there in a long time because neither of them had dated much. They had finally decided to go as each other's dates. It was a fun night.

"Like I said, you guys will get a four-hour head-start. The idea is to get as far as you can in that time. You were told to bring outdoor gear and a comfortable pair of running or hiking shoes."

Oops! No one had mentioned that to Roxy. Good thing she'd packed an old pair of sneakers on a whim.

"You can choose to stay in one big group or go your own separate way. It's up to you. I would suggest maybe splitting into two groups. You don't want them to find you too quickly. What you ideally want is for a group of males to break out ahead of the others. A smaller group means a smaller fight. Also, the royals are quicker and seem to have a lot more stamina. There are still three kings who have yet to find a mate, and quite a number of princes. Not that there's anything wrong with the warriors but it would be nice to snag royalty, don't you think, ladies?"

"Hell yeah!" Sue yelled.

"Queen Lily, Her Royal Highness . . . it has a certain ring to it." The strawberry blonde was grinning from ear-to-ear.

Funnily enough, titles didn't matter to Roxy. All she hoped was that she would find a guy who appreciated her. Who cared for and loved her. It sounded clichéd but it was true.

"You don't want to make it easy on them. They need to work for you," Julie went on.

"Bring it on!" Darcy looked pumped.

"Dragon shifters fight hard. They don't take prisoners," Julie looked at each one of them in turn. "They have all been briefed that they need to always put your safety first. They know that we humans are pretty frail and breakable, so they will do their best to keep you out of harm's way but it's important that you stay away from the action. Keep yourselves at a safe distance when the fighting breaks out. This is especially true for larger groups of males. These guys are desperate for mates. They might forget their training in the heat of battle. Dragon shifters are a strong species." She gave a little chuckle. "Back when my mate was trying to impress me—this was before he became my mate—he picked up huge boulders with one hand and twirled a ginormous tree trunk like it was a small baton." She rolled her eyes. "Males!" she huffed. "Make sure that you stay away from them while they are locked in hand-to-hand combat, it would be terrible if one of you got hurt or even worse . . ."

They all nodded.

"Do any of you have any more questions?"

"What happens after?" Sue asked.

"The dragon shifters are spread over four kingdoms. This is the fire castle. The others are air, earth and water. Depending on which dragon wins you, will depend on where you end up going. Once you arrive, you'll get to know your dragon. You'll spend time with him. Date a little. They don't truly understand the concepts of dating so you might have to help them with that. Please remember that although they have interacted with humans, they still don't really understand our ways in other aspects as well. You won't be forced to do anything you're not comfortable with though."

"What if we spend some time with, whoever it is

who . . . wins . . ." Sue looked like she had trouble saying the word, " . . . um . . . wins us and we're not happy? What if we just don't like him?"

"If that happens and you are truly unhappy even though you've given it a chance, other males within the kingdom would be permitted to fight for you. It would be the high-ranking males. Then you would get a chance to get to know the new guy and if you didn't like him then they would fight for you again, and so on and so forth until you found the right person. Apparently, it's very rare that a male and female are not compatible but then again, we haven't had much experience with human dragon shifter matings, so anything is possible."

"If we find that we're really unhappy here," it was the lady with the curly hair. "Do we get to go home like we were promised?"

Julie nodded. "Yes, you do. All we ask is that you stay for two weeks. Get to know the dragon shifters. See it as a vacation. If at the end of two weeks you are not convinced that this is the life for you, then by all means, you can go back home but you can never breathe a word of this to anyone."

"That wouldn't be easy," Roxy blurted. Her mouth flapping before she had a chance to stop it.

"No it wouldn't, but it's very necessary that we respect the dragon shifters and their need for secrecy." Julie's eyes widened for a few seconds. "I forgot to tell you a couple of important things."

"Once a dragon shifter male wins you, he will need to

claim you. This means getting his scent on you so that the others know that you're taken."

"How will he get his scent on us?" Lily asked. Within seconds her face was a bright red. "Oh never mind, I can guess."

"It's nothing too hectic." Julie smiled. "Maybe a hug, definitely a kiss."

"I'm game," Darcy chuckled.

"Why the hell not? There are worse things." Sue was grinning broadly.

"Something else to note, you won't be able to just wander around the castle when you get back. Not without your dragon shifter. Other potential suitors would be able to claim you at least until you've been officially and fully claimed by your dragon shifter."

"Okay." Sue lifted her brows. "Fully claimed as in . . ." She let the sentence die.

"Sex," Julie's lip twitched like she was trying to hold back a smile. She really did look far too happy. "Once you're having sex, it's essentially like staking a real claim. No other guy can run off with you unless you publicly renounce your ties to your dragon shifter. Be really careful about doing that in the heat of the moment because it might come back to bite you." She sounded like she had experience in the matter.

"The good news is that they're really good in bed. They have experience with human women since they make a run into one of the neighboring towns twice a year. When I say experience, I mean they pick them up for hook-ups, not that they know how to interact well with us. At least they have some experience," Julie went on. "They're pretty free about sex and talking about it. Don't let that alarm you."

"If we have sex, are we then mated to them and stuck with them? What if it still doesn't work out?" The girl with the dark complexion tucked a strand of hair behind her ear.

"No, Emma. You can have sex and if it doesn't work out you can still leave or have the males fight for you again. Be very sure about going that route because once someone else has claimed you, you can't just change your mind and go back. The male who claims you would need to be willing to give you up and that's not going to happen easily. These guys are desperate for women. All they want is someone to love and to have a family with. They will do everything in their power to convince you to stay. To make you fall in love with them."

It sounded perfect. Too perfect. They were desperate for women; did that mean that they would settle for just anyone though? Roxy wanted a partner who was attracted to her. Not just her body but also her mind. She wanted to be that person's world and have them be her world right back. A desperate guy willing to do anything for a girl, any girl? That didn't work for her.

"Any more questions?" Julie asked.

"The hunt is tomorrow, right?" Sue folded her arms.

Julie nodded. "You'll be dropped off at eight and the guys will set off from here at twelve o'clock, so essentially you will be given a double head-start. Don't be too worried about it, you're all fit and healthy; you'll be given everything you need for a day trip. We'll talk about it more in the morning before we head out, that way if you have any more questions for me then I can answer them for you. We can also talk later at dinner."

"I'm quite excited," said Darcy, clapping her hands together.

Lily swallowed thickly, her freckles were more pronounced because she seemed to have paled. Sue gave a little jump and a yell, clearly excited about the prospects of nabbing a dragon shifter. Emma looked like she hadn't made up her mind either way.

"You guys are sharing rooms," Julie said. "We thought that you might not want to spend your first night alone. Putting the three of you in one room," she gestured towards Lily, Darcy and Sue. "And you two in another room," she looked Roxy in the eye before turning towards Emma.

Julie huffed out a breath and moved to a standing position before she smoothed her dress, once again, allowing her hand to linger over her belly. A strange expression came over her face. A softening of her eyes. "Let's get you guys settled and ready for dinner. There will be someone posted at the end of the hallway, a guard, but please do remember no mingling with any of the males. It's part of their traditions and rules. Stay in your room until I come and collect you. You've got just over an hour, which should be more than enough time."

Roxy felt her stomach clench as a whole horde of butterflies took flight. At least that's how it felt. Her hands were clammy so she opened and closed them. She was happy that she was getting a chance to see these dragon shifters before tomorrow. They were bigger than the vampires. She couldn't imagine that. Vampires were huge, muscled, tall and imposing. A frisson of excitement rushed through her, followed by another clench of her stomach. *You've got this, Roxy.*

CHAPTER 6

Blaze didn't like the idea of the females being paraded around in the great hall. It was certain to rile the males. To fire their blood. There hadn't been many hunts over the last century or so, with females being so scarce. With competition being so fierce, many males had been seriously injured in the past and there had even been a few deaths. There were rules in place to prevent fatalities, but rules were easily forgotten in the heat of battle, especially when the prize was so revered.

Human females. Beautiful and lush. A prize indeed. Though he felt his own blood run cold at the prospect. He looked about his chamber. It was a place of solace, his sanctuary. It wouldn't be his for much longer, not really. He was going to have to share it with another. Tomorrow he would win a female and take her as his mate. He would do it for the good of his people. It was on him to produce fire-breathing, royal heirs and not only for the fire kingdom but for all four kingdoms. Bile rose up, tasting bitter in his mouth. Blaze would do this for his people but he would hate every minute of it. He was duty-bound, oath-bound, blood-bound.

Even now, duty called. Blaze sighed as he pulled on a pair of pants. Then he ran a hand through his damp, hair which was overgrown, before scrubbing his fingers over the week-old growth on his jaw. For a second he contemplated shaving. Fuck it! This wasn't a beauty contest. He might need a mate but he wasn't out to win anyone's heart.

He was going to the great hall to ensure that everything went according to plan; most of all, to ensure that everyone followed the rules. Unlike every other red-blooded male dragon shifter within the four kingdoms, he wasn't going to appraise the humans. He definitely wasn't going to earmark a mate.

There was a knock at the door. "Yeah," he growled.

Coal walked in. There was a smirk on his face. This wasn't what he needed right now.

"Don't look so happy," his brother grinned.

"You're loving every minute of this, aren't you?"

"You'd better believe it," Coal chuckled. Not so long ago, the male had been in his shoes. Coal had dreaded taking a human mate and now he couldn't be happier. Julie was carrying his brother's child. The two of them were so in love that it was sickening to be around them.

"It's not going to be as bad as you think," Coal rubbed his chin and made a mocking humming noise. "I'm sure, if memory serves, those were the exact words you used on me a couple of weeks before my hunt."

"But there's a very big difference between you and me,"

Blaze narrowed his eyes at his brother. "You had never mingled with human females before. I knew that once you got a taste for one, you'd be sold. I know all about humans, especially the females of their kind. I've been there and done that. I'm not interested."

"Who knows, you might find the female of your dreams. Someone who will change your negative perspective."

Blaze snorted. "Like hell that's going to happen."

"You never know, brother," Coal slapped him on the back." You need to have a little bit of faith and keep an open mind."

"Whatever. Let's get this over with." Blaze walked towards the door. This was a conversation he and Coal had had before. It was old and he was sick of hearing how he just needed to meet the right female. That wasn't about to happen.

He and Coal navigated the various hallways in silence. Thank God the male seemed to have dropped their earlier conversation. He could already hear the whole chorus of voices coming from the great hall. Hundreds of males would be assembled within its walls, all hoping to catch a glimpse and a noseful of the human females.

The noise grew louder and louder until eventually they reached the large, double doors.

Coal turned to face him. He was grinning wildly. "You ready?"

Blaze gave a nod. "I won't be sitting at the royal table."

"Why not?" Coal frowned.

"I'm not interested in parading around. I'm here to ensure that nothing goes wrong. I will be winning one of those females tomorrow but I don't particularly care which one. I'll be at the back of the hall if you need me."

Coal shook his head, still frowning. "Suit yourself. You enjoy your evening, brother. Whatever you do, make sure that you hit the sack early." That shit-eating grin was back. "We want you at your best tomorrow." His chuckle was overrun by the loud noises of the hall as Coal opened the door and headed inside.

Blaze sucked in a deep breath before moving through the doors himself. Instead of heading further into the crowd, he walked to the side, taking up a position where he could observe. There were many tables arranged around the bustling hall. There were also large groups of males standing between the tables. On the raised dais in the far corner, away from the crowds, was the table where the females sat. Despite the scent of testosterone, musk and foods of all kinds, there was the distinct scent of human female.

It was a delectable scent. One that had his mouth watering, his blood rushing to his loins. It happened completely against his will. It was a purely instinctual reaction, one he was helpless to control.

Blaze gritted his teeth and tried to breathe through his mouth. The scent also brought back some memories, memories he preferred to keep buried. Despite his best efforts, his gaze was drawn to the females.

They were talking amongst themselves. Every so often

one of the females would look up and scan the busy hall.

"Wow!" one of the females giggled, she was very tall for a human female. She had her back to him, making it impossible for him to see her facial features. Not that he was interested. "These dragon shifters sure are something." she chuckled, eliciting laughter from one or two of the others.

"I can't wait to have one of them get his paws on me." This female had curly hair; she also sat with her back to Blaze.

"There are a ton of them with golden chests," the tall one said.

"Yeah, it's really exciting!" the curly-haired one piped up.

"Royalty," a very pale female with light colored hair spoke next. "I really want to nab myself one of those. What do you say, Roxy?"

Four females turned towards a dark-haired beauty. He immediately regretted thinking of her in those terms. She was a human. The female was of average height which made her very small by dragon standards. She shrugged. "It doesn't really matter to me either way."

The curly-haired female gasped. "You can't be serious. Don't you want a king? Or at the least, a prince?"

"This is going to sound really corny but all I want is a really nice guy. One who cares for me. That and . . ." She lifted her eyes in thought for a moment before shrugging again. "Nope, that's it. The royalty thing doesn't matter to me."

"What about you?" The curly-haired one asked the fifth female.

Once again all eyes turned to this female. "I guess royalty would be nice, but I'm with Roxy, I don't really mind as long as there's a spark there between us."

"A spark is important." It was the beauty. Fuck! He needed to stop thinking of that one in those terms. It didn't matter that she was beautiful. All that mattered was that it irritated the fuck out of him. One thing was for sure, he would stay away from her during the hunt. He wished once again that he could stay away from all of them but it was not to be.

Thankfully, Roxy was used to being on her feet all day. She was also used to running up and down and making plenty of trips to the back. She lived on the first floor of an apartment with no elevator, so having to run up and down a flight of stairs and sometimes with bags of groceries was all too common as well. Having said that, they were four hours into the hunt and her back was killing her. All she wanted to do was to take a break. Her brow was sweaty and her T-shirt clung to her body.

They had followed Julie's advice and had broken into two groups. It was difficult to decide who would go with who, so in the end, they had drawn sticks. The people who drew the two short sticks would go off in one direction while the remaining three would go off in another. Darcy and Emma had drawn the short sticks and headed northeast and the rest of them had headed northwest. Her roommate's name was Emma and she'd turned out to be extremely sweet. She was a little concerned that this wasn't for her while the rest of the ladies couldn't wait to meet their future shifter. They'd gushed about how sexy the dragon shifters were and ogled them non-stop.

Roxy had to agree, the dragon shifter men were extremely good-looking. They were ridiculously tall, ridiculously built and most of them had the most amazing eyes: bright blues and greens and even the most amazing bluish purple color. Some of them had really dark eyes, almost black. They had a very intense way of looking at you. They all walked around in loose-fitting pants and nothing else. No shoes and no shirts. Serious eye candy like she'd never seen before. Although it was important to be attracted to someone you were going to spend the rest of your life with, looks were not the most important thing to her.

"Come on," Sue kept marching on ahead. "We need to keep moving. At this rate they are going to catch up with us too quickly." She heard Lily suck in a deep breath and the other woman picked up the pace, scrambling over uneven ground, making her way through the tall grass. Lily and Sue had both decided that they wanted royalty and were therefore hoping to get as far away as possible to ensure that it happened. Julie had told them more than once that the higher a dragon shifter's rank, the more stamina he had and the faster he was. She said if they got far enough ahead, they were almost assured a royal mate.

Roxy had a different motivation. She didn't like the idea

of hordes of those big burly guys going head-to-head with one another. She could certainly imagine how a person could get hurt in amongst all of that. That was pretty much her only motivation for putting one foot in front of the other at the moment, self-preservation. Roxy sighed in relief as they hit a forest of trees. Walking in the blazing sun during the hottest time of day had been grueling. She immediately felt herself cool in the shade. It would also be easier going with less vegetation and they wouldn't be as easy to spot.

All three of them picked up the pace with renewed vigor and they carried on in silence for at least another half hour until Lily bent over grabbing her side. "I've got a stitch!" She raised her head, her mouth was contorted in a grimace, a sheen of sweat covered her face. Roxy rubbed her own forehead with the back of her arm. She could feel how escapee tendrils of hair stuck to her face.

"Okay," by the frown Sue was sporting, she didn't look happy. "We'll take a five-minute breather."

"I might need more than that," Lily grit out between her teeth. "It really hurts and I'm exhausted. I know I'm quite petite, but I don't work out, as in, not at all." She was breathing hard. "I have a desk job and I'm really, really unfit."

"Don't you want a king?" Sue widened her eyes.

Lily nodded. "Yes." She tried to pull herself upright but ended up buckling back over with a loud groan.

"Don't worry about it," Roxy said, smiling at the other woman. "I needed a breather myself. We'll take a few minutes. You can't go on like that."

Lily gave a nod and collapsed into a heap on the ground. "I feel better already. I think I was getting ready to faint." She was still breathing hard.

Sue remained standing, hands on hips. She glanced at her watch. "Four minutes, ladies, and then we're out of here."

"You heard Lily, she needs a bit more time."

"If you guys don't mind, I think I'll carry on, on my own" said Sue. That wasn't very nice.

Roxy didn't say anything though, she just nodded. "Sure, if that's what you want."

"Thanks for understanding," Sue whispered.

Julie had told them that the dragon shifters had excellent hearing, hence all the whispering.

"It's fine. We'll manage," Roxy said.

Lily gave a nod. "I'm too pooped to carry on. I need a little while," Lily's voice was muffled because her head was between her knees.

"Please be sure to send the royalty my way," Sue grinned, looking far too chipper for Roxy's liking. She had mentioned that she jogged every single morning, it was obviously helping her now.

Note to self, start jogging, thought Roxy. Lily lifted her head for half a second, locking eyes with Sue, before dropping her head back down between her knees. "I'll keep him for myself," she mumbled.

"Don't you dare!" Sue responded as she turned in the direction they had been moving.

Roxy watched Sue as she moved quickly between the trees. The woman was a machine. She continued to watch her for a couple of minutes until she disappeared altogether.

Roxy removed her backpack and sat down next to Lily before unzipping her pack. She withdrew a bottle of water and unscrewed the lid. She gave Lily a nudge on the arm with the bottle. "Here."

It seemed to take some effort for Lily to raise her head. She glanced first at Roxy and then at the bottle of water in her hand. "Thanks." She gave Roxy an exhausted smile and took the bottle before taking a tentative sip and then trying to hand the bottle back.

"You should drink more," Roxy said, not taking the bottle.

Lily nodded, she put her mouth to the bottle once again, this time taking a decent slug before handing the bottle back to Roxy.

Roxy drank deeply.

"Thanks for staying with me."

"Yeah, no worries."

Lily sighed. "I'm sure if you left now you'd still be able to catch up with Sue. It's just that I needed more than five minutes. I'm sorry for dragging you down." Aside from looking really tired, she also looked concerned.

"Hey, don't worry. I meant it, I also needed a bit of a break. I don't blame Sue for carrying on, on her own but at the same time it was a bit of a dick move."

Lily smiled. "It was, wasn't it?"

"Definitely. We're in this together and therefore we should stick together." Roxy meant every word.

One second they were sitting there whispering softly, sharing their water and the next they were no longer alone. The freaky thing was that Roxy hadn't even heard the dragon shifter males approach. There was no cracking of twigs, no rustling of leaves, there was no crunching of dirt even. Then again, the forest had become eerily silent. If she'd been paying attention she would have realized that something was up.

Roxy had just been offering Lily another sip of water when a voice sounded behind them. "I'll take the dark one." It was deep and gruff. Definitely not human.

Roxy dropped the water bottle, which landed between the two of them with a dull thud. It fell onto its side and water spilled out. Neither one of them made any attempt to right the plastic container. Their focus was on the men. The huge, larger-than-life shifters. They seemed bigger somehow in this setting.

Roxy jumped to her feet. Lilly remained where she was but her whole body tensed up.

There were two of them. One of the guys growled in response to the other one's statement. Her father had once owned a Rottweiler. A big, pedigreed bitch. She was extremely affectionate and loving. Roxy remembered spending hours playing fetch. She loved it when you scratched her stomach and would lie on her back, all four paws in the air. Roxy couldn't have been older than six or seven at the time, and had insisted on calling the animal

Sharkey. This on account of her mouth being full of sharp teeth. Thing was, as much as she loved the dog, and as sweet to Sharkey was, she was also a little afraid of her. Sharkey was extremely protective of the family. That meant barking and on occasion even a growl or two. Now Sharkey had a growl on her that never failed to elicit goosebumps all over Roxy's body. It didn't matter that the aggression was never towards her. The sound was still terrifying.

This guy's growl was ten times as menacing and infinitely lower and deeper. Roxy's first instinct was to hide behind a tree but thankfully she managed to suppress the desire because that would have just been stupid. There was nowhere to go and nowhere to hide. One of them was going to hone in on her and then it would be game on. She puffed out a breath, thinking that maybe this hadn't been one of her brightest ideas to date.

Roxy looked over the shifter's shoulders and as far as the forest would allow, which granted, wasn't that far. The trees were pretty tightly packed. It didn't look like anyone else was coming. It didn't sound like it either but then again these two had managed to sneak up on them very easily. For now, there were only two of them. Two was more than enough.

The one guy was looking at her, the guy with the deep growl. No, he wasn't just looking, he was all-out staring. His eyes were an emerald green. They were bright and beautiful. He had a wildness about him, from his unruly mop of hair to the hair on his jaw. She couldn't help but

to notice that both of them had golden chests. The guy
with the green eyes had golden markings and the other
one had blue flecks mixed within the gold. The guy with
the flecks of blue had the most beautiful amethyst colored
eyes—more purple than blue. He was the better-looking
of the two and yet she couldn't take her eyes off of the
other one. The dark, wild one. The intense, dangerous-
looking one. The one that was no good. He was too
menacing, too serious. So uptight that she felt like telling
a stupid joke just to break the mood. She had a feeling that
he wouldn't laugh even though she would, hysterically and
then he would think she was mad. Her internal dialogue
with herself was getting out of hand. It was her nerves
getting the better of her. She sucked in a deep breath and
willed her mind to be silent so that she could pay attention.
Something told her that she needed to keep her wits about
her.

"Why all the growling? You said you didn't care either
way," Amethyst Eyes said; there was a hint of annoyance
in his voice. "Choose quickly, the others will be here
soon." It looked like Amethyst Eyes was giving the other
guy first dibs. Really? That didn't seem right. A gentleman
would ask the lady who she preferred. Roxy quickly
reminded herself that these were no gentlemen, they
weren't even men and there was nothing remotely gentle
about them. Green Eyes was still looking at her . . . staring.

Pick me. It was a ridiculous thought. She didn't even
know this guy. His eyes held a haunted look. Every muscle
on his ridiculously large body pumped, primed and ready.

He may not be the better-looking of the two, but he was definitely the more attractive one. Roxy could sense enormous strength rolling off of him but she could also sense an underlying vulnerability.

Pick me.

His gaze moved to Lily who was hugging her legs. *No! Not her. I can see that you want me.* The moment the thought entered her mind, she struggled to shake it. The green-eyed, intense one wanted her. She had seen it burning in those amazing eyes of his, yet he seemed to be ignoring it. Then again, she was probably just reading too much into it.

He shrugged. "Whatever! A female is a female." It was an asshole thing to say. Once again though, she couldn't help but sense a tiredness . . . no it went beyond tired . . . a weariness and still that vulnerability.

The amethyst-eyed guy smiled broadly, it made him even more handsome. His good looks had no effect on her. She felt infinitely drawn to the other one. Why though? It was just like he had stated, it shouldn't matter either way. They didn't know one another at all. Her heart was beating wildly and she still struggled to take her eyes off of him. Green Eyes might be acting indifferent but he wanted her. She knew it. Moreover, she felt a strange connection to him even if they had never met before.

On some fundamental level, maybe this was her soul telling her that the green-eyed guy was the one for her. Call it a gut feeling, call it a sixth sense. The more she thought about it, the more she felt that it was true.

The amethyst-eyed shifter advanced on her while the other one remained motionless. His muscles bunched and his jaw tightened. It was like he didn't really want his buddy to claim her. Maybe he felt it too. No, she was sure he felt it too when his stunning green eyes drifted over to her once again. Something flared in their depths. Something that she couldn't quite decipher, she only knew that she didn't want Amethyst Eyes to claim her. Then again, maybe it was just wishful thinking on her part.

"You females were briefed." It was only when the amethyst-eyed one spoke that she realized how close he was to her. Only a few feet separated them. Thankfully he stopped moving. "I'm going to claim you now, please do not be concerned. I will hold you and kiss you. The more of my scent I can get on you, the better." He grinned and out popped a couple of dimples. He sure was a charmer. Totally not for her. Ben had been a charmer, full of stories . . . full of shit more like since nothing ever panned out. All those promises had amounted to exactly nothing. Eight lost years, maybe, but that was it.

"I don't think—" She began but was cut short.

"I'm sorry, female, but there's no time for small talk. A group of males is close behind us; they will be here soon. There is plenty of time for talking later. Then again"—he chuckled—"maybe not."

Oh shit! Was he referring to sex? She sure as hell hoped not. It felt like her insides were in knots. Her eyes flashed back to the other guy who still stood riveted to the spot. Their gazes locked and his jaw tensed. His whole frame turned rigid. If she thought that every muscle was ripped before she was wrong. They all came out to play right now. Oh lord! Her mouth turned dry.

The other guy gripped her by the waist and pulled her against him. Roxy gasped. *What the hell!* She tried to break free but the big oaf wouldn't let her go. "Hey! No!"

Roxy wasn't afraid but she was pissed. Sure they had signed up for being hunted and to get to know the dragon shifters but surely they had some say in who they ended up with.

Pretty boy over here didn't seem to think so. His gaze was zeroed in on her lips. He wasn't listening to her protests. He was closing the distance between them and fast.

"No!" She groaned, squirming some more but he didn't slow his roll.

It wasn't her fault he was deaf.

It was an accident.

A total mistake.

It just kind of happened on its own. It was like her leg acted before her brain could intervene. One second she was trying to get free and the next she nailed pretty boy square in the nuts with her knee, which shot up without her consent. It served him right. She wasn't sorry.

His eyes widened with surprise before clenching shut. His face reddened and turned sweaty in an instant. A loud, drawn-out moan was pulled from him as he hunched over. The poor guy even fell to one knee.

Roxy felt guilty for a second or two before reminding

herself that it was his own fault for not listening. "Oh God!" she whimpered. "I'm sorry, but you should listen when a girl says no," she added, before locking eyes with her shifter. Thankfully, he was still standing in the same spot. His mouth hung open in a gape. It was like he couldn't believe that a girl could take down a big shifter.

Well, get with the program, she thought to herself. Just because we're human and much weaker doesn't make us completely useless. Before she could talk herself out of it, or over think it, Roxy ran to the astonished looking warrior. She launched herself at him and luckily, he caught her.

She refused to believe that he did it as a reaction but liked rather to think that he caught her because he wanted her. Then she threw her arms around his neck and wrapped her legs around his waist. Shit but he was well-muscled and his skin was soft. Oh hell, but his eyes were even more beautiful up close. There were golden flecks around his irises.

He didn't exactly hug her but neither did he toss her away.

He looked bewildered, frozen in place. His mouth still hung open, a condition she decided to take advantage of. Roxy cocked her head to the side and closed her mouth over his.

Oh heavenly father, thank you. Oh sweet, sweet bliss. His lips were soft, his mouth hot. Roxy crossed her legs behind his back and tightened her arms around his neck. It was a good thing she did because he let her go on another one of those deep growls. His chest vibrated against hers. It vibrated against her nipples which turned to little pebbles, and against her clit which was somewhere in the vicinity of his rock hard abs. The little bud of nerves woke up immediately. Instantly on full alert. She felt a zing between her legs. It was most likely a simple case of not having touched a man for so long, but then again, it could be more.

Roxy groaned and so did the shifter.

CHAPTER 7

The female was more exquisite up close. Dark tendrils of thick hair fell about her face. Her ponytail barely contained the rest. It fell down her back in a thick cascade. Her eyes were soft blue, like the sky on a crisp winter's morning or freshly melted snow as it trickled down a winding, pebbled brook.

Blaze gave his head a shake. He needed to get his mind out of the gutter.

"I'll take the dark one," Thunder announced.

It didn't matter that he'd told the air king moments earlier that he could choose whichever female he wanted. Blaze bristled anyway. Every hackle went up. He felt his scales rub just beneath his skin. His gums ached where his fangs pushed against them. Blaze couldn't help the growl that was torn from him.

The other male looked pained for a split second and then Thunder lowered his head a fraction as a sign of submission. Good!

Then the air king's gaze locked with Blaze's. "What? You said you didn't care either way." There was a slight growl to the male's voice. "It's up to you, just choose quickly, the others will be here soon."

Blaze felt a snarl build inside him but managed to stop it before it erupted. Only because the other male was right. He had yet to take his eyes off the delectable female before him. Fuck! If only this was a rutting expedition, he would take her in a heartbeat. His loins tightened at the prospect. Unfortunately, this was an event designed to find a mate and he knew all too well that attraction between two people could complicate things and in a big way. It was a complication he didn't need or want.

The female was eyeballing him like there was no tomorrow. If eyes could fuck, he'd be on his third orgasm.

No way.

This female was not for him.

Blaze forced his gaze from the dark-haired beauty and took in the human sitting on the ground at her feet. Her eyes were darker blue, her hair light-colored, it was tinged with red. She was much smaller and not nearly as curvaceous. She was pretty but didn't put fire in his veins like the other one. She would do just fine.

He shrugged. "Whatever! A female is a female." Blaze tried to sound indifferent and was surprised to find that he pulled it off.

Thunder gave him a shit-eating grin. The male looked pleased and Blaze had to clench his fists to stop himself from removing a few of the air king's teeth. He had to remind himself that the male had done nothing wrong.

Thunder moved towards the human, wasting no time.

Blaze couldn't help but to lock eyes with the dark-haired female. He was surprised to find that her gaze was still trained on him and not on Thunder as he had expected. It almost felt like she was pleading for him to rescue her, to come for her, to do something. That couldn't be it. Or could it?

One thing was for sure, she didn't look happy.

"You females were briefed," Thunder said. The female's eyes snapped to the other male's, they widened in shock and possibly . . . fear. Surely not. These females were willing. They hadn't been abducted like the previous hunt. Was Blaze reading too much into this? Most likely. "I'm going to claim you now, please do not be concerned, I will hold you and kiss you. The more of my scent I can get on you, the better," the asshole king grinned and the female frowned.

Fuck but did his scales grind inside him! Blaze wanted nothing more than to go over there and take the human for himself.

No!

It was irrational thinking and that very thing was what had gotten him into trouble in the past. This mating would be a business transaction and nothing more.

"I don't think—" The human started to talk but the dickhead air king cut her off.

"I'm sorry, female, but there's no time for chit chat. A group of males is close behind us, they will be here soon. There is plenty of time for talking later. Then again—" he chuckled, "—maybe not."

The fucker had no finesse. None whatsoever. From this angle, Blaze could only see Thunder's back. He wouldn't be surprised if the male had winked suggestively at the human as he said that line. Didn't he notice her discomfort?

Then again, this was the hunt and Thunder was right when he had mentioned the group of males closing in. They couldn't be more than a minute behind them. Blaze needed to move himself, needed to get his ass over to the other human. Needed to claim her and right now. The thought left him cold. Good! It meant that she was perfect.

That might be the case but he couldn't take his eyes off the luscious one. The one that Thunder was about to make his. Everything in him hardened. Adrenaline coursed through his veins. The need to act rushed through him. Blaze clenched his teeth and clenched his fists to stop himself from moving forward and putting a stop to what Thunder was about to do.

"Hey! No!" the female yelled, as Thunder gripped her waist.

Thunder didn't seem to notice or maybe the male didn't care, because his hands tightened on the human's hips and he leaned forward, clearly intent on following through on his kissing threat.

Leave it alone, Blaze. Just leave it the hell alone. This female was not for him. The sooner Thunder claimed her, the better. Why was he torturing himself by watching it go down?

He had to suppress a growl when she groaned out the word 'no.' The female had her hands locked around Thunder's wrists and was squirming, trying to free herself. What was wrong? Females loved the air king. They considered him to be very good-looking. Why was she fighting him so much?

Oblivious to her turmoil, Thunder closed the remaining distance, but just as his lips were about to lock with hers, the human kneed him right between the legs. Bulls-fucking-eye. There was a loud thud as her leg connected with the most sensitive parts of the air king's body. Blaze could almost feel the other male's pain as Thunder sucked in a ragged breath.

There was a second or two where time seemed to freeze and then Thunder let out a loud, drawn-out moan. He hunched over, cupping his junk with one hand. The pain the poor male must be feeling. It had to be agony. Thunder collapsed onto one knee. Blaze couldn't believe that the tiny human had managed to bring a royal dragon shifter to his knees. Then again, whether human or another species, balls were balls. The pain was the same.

The female's eyes widened for a few seconds. "Oh God!" she whimpered. "I'm sorry." Then she locked eyes with Blaze and the look of remorse evaporated, it was replaced with . . . determination.

What the hell was she up to?

Part of him felt bad for Thunder, though another bigger part of him agreed with the human. The male should've listened. He should have given her a chance to talk.

Hang on just a minute. The human was making her way to him—although making her way was not the right term, she was jogging. Then she gripped his shoulders and jumped right into his arms. He caught her. It was an accident. When someone jumped into a person's arms, the natural reaction was to catch them.

Blaze needed to let her go now. He really did, but his arms stayed around her body. One hooked under her ass and another across her back.

The female looked him deep in the eyes. Her pupils dilated. *Oh no! No!*

Her arms snaked around his neck and her lush thighs wrapped around his hips. Her lips, lush and soft, closed over his.

Motherfucker!

She tasted of everything he had been avoiding. Of everything he needed to stay the hell away from. She tasted far too fucking good for his own sanity. Her scent was of fresh-cut grass and spring mornings, candied apples freshly made with a hint of baked cookies. Wholesome and clean, yet sexy as fuck, a toxic combination. At least, to him it was. This female was no good. She wasn't for him. No fucking way.

His cock had decided otherwise. It wanted into the cookie jar. There was a certain candied apple it wanted him to eat. It wanted that sweet wholesome mouth to scream his name. What the hell was he thinking? He wasn't, at least not with the head that was on his shoulders. Irritation coursed through him and he growled. The little minx ate up the sound with her hungry little mouth, which continued to devour his.

No fucking way. Her full breasts were mashed up against him. The moment the growl had left his throat, her nipples tightened. Her arms tightened and she locked her ankles behind him, rubbing her sex against his abdomen. The scent of her arousal hit him hard and fast. His dick twitched. His whole body prepared to rut. His skin grew tight, his cock hardened up some more.

Blaze didn't need this kind of shit in his life. His body didn't seem to be listening to him though. He was a male in his prime, dammit, no longer a teenager ruled by his dick. Blaze tore his hands from her. Unfortunately, she clung to him. Not that he would've let her fall but he needed to get her off of him. He needed to tell his mouth to stop kissing her back.

When the female groaned, it solicited a matching groan from him. Blaze hadn't had sex in forever so when she sucked on his lower lip and stuck her tongue in his mouth, it was all he could do to stop himself from shoving her up against a nearby tree and grinding his engorged member against her pussy. He could scent that she was wet. Dripping fucking wet.

Enough!

He stepped back and pulled her off of him, setting her on her feet. Using a hand on her hip, he spun her around so that her back was to him. This needed to stop. The human glanced at him from over her shoulder, Blaze couldn't help but to notice how swollen her lips were, they glistened. Her eyes were glazed over, her lids heavy and at half-mast.

It doesn't matter.

Her chest heaved and oh what a chest it was.

Stop!

Blaze averted his gaze, seeking the air king. The male was no longer in his kneeling position. He was sitting in front of the other human. His face was still shiny with sweat and his eyes still held a pinched look but otherwise he looked fine.

With horror, Blaze could see that the male intended to claim the other female.

"What are you doing?" he growled. "I thought you wanted this one."

The dark-haired female shook her head and gave a disapproving growl before giving him a dirty look over her shoulder. The look was a mixture between *what the fuck* and *fuck you, you asshole.*

Thunder chuckled. "No thanks. The human has clearly decided which male she would prefer. I think I kind of like this one." He winked at the other human. "I like her a whole damn lot."

"You wanted this one though," Blaze gestured towards the human in front of him. His argument sounded thin, even to his own ears. What else was he supposed to do, insist that Thunder take her when she clearly didn't want the male back?

What the fuck was he supposed to do with the female?

"You said that you didn't mind either way. Take that one. Besides, our time is up." Thunder gave another chuckle. He turned his attention to the female on the ground. "I'm going to kiss you now, do not be alarmed and please whatever you do, do not kick me in the nuts."

"I won't," the female smiled at Thunder just before he proceeded to tongue-fuck the hell out of her.

That's when Blaze heard them, the group of males that were tracking behind. Higher-ranking warriors. If he ran now, he would catch the female up ahead before any of them. He didn't have to settle for this one. The most attractive of the bunch. The most dangerous.

The female turned, staring daggers at him. Then she did something strange, she sniffed at her armpits. "Do I smell?" She ran a hand over the top of her head. "Or did I suddenly sprout horns? Maybe I'm just not your type? Is that it?"

Shit, from the noises in the undergrowth, the males were drawing closer, they were almost upon them.

If he left now, he could still beat them to the third human. The only problem was that the thought of any of the non-royals taking this female irked him. No, more than just irked him, it pissed him the hell off. He'd experienced love before and knew it wasn't for him. Blaze was sure that he could keep that part of himself locked up tight.

Maybe it wasn't such a bad thing that he would be compatible with his future mate. Both good sex and a business relationship, it was possible.

"The others will be here soon," he said. The human seemed unaware of the approaching males.

She gasped as she heard the noises and registered what he'd just said, her luscious mouth fell open.

"Do not say anything, unless you wish for one of them to have you." He put an arm around the female and drew her towards him.

She instantly stiffened and tried to pull away.

"I find you highly attractive. I believe that we will be compatible." Blaze would be honest with his future bride.

Her eyes narrowed and she frowned. "Why did—"

"We will talk more about it later. Do you wish to explore a possible mating or would you prefer it if one of the others claimed you?"

"I know what I would prefer," Lava said. Their time was up, a group of about eight males congregated around them. Their attention was fixed on the female at his side. Thunder was still having an epic make-out session with his female so none of the males were interested in pursuing that avenue. The male sniffed and frowned deeply.

Yes, fucker, that's my scent all over her.

"The female is mine," Blaze growled. He pulled her even closer still, turning her so that her chest flattened against him. *Fuck, but she felt good.*

Lava was the most senior of the males, most of whom, he noted with pride, were fire dragons. "I think the female can speak for herself."

Blaze felt her shiver in his arms but then she stood taller, looking back over her shoulder so that she could look Lava in the eyes. "He claimed me. I think I'll go with him . . . thanks."

"More like the female claimed you," Thunder chuckled, lifting his female into his arms. "Anyone care to challenge me for my human?"

"A female can't claim a male. Maybe she's still up for grabs after all," Lava put his beady eyes back on the human female in his arms.

Blaze couldn't help but smile even though he wasn't feeling particularly amused right now. "Say the word, fucker, and I'll smear you all over this forest."

The female shivered again but she curled her hand around his bicep and pushed herself more firmly against him.

"That goes for all of you," Blaze added, allowing his gaze to drift across the group of males. He'd make sure that the female was at a safe distance and take the fuckers out.

Sensing defeat, two of the group broke away sprinting towards the third and final female.

Lava snarled like a child who had been denied his favorite toy and then followed closely on their heels. The others dashed away as well, and within seconds it was just the four of them and the sounds of the forest. The female pushed her hands against his chest and gave a shove. It seemed she hadn't forgiven him for trying to pawn her off on Thunder. Blaze released her.

"Well, damn," Thunder announced, still carrying the female in his arms. "I had hoped for more of a show."

"Sorry to disappoint, asshole," Blaze muttered the expletive.

Thunder walked over. His female looked comfortable, snuggled up against the male's chest. Thunder smiled. "We can travel together, at least for part of the journey."

Blaze shrugged. It didn't matter either way. "Yeah, why not." He bent over to pick up the human beside him but she took a step back and raised her eyebrows. The look quickly morphed into one of those scathing looks she could do so well.

"Not so fast. Although I agree with you, he is a bit of an asshole," the female pointed at Thunder, who grinned in response. "I think if there was an asshole award going around here, you would be the one to win it."

What the hell! What was she on about?

"I can see by the look on your face that you have no idea why I said that. Typical!" She shook her head. "Did no one ever tell you when a woman practically throws herself at you, it's impolite to try and hand her over to someone else?" She cocked her head, putting her hands on her hips and raised her eyebrows some more.

His dick was loving her fiery attitude. There was a familiar tightening between his legs. *Not now! Not fucking now!* It didn't help that he hadn't had sex in the longest time. "I'm sorry. I panicked," he scrubbed a hand over his face.

Thunder burst out laughing. "Okay, so maybe a show isn't completely out of the question after all." He looked down at the female in his arms. "It's a pity we don't have any popcorn. That's what you humans like to eat during a show is it not?"

The female nodded and giggled. "I guess." Her voice sounded breathless. She was totally falling for Thunder's bullshit.

"Can you give us some privacy?" Blaze gritted his teeth.

"What, and miss all the fun?" Thunder grinned.

Fucker! His scales rubbed like mad. "Now," Blaze growled.

Thankfully the male nodded. "Don't get your scaly tail in a knot. My female and I will be over there getting to know each other better. What's your name, sweets?"

"Lily," the female smiled up at him. She didn't seem to care in the least that she wasn't Thunder's first choice.

His human felt very differently.

"Explain the whole 'I panicked thing.' I find it hard to believe." Her stunning blue eyes narrowed on his. "Why did you act like I have the plague? Are you sure I don't smell?" She sniffed at her armpits again.

"Stop doing that!" Blaze took a few steps away from her before spinning back to face her. "You smell fucking great," his voice turned husky and blood congregated south as he was reminded of how sweet her scent was while she had been momentarily aroused.

She frowned. "What then? This is confusing." She shook her head.

"The problem is that I'm too attracted to you."

"That doesn't make any sense."

"You're right," he said. "I've since decided that it's a

good thing if we are to be mated."

"Mated? That's a very big maybe," she mumbled. "I don't even know if I like you yet."

"We do need to get along," he nodded.

The female smiled. "Yeah, at the very least."

"Look," he huffed out a breath. "We got off to a bad start. I'm very attracted to you. I am sure that we will be compatible."

"Compatible?" Her cheeks turned pink and her eyes darted to the floor.

"Yeah, the fucking will be really good," he added, just in case she didn't fully understand what compatible meant.

She swallowed hard and made a strange noise in the back of her throat. "When Julie said you guys were open about sex she wasn't messing around."

"We are open about sex. We're open about everything."

Her stunning eyes caught his once again. Her cheeks were still flushed. "That's a good thing. Okay, so you panicked because you were attracted to me but have since decided that it is a good thing. It still really doesn't make sense."

"A major attraction between people can complicate things," he said, choosing his words carefully. Blaze didn't want to piss her off again.

She frowned. "In what way? Being attracted to your partner is a good thing, isn't it?"

"Yeah, it is." *Maybe!* He sure as hell hoped so. There was no way he was falling for this female or any other for that matter. "Let's just get to know each other a bit better." He shrugged. "I should never have tried to hand you over to Thunder."

She pursed her lips. "It wasn't very nice."

"I'm sorry," he quickly added. *Fuck!* He'd forgotten how much work this was. "Please, can we start over? Let's test compatibility and get to know each other. We might not even be suitable as mates."

The female pondered his words for a time. "Mister Negativity. Don't you mean get to know each other and then test . . . you know . . . if . . . you know . . . ?"

Blaze shook his head.

CHAPTER 8

H oly hell!
Crap sticks!

He wanted to have sex with her and he didn't even know her name. "I'm Roxanne," she blurted. "My friends call me Roxy. I suppose you can call me Roxy. No, you should definitely call me Roxy." It was her turn to panic, as in seriously panic, as in heart racing and blood pumping, serious as shit panic. "I work in a bakery. My best friend owns said bakery. It's called Sweet Treats. Oh my God, you want to have sex." The crazy thing was, she felt excited at the prospect. What red-blooded woman wouldn't be? The guy in front of her was a dreamboat. A tall drink of delicious with a side order of muscles. His abs seemed to go on forever and he had that whole 'v' thing going on just above his pants. Don't even talk about those pecs or how thick his biceps were. Those forearms were a thing of beauty as well. His hands, and my God his hands. She could only imagine what he could get up to with those.

The shifter gave a single bark-like laugh. Oh shit, her eyes may or may not have been roaming freely across his body. When she looked back up, he was smiling. Well sort of smiling. Hello, hottie! Why did he have to look even better smiling? Why, oh why? "My name is Blaze."

Even his name was freaking hot. For a second there, Roxy felt like fanning herself.

"To answer your question, yes, I wish to have sex with you but not right now. We have a long journey ahead of us. It will take us most of the night to get back to the fire kingdom."

"Oh!" She felt dumb. So very, very stupid. "Of course. I didn't mean right now. I mean, I don't even know you and well, I don't just have sex with guys I've just met. It's been so long since I had any . . . sex that is." Why the hell did she say that?

"Why not?" Blaze asked. "You are a highly attractive female."

"Sure, I could get sex. Any time I wanted. That's all the guys on the dating websites want, but I'm a relationship kind of a person. That's why it's probably better that we get to know each other first, if that's okay with you. Just to be sure that we like each other and get along and . . . you know . . ."

The big shifter frowned. "If you haven't had sex in a very long time, it would be better to ease some of the tension you're feeling. It will make the getting to know each other part easier, but if you wish to wait, I'm okay with that also. Let's not over-complicate things."

What did that even mean? No over-complicating things. Then again, complications within a relationship were bad. It seemed that he'd left the ball in her court. She could live with that.

Roxy finally nodded. "We'd better get going then."

They walked in the direction that the other big shifter and Lily had taken. It didn't take them long to catch up. Oh God! The big guy had Lily pushed up against a tree. They were seriously making out. The shifter was dry humping her and it sounded like Lily was well on her way to . . . well, to having a party in her pants . . . That, and he had his hands up her top, as in both hands; he was squeezing her boobs in tandem. These two hadn't wasted any time.

"Stop mauling that female," Blaze growled.

"My name is Lily," she said, as the shifter came up for air. She was panting heavily as well.

"I'm Blaze," he introduced himself to Lily. Then he glanced down at Roxy. He was huge. Roxy was average height for a human, which meant that she barely made it halfway up his chest. "That's Thunder." Blaze pointed at the Casanova shifter. "He's king of the air kingdom."

"Oh my God!" Lily shrieked. "I knew you were royalty but you're the king of the whole kingdom."

"You better believe it, sweetness," Thunder winked at her. She shrieked again as he lifted her into his arms. "Lily and I had a discussion."

"I could see that," Blaze gave a half smile.

Thunder grinned. "She's tired and hungry. They gave the humans shitty tasting protein bars for the hunt instead of any real food." The shifter king pulled a face. "We're going to walk until nightfall and then set up camp, closer to the river. My female wants some roast meat. You're welcome to join the party."

"I don't know," Blaze said. "I'd like to get back."

Thunder was right, although the protein bars hit the spot, they weren't very appealing. The thought of sinking her teeth into freshly barbecued meat, dripping with fat, made Roxy's stomach growl.

The air king laughed. "It looks like your female likes the idea." Oh shit! Had he heard that from way over there? Of course he had. The guy was a shifter.

Blaze turned to her. "Do you want to camp out with them?" He didn't look happy about it.

The thing was, the thought of being alone with him so soon nerve-wracked her a little bit. On the other hand, sleeping out in the wild wasn't all that appealing either. At least they wouldn't be alone. Roxy had already thrown herself at him once before and with all this talk of sex and him wearing those leave nothing to the imagination pants—not to mention her very long, extended dry spell—had left her feeling rather horny. No! Alone time with Mr. Brooding & Delicious-piece-of-ass-shifter was not a good idea right now.

"I'd like to camp, if that's okay with you? I'm hungry and tired. I'll never be able to walk all night."

Blaze frowned, those beautiful green eyes of his bore into hers. "I would never expect you to walk. I'd carry you."

She snorted out a laugh. "What? The entire way? Don't

be crazy."

Blaze remained perfectly serious. "I'm not a human. I'm a dragon shifter and a fire breather at that. I can carry you to the other side of the continent with one hand tied behind my back and still not break a sweat."

"You don't have much of an ego, do you?" The words just came out.

"This has nothing to do with ego." Deadpan.

"Oh! Okay." Maybe he could carry her. "If you say so."

"I do." It came out growly. "I'm carrying you."

"Bossy as well I see. Do you plan on telling me what to do all the time?" Roxy was being a little hard on the big shifter but this relationship was not going to work if she just let him walk all over her and make all the decisions. It would be like being with her ex all over again and that hadn't ended well at all.

"I'm not bossy." Blaze looked put out.

"You pretty much are," Thunder chimed in.

"Who asked you?"

Thunder held Lily in one arm—okay so maybe shifters were really strong, not that Lily was big or anything—he raised his free arm as a sign of apology. "Forget I said anything."

Blaze sighed loudly. "Please, let me carry you. I assure you that I can handle it. We need to make ground before nightfall. Unless you feel you can keep up."

"Now, that wasn't so hard was it?" Roxy knew that she was busting his chops but at the same time they hardly knew each other. She didn't want him to think that he could order her around and that she'd be fine with it.

Blaze rolled his eyes. So far, this was going along swimmingly. As in not so much. She had thrown herself at him. She wasn't so sure she bought his whole I find you highly attractive thing, or his whole I panicked story. Relationships were all about chemistry, at least they were in the beginning. Had he really planned on picking someone he didn't have those kinds of feelings for? Why would he do a crazy thing like that?

She'd have to wait and see.

Lily slumped back against the tree trunk; she gave a loud moan and patted her belly. "That was the best steak I've ever had in my whole entire life."

Roxy made a sound of agreement and rubbed her own distended belly. "I couldn't eat another bite even if I wanted to." They had all eaten like there was no tomorrow.

The whole set-up was rustic. They had grilled chunks of meat on long pieces of stick and then proceeded to eat their dinner right off the makeshift skewers. It was the best thing she had tasted in the longest time.

"I'll hunt for you anytime, sweets," Thunder pulled Lily against him. Roxy was still jealous at how well the two of them were getting along. They seemed completely relaxed in one another's company, like they'd been dating for a long time.

Lily made a disgusted noise. "Hunted? As in you butchered an innocent animal?" She crinkled her nose in clear disgust.

Thunder frowned. "Yes. How did you think we got the meat?"

"It's not like we have a store or a butcher shop around here," Blaze added.

"Eeeeew!" Lily pulled a face. "What did I just eat anyway? I thought it was beef."

Thunder laughed. "Beef? No damned way. That was cane rat. I bet you never knew that rodent tasted so good?"

Lily slapped a hand over her mouth and made a choking, gagging noise. Her eyes turned watery and she looked like she was going to barf any second.

"I'm only joking, sweets," Thunder laughed. "You should see your face right now."

"That's not funny," Lily mock punched his arm. Her face looked more pale than usual.

"Those were a couple of deer steaks." Roxy could hear that Blaze was smiling but, when she glanced in his direction, the smile turned to a frown. He turned serious the moment she laid eyes on him. He even scooted a little bit away from her. What the hell? She had to stop herself from giving her pits another whiff. She may have been walking half the day in the blazing sun but her antiperspirant had done its job. At least, she hoped it had. A person couldn't always smell BO on themselves.

"So, what did you think? Did you enjoy the meal?" He looked unsure of himself.

"It was really good." Her hand was still pressed against her belly. "I love deer steaks."

"Good." He paused. "I take it you don't mind that we tracked down a deer and killed it for your supper?" It felt like he was testing her, but at the same time, it also felt like he cared about her opinion. Maybe she didn't smell after all.

Roxy shook her head. "No. My father used to hunt sometimes back in the day. We had our fair share of deer steaks, not to mention rabbits, grouse and whatever else he could rustle up."

"So he doesn't hunt anymore?" Blaze asked, there was genuine interest reflected in his eyes.

"My dad died while I was still in high school. Heart attack."

"I'm sorry. That's shitty," Blaze frowned.

"Yeah, it was. I still miss him. He wasn't there when I graduated, he won't be there when I walk down the aisle . . ." What was she saying? It seemed like her mouth wouldn't shut it. "Or when I have babies, but hey . . ." Roxy shrugged. "I've come to terms with it."

They sat in silence for about half a minute.

"What's your air kingdom like?" Lily changed the subject, Roxy was grateful. Talking about her dad made her feel a bit sad and nostalgic. Especially when so many things were up in the air about her life right now. She was sitting in the middle of nowhere with a couple of shifters for crud's sake.

"My kingdom is amazing." The flames illuminated Thunder's face. The guy looked like he was beaming. "We live on the highest peak and have the best views."

"What about your lair? Is it as big and beautiful as the fire castle?" Lily's eyes were wide and bright. She seemed genuinely excited. Then she turned to face Roxy. "Lair is another name for castle, in case you didn't know."

Roxy nodded.

"Not as big, no. Nearly though," he winked at Lily. "As rulers of the four kingdoms, fire has the biggest lair." Thunder shrugged, there was a smirk on his face. "My pad is way better though. Blaze might live in a bigger castle but I'm bigger where it counts."

Lily covered her mouth with one hand and giggled. Roxy had to suppress a gasp.

Blaze chuckled and shook his head. "You wish, fucktard."

Thunder laughed. "I don't have to wish, I know. What is a fucktard anyway? You've spent way too much time with humans, you sometimes even sound like one of them."

That shut Blaze right down. His jaw tightened and his eyes hardened up. It went from fun and lighthearted to *watch out a hurricane is coming* and in under three seconds.

By the look on Thunder's face, he could tell that he'd said the wrong thing because he put up both hands. "Forget I said anything. I didn't mean anything by that."

Blaze didn't say anything, he kept his intense gaze on Thunder. Roxy got the distinct impression that if they weren't there, he'd be beating the air king right about now.

"Come on, sweets," Thunder tightened his arm around Lily. "Let's give these two some space."

"Um . . . I'm cold. Maybe it would be better if we stayed by the fire."

Thunder's gaze turned molten. Roxy felt like she was intruding, so she looked away. Blaze was looking at her but he still looked angry so she quickly faced the other way. Was he still angry with Thunder or was it something she had done? It seemed that Blaze was a complicated guy.

"I'll keep you warm, honeybuns . . . Don't you worry about that." The big oaf was trying to whisper into Lily's ear but his voice was so deep and so loud that everyone could hear.

Lily sighed. "If you think it'll work."

"Oh, it'll work all right."

Blaze snorted but didn't say anything. Oh shit! Were these two about to disappear in order to have sex? Probably. No, definitely, judging from the massive erection in Thunder's pants. She'd purposefully chosen the camping option so that she wouldn't have to be alone with Blaze too soon. This was awkward. She realized that her focus was still on Thunder's erection even though she wasn't really looking at it.

Roxy quickly looked away, her eyes moving automatically to Blaze's crotch. There was nothing happening there.

Blaze cleared his throat.

Oh damn! Busted! She pretended to look past him into the darkness beyond. Maybe he hadn't noticed the staring.

When she finally looked him in the eyes, his mouth did this twitch thing like he was trying to suppress a smile. She was so busted. This was so embarrassing.

"So," she blurted, her voice a little high-pitched. "You're royalty; you have a golden tattoo."

"It's not a tattoo, it's a marking." He rubbed his hand over the golden swirls on his amazing chest. His lick-worthy chest.

Her eyes tracked the movement for a few seconds before she quickly looked away. Shit! He must think that she was some desperate hussy. She couldn't stop ogling him. "How many princes are there in the fire kingdom?" She needed to try and make some conversation. There was this weird vibe between the two of them. It certainly wasn't relaxed and carefree like Thunder and Lily. Far from it.

Blaze almost smiled. "I have two brothers and a sister."

"You're lucky, I'm an only child. There were complications when I was born. It's a condition called *placenta previa*. I almost died, my mom almost died as well. She was bleeding out so they had to remove her uterus."

His eyes widened and he looked distinctly uncomfortable.

"Let me guess, too much information? Sorry, I have this bad habit of over-sharing and talking too much when I'm nervous."

"There is no need for you to be nervous. Not with me." His eyes looked dark in the firelight. They were so intense, especially when focused solely on her.

She nodded. "Okay. I'll try and relax. This is just, so different."

Blaze licked his lower lip. Even such a simple thing was ridiculously sexy on him. "We'll either be compatible or we won't." His voice was deep and husky, like he was thinking about having sex with her right then. "Either we'll get along or we won't. It's really quite simple, Roxy."

Holy shit, hearing him say her name was just about the sexiest thing she ever heard in her whole entire life. Maybe he was right, maybe having an over-the-top attraction for another person wasn't such a great idea.

She needed to change the subject and right now. "One of your brothers is Coal right? Julie mentioned that she's mated to him."

Blaze nodded. "Yup, and then there's Inferno and my sister Ruby."

Roxy tucked her hands between her thighs to try and get them warm. The fire had died down. Blaze must have noticed because he leaned forward and threw a couple of logs onto the dying flames. A few sparks flew and there was a cracking noise as the new wood began to kindle. "Inferno," Roxy murmured, almost to herself. "I'll have to try and remember that. You'll need to point him out to me so that I don't embarrass myself."

"Ummmm . . . okay . . . sure." Blaze frowned deeply.

"Does the king wear a crown or something? Will I need to curtsy to him?"

Blaze chuckled.

"What's so funny? I don't want to look like an idiot or anything in front of the king."

Blaze all-out laughed, a ton of the tension he'd been

carrying seemed to dissipate, he even leaned back onto his elbows.

Oh god but his abs were a thing of pure beauty. Her mouth actually watered for a taste. Not going there. She quickly looked into the flickering, lashing flames.

"You did just fine." He finally murmured, in that deep baritone he was so good at.

"What?" Roxy frowned, not sure what he was talking about.

"Introducing yourself to the king, that is. You did just fine."

"I don't understand what you're talking about." She felt her frown deepen.

"I wouldn't have minded a curtsy but jumping into my arms and sticking your tongue in my mouth was good too," Blaze winked at her.

Oh shit! It finally dawned on her what he was saying. Blaze was the king. Blaze was the freakin' king. The guy in charge. The head honcho. The freaking king of all the dragons.

Roxy felt her mouth drop open. "Oh . . . oh. . . . Um . . . right . . . I didn't know." She shook her head so hard that her ponytail bounced around. "I'm okay with you being the king." Her voice had that high pitch to it. Definitely a tad panicky. "Um . . . not that it matters to me either way. It doesn't. I mean it's great and everything but it's . . ."

Blaze gave another chuckle. "Relax. It's not a big deal."

"Well it kind of is. Am I supposed to curtsy to you or treat you differently or . . . I mean, this isn't going to work for me if that's the case. I'm looking for a partnership, equal ground, is that going to be a problem?"

Blaze turned serious and shook his head. "No, as my mate you would be the queen and a partner in all aspects of the word. Don't treat me differently. I like how you stand up to me."

"Well, no wonder you're so bossy and so arrogant." Dammit! She hadn't just said that, out loud. Had she?

Blaze cracked up laughing. He raked a hand through his hair. "I guess I'm used to getting my way."

I'll bet. She managed to keep it to herself. Roxy nodded.

"Don't treat me any differently now that you know. I would prefer to keep things open and honest and as uncomplicated as possible."

"That would work for me. Besides, I tend to say things before thinking them through anyway."

"Mmmm . . ." Blaze gave his lower lip a lick. *Why did he keep doing that?* "I had noticed."

"It's got me into trouble over the years."

"I'll bet." At long last the tension between them seemed to ease up.

"So what's it like being the king?"

"It's hard work. It often means putting my own personal wishes to the side. I always need to put my people first. So being the one in charge is not always easy."

"Yeah, I'm sure . . ." A loud moan punctured through the darkness.

"What the hell?" Roxy jumped to her feet.

There was another loud moan. Her heart rate jumped

up. "That sounded like Lily. She sounds like she's in pain." Her own voice was laced with panic and concern.

Without really giving it any thought she turned to face the area where the noise had come from and was just about to take off in that direction when Blaze grabbed her ankle. "She's not in any pain."

"Yes, she is. Didn't you hear . . ." Roxy felt her cheeks get super-hot. "Seriously? They're doing the wild monkey dance? Is that what you're telling me?"

Blaze let go of her ankle and gave a short chuckle. "Yup."

There were a couple of louder drawn-out moans. "Good god, yes!" The other woman shouted. Right! She felt like a total doofus. They were definitely doing the two-backed rodeo.

Lily moaned . . . again.

Roxy's clit woke up. Okay, maybe it stood to attention. She'd never heard other people having sex before. "So rude," she muttered. She didn't know what was worse, that they were doing it within earshot of other people or that Roxy was getting oddly turned on by listening to them go at it. "They must know that we can hear them." Roxy sat back down. She grabbed ahold of her thighs and pulled them to her body.

The groans had turned into high pitched cries. Why the hell was her body reacting? This was beyond embarrassing.

"I think they're beyond caring and, for the record, they're not having sex."

"It sure as hell sounds like it. How would you know anyway?" She glanced at Blaze.

"Supersonic hearing," he pointed to one of his ears.

"What is he doing to her then?" She held up her hand. "Never mind." Why did she have to ask such a stupid ass question? Lily made this loud keening noise that had orgasm written all over it. The noise went on for what felt like an age. No way in hell could a pants party last that long. She had to be faking. It didn't sound fake though. At long damn last, there was silence.

"Thank god," Roxy muttered. Her panties felt damp and she squirmed trying to stop the ache inside her. Sex with her ex had always been good, well mostly. There was the odd occasion when he got too excited, but for the most part it was good. They'd had a healthy sex life right up until they had broken up. It was one of the things Roxy missed. She didn't miss Ben, she missed orgasms with another person.

Blaze threw a few more logs on the fire. That pissed, tense look was back. "We should get some shuteye. Tomorrow is going to be a long day."

Much to her dismay, Roxy's clit was throbbing. His words disappointed her. Not that she wanted to do anything about her wet panties and achy nub, but a little make-out session would've been nice. It wasn't like they hadn't already kissed or anything. Forget the make-out session, a small sign that he was even a little interested in her would be fantastic.

"Use your pack as a pillow," he handed her, her

backpack.

"Thanks."

"That jacket looks warm." He glanced down at the garment in question. "Don't worry, we have plenty of wood, I'll keep the fire going so that you don't get cold." Blaze was frowning. He scooted further away from her, putting his back to the fire and inadvertently to her.

Roxy wasn't sure what she had expected but this sure as hell wasn't it. Body warmth was important. Snuggling up to a shifter sounded nice. Maybe he was trying to be polite. They didn't know each other. It wasn't like she would normally sleep—as in get some rest—with a guy on the first day of meeting him anyway. Even if he had offered to snuggle with her she would've turned him down, so maybe it was a good thing he hadn't offered.

She lay down, also putting her back to the fire. Two could play at this game. When he finally did make a move on her, she was totally turning him down flat. She had already jumped him once so she refused to be the first one to do it again. It was on him . . . the king of all the dragons. Shit! She hadn't really minded either way. Royalty or not. Part of her had hoped for a regular guy . . . shifter. He kept on saying that he didn't want to complicate things, yet she got the distinct impression that being with a guy like him was complicated to begin with.

There was a loud groan. Distinctly male. Sound sure did travel in the woods at night . . . unfortunately. "Oh fuck, you're good with your mouth," Thunder growled out the words.

"Really?" Roxy huffed, turning back towards the fire and giving her bag a punch to try and make it more comfortable to lie on. It seemed that hearing a guy in the throes of passion turned her on just as much as hearing Lily earlier. It was plain gross but she couldn't help it. She needed sex and badly. Roxy stared across the fire at Blaze. His back was muscular and broad.

"Ignore it and get some sleep," Blaze sounded royally pissed off—*royally pissed off, ha ha!* She'd find that funny if she wasn't so damned horny. He didn't sound like the others having sex affected him in any way. He might be arrogant and bossy but at least he wasn't a pervert. Not like her. Roxy squeezed her eyes shut—along with her thighs.

Thunder was loud and made more noise than Lily. Grunting, growling and plenty of dirty talk. He said things like *take me deep* and *suck my balls.* The guy also had a ton of stamina because it seemed to go on and on and on. His orgasm was quick and loud. A roar that echoed through the entire forest. He sounded like a grizzly bear. Not that she knew what a grizzly bear in the throes of orgasm sounded like. He probably scared away all the wild animals in a wide radius, including the grizzly bears.

A laugh slipped out. She managed to stop it quite quickly.

"What's so funny?" Blaze didn't sound happy.

"Nothing."

"Get some sleep, dammit," Blaze growled at her.

"I'm trying but it's hard with all the noise." *Asshole!*

What was his problem?

Just as she was dozing off, Lily started up again. "You've got to be kidding me!" Roxy unzipped her backpack and pulled out her spare set of jeans. She then proceeded to lay back down. Her pack wasn't as comfortable without the extra padding but at least she had something to cover her head. More importantly, her ears. It definitely muffled the cries. And then the weirdest thing happened . . . she fell asleep.

CHAPTER 9

They woke up at sunrise the next morning. Lily and Thunder were snuggled in each other's arms. *I'm not jealous!* They kissed each other continually and called each other by endearments. It was sickening. You would swear that they had been together for ages.

After a quick breakfast of deer steak, they'd set off. Blaze carried her. The guy smelled incredible. How was that even possible after spending the night in the wilderness? His arms felt good around her. Too damned good. She was disliking him more and more. He didn't speak to her. Her only solace was that he didn't seem keen on speaking to any of them and when asked a direct question his answers were short.

Within a few hours, they went their separate ways. It was a couple more hours before they reached the fire castle. They traveled in complete silence. It was such fun. The guy was as entertaining as they came. Roxy gave up trying to talk to him ages ago. His yes and no answers were riveting. They put her to sleep more than once.

Then without giving her any warning, Blaze put her

down and changed into this huge dragon. There was a cracking and a popping sound. One second a beautiful man stood before her and the next, a majestic dragon. His scales gleamed in the sunlight. Glorious shades of greens and blues. His chest was golden and reflected the sun. Not so much that she couldn't look at him but a pair of shades would have been good right about now.

Again, without so much as a warning, he flapped his wings and took to the sky. Using giant, scaly talons, he picked her up around her waist. She couldn't help but squeal but his touch was soft and careful so she forced herself to relax.

Her stomach lurched as they rose into the air with a speed. Blaze rose up over a large stone patio and then slowly descended. He released her just as her feet hit the ground. He moved to the side and landed with grace and finesse. Especially considering he had to weigh at least a ton. If not more.

There were fewer cracking noises as he changed back into his human form. *Oh lord!* His ass was a thing of sheer beauty. His glutes pulled tight as he walked inside the building through a glass side door. No tan lines. The guy had beautiful sun-kissed skin with not a tan line anywhere.

Roxy decided she was definitely a pervert because she felt disappointed that he was already dressed in another pair of those loose-fitting pants by the time she got her legs to work. She looked around the space. It was big, as in, very high ceilings and sparse furnishings. From what she had seen so far, she realized that this was normal for dragons. They liked big, open spaces. Even the hallways were high and wide.

The room was tastefully decorated. There was a desk and chair, as well as a sitting area. There was also a large bed. Her eyes were drawn to it.

"This is my chamber," Blaze didn't sound happy and when she looked at him, he was frowning. "Make yourself comfortable. Your things will be brought in shortly. I'll have food delivered."

"Where are you going?" It was out before she could stop it. It sounded like she didn't want him to go, which was partly true.

"I have things I need to attend to, four kingdoms to run." His body turned slightly towards the door.

"Yeah," she nodded. "Okay . . . fine."

"I'll be back later. Refuel, get some rest. Wash up."

She must stink. Back to armpit problems, it had to be it. And, he was the king, so it made sense. Roxy wanted to ask him when she would see him again but she didn't want to sound too needy.

"I'll see you later," he growled. He was already half out the door when he turned back. "Don't try and go anywhere without me. Someone else might try to claim you and I would be forced to kill him."

Blaze left before she could say anything. He was joking. Although, he had looked deadly serious. Okay, maybe he wasn't joking. Exaggerating then maybe. Yeah, that had to be it.

Roxy showered and changed. About a half hour later

there was a knock on the door.

"Come in," she called. The action felt a bit strange, considering this wasn't even her place.

Julie stuck her head around the jamb. "Are you decent?"

Roxy laughed. "Yeah, come on in."

Julie did as she said and put the bag down at her feet. She proceeded to put her hands on her hips and give Roxy the once-over with a strange look on her face.

"What?"

Julie smiled. "So you got Blaze," she made a snorting noise and shook her head.

"It's not a biggie, is it? I mean, maybe it is since he's the fire king and all." It made her feel a bit nervous.

"He's actually pretty down-to-earth, but he does have a giant stick up his ass. I'm hoping he'll relax a bit when he . . . forget I said anything." She gave a wave of the hand. "What would you like to eat?"

"He's pretty intense and a whole lot serious, but . . ." Roxy wanted to say that she thought he was nice but nice didn't fit the big, brooding shifter. Neither did sweet.

Julie nodded. "Yeah and he acts like he has a stick jammed right where the sun don't shine. Don't tell him I said that. We're only just starting to get along. He didn't like me at first because I didn't want children and the whole purpose for us being here is to procreate but then it just kind of happened." Julie cupped her belly which was a bit distended now that Roxy was close enough to really get a good look at Julie's profile.

"Oh wow! You're pregnant," Roxy gushed. "Congratulations!"

"It's unexpected but we're really happy about it," Julie smiled broadly. "I'm a little nervous with the laying approaching."

"Laying? As in an egg?" Roxy felt her eyes widen, she could hear the shock in her voice.

Julie nodded. "Yup. Fire dragon offspring are laid, as in, yes, there is most definitely an egg." She didn't look too sure about the whole thing.

"How far along are you?" Roxy was expecting the other woman to say that she was a couple of months.

"Two and a bit weeks." Julie must have read the shock on her face because she continued. "I will carry for six weeks and then it takes about another six weeks for the egg to hatch. Although, we're not entirely sure how it's going to go down since I'm the first human to carry a fire dragon egg. A royal egg for that matter."

"That must be scary for you."

Her eyes widened. "You have no idea. Coal is really wonderful. He's going to be a fantastic dad." She took a deep breath. "There have been human and dragon shifter births before that went well so I'm sure I'll be okay."

"Well, that's fine then."

"Yes and no. Air and water dragon females bear live young so it's very different. It's uncertain about the earth dragons who are very secretive about their offspring. We don't know for sure how earth dragon babies are born although it is suspected that they have live young as well."

"Why do you think that?" Roxy found this whole conversation fascinating and a little concerning, she wasn't sure she liked the idea of carrying an egg. Not that it was a given that she and Blaze would end up together or anything. It seemed less and less likely as time wore on. Considering that he thought she stank and that he didn't seem to like her much. She pushed the thought aside.

"Well, the whole reason we carry an egg . . ." Julie's hand went to the light curve of her belly. " . . . is because fire dragons breathe actual fire."

Roxy nodded. It was something she'd witnessed firsthand when Blaze had set the kindling alight last night for their fire. Flames had shot out of his mouth for a few seconds. It was bizarre and freaking hot—and not just the temperature.

"Their offspring already start breathing fire as fetuses. Their females . . ." she cleared her throat, "those of us carrying fire dragon offspring would get burned to ashes if we had to carry a baby to term." That weird look from before was back. Julie was scrutinizing Roxy in a way that made her feel uncomfortable. "So, are you happy about Blaze? How are the two of you getting along?"

"It's really too soon to say." *Not well at all!* She kept that thought to herself.

"Come on, give me something!" Then Julie pulled a face. "You'll have to excuse me. I know I'm being a bit nosy. You might end up being my sister-in-law. Also, I think we could be friends. It's crazy because I've never had many friends, never had many people in my life. I'm really happy and . . ." She paused, raising her eyes to the ceiling while she thought up the right word. "safe and did I mention happy?" She smiled her ass off. "I wouldn't mind a friend to share that all with. Sorry if I'm coming on too strong. If I am, you can say so."

Roxy laughed. "No, it's okay. I really miss my bestie. She and I talk about everything but she's not here and regardless if things work out or not, I won't be able to confide in her, so I'm glad you're here. I'm glad you want to be friends with me."

"Good. Now that that's out of the way, tell me about Blaze. What do you think of him? I know it's a bit of a pain that the women don't get to choose the guy, but—"

"Well, actually . . ." Roxy felt heat flood her cheeks, "he didn't choose me exactly."

"Out with it. What happened? The guys always choose the girls."

Roxy told Julie how the whole thing had gone down. The other woman went from looking shocked to laughing like mad. "You kicked Thunder in the balls?"

"I cracked his royal jewels," Roxy had to smile.

Julie laughed some more. "That's hilarious! And Blaze's excuse for not picking you was that he's too attracted to you?" She shook her head. "The guy's got everything upside down. I think he got his heart broken or something. He doesn't believe in love anymore."

"Was she a human?" Roxy blurted.

Julie nodded. "I think so. How do you know, did he say something to you?"

"It was something Thunder said about him sounding almost human because he had spent too much time with the humans. I'm putting two and two together."

"Yeah well, reading between the lines, I think the whole stick up the ass problem he has is because of what happened to him. So . . ." her eyes widened, "do you think he's hot?"

Julie must have seen something written in her facial expression because she jumped up and down. "He is pretty hot. At least he's normally pretty good-looking except he's let himself go a bit of late. His hair is overgrown and he has a semi-beard thing going. It's like he's halfway to beard but not quite there yet. He looks better clean-shaven."

"I don't know, he's pretty hot as he is."

"I'm so glad you think so. I really hope you guys work out," Julie grinned. "He's going to want to have sex with you soon. I hope you know that."

Her girl parts did a happy dance. This was followed by a rush of nerves induced by adrenaline. Roxy tried hard to remain neutral.

"Don't worry too much about it. Shifters are really good in bed . . . oh and they are really well-endowed but don't let that scare you. They have had sex with human women before so he'll fit."

"You didn't just say that."

Julie smiled. "It's a genuine concern when you first get a look at what's going on down there. Trust me."

"I don't even know if we'll have sex."

"Silly lady!" Julie rolled her eyes. "Of course you'll have sex. Sooner than you think, trust me. They're charmers in their own rough around the edges way. You only realize you've had sex after you've had it."

Roxy gave a nervous laugh; she couldn't help but looking at the huge bed. She felt both scared and excited. Just as long as she didn't make the first move. Oh, and she had to say no the first time he tried anything on her. Her stomach clenched. Her hands felt clammy.

It turned out that she needn't have worried. Blaze didn't come back that night. She had everything she needed. Plenty of food was sent to the room. She finally changed into her pajamas and went to bed.

Roxy showered and changed the next morning. There was still no sign of Blaze. She had breakfast alone on the terrace. It was beautiful but lonely. Where the hell was he? Why wasn't he there trying to get to know her? Trying to make some sort of an effort.

She had to remind herself that he was the king. He had said that he had duties to attend to but surely he could've come back at some point? Even just for five minutes. There was only one bed so maybe he was trying to be polite and give her some space. Finally, after lunch, there was a knock on the door and he entered.

She'd just been settling down to an afternoon nap. It wasn't like there was a whole lot to do in this place. Especially since she couldn't go out anywhere.

Blaze didn't look all that good. It looked like he'd been

up all night His facial hair had grown out some more. It was straggly and unkempt. His hair had also grown out and seemed even more unruly than before. His eyes were bloodshot and he had a pinched expression.

Like he really had a stick up his ass.

She couldn't help but think of Julie's words. It was all she could do to keep from laughing. He still looked gorgeous though. Sexy as hell. Bastard!

She sat up and tucked some of her hair behind her ear. It was loose, she didn't like sleeping with her hair up.

Blaze gave her the once-over, he frowned and his jaw tightened. What? Didn't he like that she was asleep in the middle of the day? Maybe he thought she was being lazy.

It couldn't be what she was wearing. A plain white top and a pair of denim shorts.

"I came to check in on you," he stayed by the door. He looked tense.

"I'm doing okay, thanks."

Blaze gave a nod. "Good. How is the food?"

"Fine . . . really good actually." She stretched and his eyes darkened. He looked . . . angry.

"Do you have everything you need? I see that you are wearing your own things so your bag was delivered."

She nodded.

"Good," his voice was rough. There wasn't even a hint of friendliness. "I'll see you later then."

"Where are you going?" *Lame! Lame!* She sounded desperate.

"I have some things I need to do." Blaze was already

on his way to the door. "Later." He turned the handle.

"Yeah, sure," Roxy said. "Later." But the door was already closing and clicking shut. What was that all about? The guy obviously didn't like her. He had to have been talking shit when he said he was attracted to her.

Wait.

Stop.

Maybe he was just really busy. She needed to give him the benefit of the doubt. He'd said that he would come by later. Maybe they could have dinner together or talk or something. Roxy started to feel better about the whole thing. It was going to be okay.

CHAPTER 10

The next day . . .

S o much for Blaze coming to see her. A lady who she
assumed was a dragon shifter because of her height
and build—bigger than a human woman—had delivered
her dinner. That was it, no one else. No visit from Julie,
no visit from Blaze. No answers to the ever-growing list
of questions.

Why did he even take part in the hunt in the first place?
Especially since he had shoved her in his room and was
ignoring her flat. What was the point of that? She thought
she was here to get to know someone, to potentially start
a future with them. It seemed that the dragon shifter had
some serious baggage. Maybe he was starting to have
second thoughts about the whole thing. She sure as hell
was. This was not what she'd signed up for.

It was late afternoon before the knock finally came.
Blaze walked in. Nothing had changed. His hair was still
an unruly mess, it looked as if he had been tugging on it
and running his hands through it. His facial hair was

getting out of hand. His eyes had a haunted look, there were black smudges underneath them. It looked like he hadn't slept in days. The one thing that irritated her the most though was how good-looking he still was. Even scruffy and ungroomed, he still managed to look edible.

His body was a thing of beauty. His muscles popped and tension radiated through him. His full lips were pursed and he folded his arms across his chest.

He narrowed his eyes at her looking . . . angry. Why would he be angry? His eyes roved over her, a deep frown marred his forehead. "You're lying down," he stated the obvious.

Roxy pulled herself into a sitting position, careful not to flash him. On a whim she had decided to wear one of her pretty summer dresses. It was a beautiful royal blue. It brought out the color of her eyes. It was one of those wraparound numbers that came to just above her knees. There was a deep 'V' in the front, so it also showed off a nice amount of cleavage. Enough to stir the imagination but not enough to give it all away.

By the look on Blaze's face, he obviously thought she looked hideous. Then she remembered his comments about her lying down. "It's not like I have anything better to do," she snapped back.

"And what the hell are you wearing?" Okay, so he clearly didn't like her dress.

"What's wrong with it?" she looked down. Guys always approached her when she wore this dress—not that she went out all that often with the intention of picking up guys. Certainly not in the last couple of months. When he didn't respond, Roxy felt anger stir. "I look fine. It's not like anyone can see me anyway. I may as well walk around naked or in my underwear." She didn't mean it. Her statement seemed to anger Blaze even more. "I'll sleep whenever I feel like it. It's seriously boring just sitting here all by myself." She had to work to keep her emotions from coming through in her voice. Thankfully she managed to sound more angry than upset. She didn't want him to know that he was getting to her. That this whole thing was getting to her.

"Julie is coming by later," Blaze said. "Is there anything else you need?"

No way! No freaking way, he took a step back and then another, clearly on his way to the door.

It was about time she gave this asshole a piece of her mind. Roxy clambered off the bed. She didn't give a damn if he saw her panties.

By the way his eyes widened and flared for a moment, she got the distinct impression that he had. She couldn't give a rat's ass.

"Where are you going?" she carried on before he could answer. "Don't answer that because I don't care. All I have to say is that you are seriously rude and you're one hell of an asshole!" Roxy walked towards him. Blaze took a step back and swallowed hard, his Adam's apple bobbed. "What's wrong with me? Actually, I should ask you the same question. In fact, I'm going to: what the hell is wrong with you? Did you bring me all the way out here just to lock me up in a room? It's been two whole days and I've seen you for all of five minutes during that time. If that." She put her hands on her hips.

"I've been busy."

His answer infuriated her and she took another step towards him, Blaze stood his ground, looking down at her. "That's not good enough. Not by a long shot. Why did you partake in this whole hunt thing if you're not interested in taking the time to get to know me? Have you changed your mind about this whole thing, is that it? You should've just let one of the others have me." Not that she wanted to go to any of the others. She'd wanted Blaze. Roxy had foolishly believed that there was something there. A gut instinct. Well, she wouldn't be listening to her gut feelings again any time soon.

Blaze made a growling noise from deep down in his throat, it was a scary sound and she had to work to stand her ground and maintain eye contact. His eyes seemed to grow even brighter, they were even more beautiful. The most vivid green she'd ever seen. "I need to go," his voice was deep.

"What the hell?" she muttered more to herself than to him. "Fine," she huffed. "Don't bother coming back."

His sexy mouth twitched like he found her statement funny and it just angered her even more. Firstly, because she still found his asshole's mouth sexy and secondly because he dared to find humor in this. She was serious. "I mean it. If you walk out that door, please don't bother coming back . . . ever. It would be a waste of time."

"This is my chamber."

"You could have fooled me. You haven't so much as showered or changed your clothes since we got back." She took another small step towards him, closing most of the distance between them and gave him a sniff. *No shit!* The guy smelled heavenly. Woodsy, soapy and fresh.

Blaze ground his teeth. "Stop that," he growled.

"I'm trying to understand how the hell you smell so good . . ." she sniffed again, "when you haven't showered in days."

"I said to stop that," an even deeper growl. "I have showered," he added. "Just not here."

"Of course not. Why would you shower here since you're avoiding me?" She gave him another sniff, just because it was pissing him off and well, because he really did smell damn fine. Quite frankly, she could sniff him all day. *Yummylishous!*

"Stop doing that," his voice was guttural.

"Why? What's the big deal?" What an ass!

"Because I'm a shifter." Those tendons on the sides of his neck popped out. *Hello, Mister Angry.* It was wrong on so many levels that he just grew even sexier the more pissed and obnoxious he became.

"So what if you're a shifter," she put her hands on her hips.

"You're taking in my scent and declaring that I smell good," his eyes narrowed.

"Yeah, and?"

"In shifter talk, that means you're initiating sex. You

may as well get undressed and go and lie on that bed with your legs open . . . it means about the same thing."

She swallowed hard. *Oops!* Then her mouth opened and said what it was thinking before she could stop it. "Well, sweaty sex would be better than the silent treatment you've been giving me. Some good old-fashioned humping would be better than sitting around all day twiddling my thumbs."

"I'm going to pretend you didn't say that," Blaze was breathing hard, he turned and grabbed the door handle.

Roxy let out a shrill laugh. "Run away! Yup, go! That's fine. Good-freaking-bye!"

He sighed, like he was relieved or something. His hand tightened on the handle.

"But . . ." she quickly added before he could leave. "Don't bother coming back. Oh yeah, I forgot this is your room. On second thought, I'd rather be introduced to someone else. I don't particularly like the idea of starting over with someone else . . ." It wasn't true but he didn't need to know that. "or of guys fighting over me but—"

Blaze moved so quickly that she only realized he had moved when his body was pressed against hers, when his hands clasped around her upper arms. "Fuck that!" Okay so maybe he hadn't been all that pissed before. He sure as hell looked it now. "You are mine." His voice was barely recognizable as human.

This guy was just too much. "I don't get you. You clearly don't want me. You have no interest in getting to know me. You won't spend any time with me. I came here in the hopes of—"

"I know why you're here. Fuck . . ." He let go of her and marched towards the other side of the room before marching part of the way back. He grabbed a fistful of his hair and tugged on it before dropping his hand at his side. "We need to get something very clear. When I said I was attracted to you, I meant it."

"I don't buy it," she shook her head. Roxy knew when to call bullshit. "You've been nothing but cold towards me. We can't even hold a conversation."

"You told me that you haven't had sex in a while."

Why did he have to bring that up? Why had she told him in the first place? "How is that even pertinent?"

"You scent strongly of arousal," his nostrils flared. "Even though I can scent anger, I can smell your need as well."

Ground, please open up and swallow me whole. She squeezed her eyes shut, praying that he might disappear when she reopened them. It wasn't the case. Roxy tried not to blush, but it was like trying not to breathe. Her heart hammered inside her chest.

"You were wet with need after our kiss and even more turned on listening to Thunder and—"

"Please, can you stop . . . ?" She held out her hand, it shook slightly. "You've humiliated me enough, don't you think?"

Blaze frowned. "Why is that humiliating? It shouldn't be. Hell, Roxy . . ." His hand went back into his hair. "I can barely think or breathe around you. I haven't rutted in fucking forever. Non-humans are highly sexual. You're fucking killing me here."

She pulled her bottom lip between her teeth. What did she say to that? Her being horny was making him angry. Was that right? Was she misunderstanding this?

"I would love to stay and chat but all I can think about is fucking when I'm around you." That's when she noticed that there was a whole lot going on in his pants. "I can't trust myself not to tear your dress off. Not when you smell the way you do, not when you look like that." His eyes drifted down the length of her body and certain parts of her puckered, as if on command.

His nostrils flared. "Don't," Roxy said. It looked like he was walking towards her but he continued to the door.

"Don't what?" He stopped in his tracks, his back stiffened. "My words are arousing you."

"I can't help it. I'm attracted to you as well."

His whole body tensed up. "I'm going to leave. We'll finish this later."

"When later, tomorrow? What will have changed?"

His big shoulders moved up and down as he shrugged. "Maybe you should take care of things."

"What things?" He was really irritating the hell out of her. "You told me that dragon shifters are open and honest. You're not doing that. You keep avoiding me or talking in riddles. Spit it out already."

Blaze turned. His intense gaze bore into hers. *Oh shit!* His hand was still on the handle behind him. "You should come a couple of times."

"You mean masturbate?" She could feel that her eyes were wide in her head.

Blaze gave a nod. "Yeah. You might not scent of . . ." he sniffed, "need and arousal all the time then. It's an intoxicating scent it . . ." He ground his teeth.

He hadn't just said that? "For your information, I got myself off last night and this morning. So there!" Why did she have to have such a big mouth? What was wrong with her?

His whole face looked pained for a second and he even made a sexy groaning noise. "I really didn't need to hear that. I need to get out of here."

"Don't go. We really need to talk about this."

He shook his head. "I meant it when I said I was attracted to you. That, coupled with your scent and the amount of time that has passed since I last rutted, is a ticking time bomb."

"What does that even mean? Why is it a time bomb? Would sex with me be so bad?" She mumbled the last. It didn't make sense.

His chest heaved as he turned and yanked the door open. "I'm sorry, Roxy. I need to leave right now. I will work this out." Then he was slamming the door in her face.

She waited for a key to turn. She had threatened to leave and find someone else if he left. There was silence. It mocked her. She should make good on her threat but he'd seemed so pained in the end. He'd actually looked afraid. Roxy knew that his fear was for her but she didn't know why.

She walked over to the bed and on a sigh, she threw herself onto the soft mattress. What had she gotten herself into? Hopefully he would come back really soon so that they could talk some more.

Roxy spent the next two hours playing their conversation over and over in her head. What could he have meant by ticking time bomb? Was he talking about having sex with her? What was so bad about having sex? She wasn't a prude or anything but neither did she hop into bed with a guy she hardly knew. She'd had a one-night stand or two. Who hadn't? Her relationship with Blaze—if you could even call it that—was still really new. Having said that, she was ready to take the next step. They were both hot for each other, so why not just have sex and get it out of the way?

He said it himself when they first met, what had changed?

There was a knock at the door. "It's me." It was a woman's voice and could only be Julie.

"Come in."

Julie entered the room frowning deeply. "What's going on? What happened between you and Blaze?"

"I'm not sure." Roxy relayed the events that had taken place between them.

"That explains things," the other woman shook her head, looking worried.

"What's wrong? Is something wrong? Did something happen?"

Julie was silent for a long time. Roxy began to worry more and more. Her stomach clenched. It felt wound up in knots. "Please just tell me."

"Blaze came by," she paused. "He asked to speak to Coal alone. By the way, he's really looking like shit."

"Okay so scraggly beard and overgrown hair is not his normal style then?"

"No, definitely not. He's freaked out about you," Julie smiled for a few seconds but quickly grew serious.

"Why?" She could only pray that Julie confided in her. "Please tell me what's going on. I really need to know. I deserve to know."

"I really shouldn't," Julie licked her lips. "Coal told me a couple of things after Blaze left. Shit." She scratched her forehead and looked at the floor for a few moments. "I shouldn't tell you."

Roxy could see the other woman wrestling with the decision of whether or not to confide in her. "Please just tell me what's going on. I beg you."

Julie lifted her eyes to meet Roxy's. She sighed. "Okay, but I'm probably going to regret this," she mumbled to herself. "Blaze is worried about hurting you."

Roxy could feel herself frown. "Why would he be worried about hurting me?"

"Dragon shifters are big and strong. Like super powerful. Blaze told you that he hasn't had sex in a really long time. To put it bluntly, you make him so horny that he's worried he might hurt you during sex. He does have a point since you are a human. We *are* breakable."

Roxy was trying to process this information. So that's where the ticking time bomb analogy came in. He was afraid, literally, of hurting her or possibly killing her. Roxy swallowed hard, suddenly feeling a little nervous.

"This is where things get a little hairy," Julie scratched the back of her neck and looked back down at the floor for a few moments. "Don't freak out when I tell you this."

After about a half a minute of silence Roxy finally grew impatient. "Tell me already."

"He's thinking of having sex with one of the dragon shifter women."

Roxy's mouth fell open in an all-out gape. At first it felt like the blood was rushing from her face. If she looked in the mirror, she would probably be as white as a ghost. It didn't take long however for her blood to really start pumping as anger coursed through her veins. Pale was quickly replaced by blood red. "What the hell! You can't be serious?"

"It might be safer if you let him . . ."

"Are you serious? Are you telling me that I should be okay with it if he has sex with some other woman?"

"You've only just met him, it's not like—"

"That's bullshit!" Roxy yelled. "I'm here to date him. To possibly marry the asshole. He's made it very clear that he's not going to share me, so why the hell should I share him?" The more she spoke, the angrier she became. "How would you have felt if Coal had won you during the hunt and then proceeded to screw the brains out of another woman?"

Julie's eyes narrowed.

"How would you feel if he had hopped out of one of their beds and into yours?"

"I would've told him to go to hell," Julie blurted. She sucked in a deep breath. "You're right. Blaze would be making a mistake. He really thinks you're in danger though. He made it clear that he doesn't want to have sex with one of them," her eyes widened. "I shouldn't be telling you this either but according to Coal, Blaze has never had sex with a dragon woman before."

So, Blaze was just going to go behind her back and have sex with another woman? It felt wrong even though he hadn't made any promises to her. They weren't really together, but it still felt really wrong.

"He's thinking it over right now. He told Coal that he was going to his office. I think if he's going to go through with it, it's going to be soon. Do you want me to go and talk to him? Maybe I can talk him out of it."

Roxy shook her head. *Stuff that!* "I'm going to give that asshole a piece of my mind."

Julie's mouth fell open. "What do you . . . ?"

Roxy didn't wait to hear the rest of what Julie had to say. She raced to the door and tugged it open. Blaze always went to the right just before he shut the door, so it made sense that, that was the direction of his office. At least she hoped it was. Heaven help any shifter male that tried to come near her, she'd break his shins and crack his balls. It didn't take long before she passed one of them.

His eyes widened. "Are you lost?"

"Where is Blaze's office?" she tried to stay calm.

He frowned, looking really confused. His nostrils flared. "You shouldn't be walking around like this. I can scent that my king has not fully claimed you yet. Another male might try and claim you for himself," he pulled a face. "That could end up in disaster. Go back to my lord's chamber. Go quickly."

"Listen, buddy, I need to find Blaze and I need to find him right now."

Julie came running up behind them. "What are you doing? You need to go back."

"That's what I was just telling her," the big shifter said.

Julie looked worried. "Don't you dare touch her or . . ."

The shifter held up his hands. "Don't you worry about that. I happen to like my balls. I'd also like to keep breathing."

Roxy wasn't sure what he was on about. "I get that you're both afraid of what might happen with me running around the castle. I know it's not safe." A shiver of fear raced through her but she pushed it down. She needed to see Blaze and right now. "Take me to him. Do it now! Otherwise I'm going to have to try and find his office on my own and that would probably mean running into a whole lot of shifters."

"I should never have told you," Julie moaned. "I'm such an idiot. You've made up your mind haven't you?"

Roxy nodded. "Please help me, before he does something stupid. Call me a complete idiot but there's something about him . . ." It was that whole gut instinct thing again. A little voice inside her that told her that Blaze might just be the one. It was probably just her being overly romantic and looking for the sunshine and rainbows where there weren't any. Looking for a happy ending where there probably wasn't one. Roxy was just being an idiot but she couldn't help it.

Julie's whole demeanor softened. "I think you're just what he needs. A human capable of whipping him into shape," she smiled. "I'm going to get into such shit for this, but come on."

The three of them ran, much to the astonishment of those they passed. Thank god none of the shifter men tried to approach her or tried any funny business. They were probably too shocked, judging by the expressions on their faces.

Less than two minutes later, they stood outside Blaze's office.

"Thank you," Roxy whispered.

"You should go in now, you're in danger," the shifter looked worried, he kept looking up and down the hallway.

"You should get out of here," Julie looked at the dragon shifter. "You're the one who's in danger," she whispered. "If Blaze catches you anywhere near his female . . ."

He nodded and left. "Thanks again," Roxy said to his retreating back.

"Good luck," Julie whispered. "Don't be too hard on him."

Roxy had to fight not to roll her eyes. She nodded, took

a deep breath, squared her shoulders and walked in.

Blaze's back was to her. It looked like he was staring at the view. His whole stance immediately stiffened. "Who the . . ." he growled as he turned, then his eyes locked with hers and they widened before narrowing. "How did you get here?" he went on before she could answer. "Do you have any idea how much risk you put yourself in to come here?"

Roxy slammed the door behind her. "Do you know what a gigantic asshole you are?"

"So you keep telling me."

"No really! Did you think you could go off and screw some other person and think that I would never find out? God!" She pinched the bridge of her nose for a second. "Why am I even here? I think it's unacceptable. You can't bring me here to get to know me with the intention of marrying me . . . maybe . . . and then go and sleep with another woman. It's just not right. It's not how humans do things. If that's how shifters go about relationships, then I made a mistake coming here."

If he was shocked or upset, he didn't show it. "It's not how we do things either."

"Why then? I know we don't know each other and that you don't owe me anything but I think it's in bad taste and . . . I think you at least owe me an explanation."

He didn't answer her.

"You know what, forget it. I don't want to try and start something with you anyway. Not if this is your attitude. You don't want me messing around with other guys but you will quite happily sleep with another woman."

He growled, his hands curled into fists. "You are mine."

What an asshole. "See!" she pointed at him, "my point exactly. You said that I was yours earlier as well. You keep laying claim to me like I'm some kind of possession yet you'll go and quite happily fuck someone else. That's not cool."

"It wouldn't be happily," he growled, looking pissed—nothing had changed there. "I can't see any other way around it," he sounded anguished. "The things I want to do to you," his throat worked. "I don't have much control. I could hurt you so easily. I *will* hurt you." His eyes had this pleading look. "I don't want another female, but I'm not sure I have a choice. I'm not sure that *we* have a choice." It was the first time he'd referred to them together. His words warmed her, gave her hope. She was an idiot!

Blaze was huge and imposing. Raw power radiated off of him. She had to suppress a shiver.

"You're afraid. I can scent it. You *should* be afraid of me." He flexed his muscles and his pecs did that bounce thing.

Roxy nodded. "I *am* afraid," she whispered. "But, I'm not a coward and neither are you. We're attracted to one another in a big way." She walked towards him. "I, for one, really want to see where this leads. If you feel the same, then we need to get through this together. Come up with a plan together."

Blaze shook his head. "I can't think of anything. I've

been wracking my brain, but . . . I meant it when I said I don't want anyone else. For what it's worth, I had already decided not to go down that road."

Something eased in her. She tried not to show her relief.

"The only reason I would've done it is to protect you. You need to understand that," his eyes shone with sincerity. Roxy believed him.

"The only other option is to send you home. This," he motioned between them, "is a ticking time bomb. I don't know how much longer I can keep my hands off of you."

Holy hell! Hearing him say that made her want him more. "I'm not going anywhere." There was only one thing to do in a situation like this. Not that she'd ever been in a situation like this. She dropped to her knees in front of him. "You have to promise to talk to me in the future instead of running off on your own."

"What are you doing?" Blaze half-whispered. His hands clenched at his sides, to keep from touching her maybe?

Her eyes focused on his erection. Shit! He was big. The loose, cotton pants tented.

"Female," it was a low growl. "I'm not sure . . ." he sucked in a breath as Roxy pulled down his pants. His dick sprang free. It strained from his body.

She made a squeaking noise. "Holy mother of . . . they weren't lying when they said you guys were well hung. It was an understatement." Blaze's . . . member was thick as well as being a good length. Definitely an understatement.

"You're playing with fire. You . . ." he hissed as her hand closed around him.

He was as hard as nails, yet, his skin was silky smooth. The area was hairless, which made him look even bigger. A drop of pre-cum beaded on the head and his dick throbbed in her hand. His heavy sacs were drawn up against his body. "There's only one way to deal with this. I'm going to blow you," she licked her lips. "Relieve some of *your* tension."

He choked out a strangled laugh. "Even if you made me come five times with that pretty mouth of yours, it wouldn't help. My cock wants inside your pussy and nothing else is going to ease this raging inferno inside of me," his voice was a smoky rasp.

She'd never had a guy talk dirty to her before. Not like this. Although, Blaze wasn't technically talking dirty. He was just saying it like it was, which somehow was even hotter. Roxy felt her nipples tighten, her clit pretty much went onto both knees and begged for attention.

Blaze sniffed. "You like the thought of my cock inside you," he frowned deeply. "Even though I could hurt you? I could kill you, Roxy." He probably didn't realize it but Blaze gave a small circling, thrust of the hips pushing his cock further into her fist.

She looked at his head longingly. "Just for the record, I don't normally offer to blow guys I hardly know." Roxy wanted his manhood in her mouth but today was not the day.

She let go of him and got back up onto shaky legs. She couldn't believe she was about to say this. "You won't hurt me. I trust you, Blaze. Let's just get this out of the way so that we can move on. I have a feeling we're going to get along just fine." Gut instinct—she felt like giving herself a hit upside the head, yet she couldn't shake the feeling that she was right. "That is, if you don't try to pull one of your dick moves again. By dick move I mean leaving me locked up, having sex with another woman or just being plain pissy."

He frowned. "Males don't get pissy."

"Fine, bad tempered then."

Blaze's mouth twitched. "I have been a bit bad tempered."

"Big time. I shouldn't even want to have sex with you, but for some reason I do."

"Fuck," he whispered as he ran a hand through his mop of hair. "I don't know, I . . ."

"Look, either we have sex or we end this now."

"You're right, I'm an asshole," he scrubbed a hand over his half-grown beard. "I can't let you go. I really fucking should but I can't. I might kill you." His eyes were heated. A whole lot of need reflected in their depths. They were mesmerizing. He took a step towards her and then another one.

"You won't hurt me. Don't ask me how I know, I just do."

He squeezed his eyes shut for a second. "You need to do everything I tell you."

She nodded. "Okay."

Blaze picked her up. "Every single thing. No arguments." His breath was coming hard and fast. He kept walking, her feet dangled off the ground. His eyes were trained on something over her shoulder. Blaze put her down and leaned past her. There was the sound of clattering followed by a loud bang.

In one quick move, he turned her around, coming to stand flush behind her. His erection dug into her back. *Oh shit!* At this point, she was breathing heavily as well. He crouched a little so that his mouth was next to her ear. "Are you sure about this? Be very sure, Roxy."

"Yes," it came out sounding like a half moan. "I'm very sure," she added when he didn't make a move. It was nuts, but she'd never been more sure about anything in her life.

"Once I'm inside of you there'll be no stopping," his husky voice caused shivers to race up and down her spine. It was such a cliché but she found herself squeezing her thighs together to stop the ache that was building there. "I'm going to fuck you hard. It might even hurt but you can't fight me. Do you understand that?"

"Yes," a breathless moan.

He leaned down and grabbed the bottom hem of her dress. There was a loud tearing noise as he ripped her garment to somewhere above her ass.

There's something so sexy about a man ripping your clothes off. Roxy loved this dress yet she couldn't muster any other reaction other than excitement. There was a hard tug and another rip and her panties, or what was left of them landed around one of her ankles.

Using his knee, he shoved her legs open. "I've wanted you from the moment I first saw you," he rasped, as both of his hands closed over her hips. "Lying just on the other side of that fire the first night was like torture. Seeing you on my bed yesterday . . ." He made a groaning noise.

Oh god! So that's why he had looked so angry. "That's why you ran away."

She felt him nod his head. The one hand on her hip slid around and between her legs, zoning in on her clit. With just the tip of his finger, he circled her clit a few times. Roxy threw her head back and moaned. That's when she realized that Blaze was shaking, his whole body vibrated. "I'm barely holding it together." He slipped a finger inside her and pumped. "So wet for me," he moaned.

"Yes." It came out sounding strangled. Her own legs shook a little as he used his thumb to stroke her clit while plunging his finger in deeper. Her breathing turned a little ragged and her nerve-endings caught alight. She wasn't going to last long. It had been so damned long since someone had touched her like this.

"I'm going to bend you over this table and fuck you."

She moaned, so on the verge of coming it was scary. She rocked her hips in time with his finger.

"I'll probably cage you in with my body." His finger slid in and out of her. That thumb of his had to be magic. "I might bite you, don't fight me please. Stay still and stay calm." There was an edge of worry to his voice.

"Bite me?" Her voice was husky and she sounded out of breath. She couldn't be blamed since he was still finger fucking the hell out of her. Had someone turned up the heat in there? Where had all the oxygen gone? *Holy* . . .

hell . . . holy . . . she moaned.

"I'll try not to hurt you," he sounded pained. It wasn't much of a consolation.

The only response she could give was to groan in utter bliss. What was wrong with her? She should be running away and as fast as her legs would carry her. Instead, she was bouncing on his hand, about to come.

Blaze took a shuffling step forward until her thighs hit the mostly cleared desk. She looked down, noticing that there were still a couple of papers and a thin folder on the desk but otherwise everything was strewn across the floor along with an upside down laptop computer.

"Oh . . . oh . . . oh . . ." *Bounce . . . bounce . . . bounce.* Any second now.

Hopefully his computer wasn't broken. It was such an irrational thing to think, especially considering what was about to go down. Roxy's whole body felt tight as her pending orgasm drew closer and closer. She was moaning with every thrust of his finger.

Blaze placed a hand on her back and pushed her over the desk until her cheek was flush with the dark glossy wood. He wasn't exactly rough but there was a definite sense of urgency.

He pulled his fingers out of her and she groaned in frustration. Five more seconds and she would've been tickets. He kept his hand on her back using the other one to grab her hip. His leg was still between her thighs, he used it to widen her stance. "So damned sexy," he muttered.

His cock nudged up against her opening and Roxy held her breath. He was still shaking. "Last chance," he sounded like he was talking between clenched teeth. Like he was using every ounce of strength to hold back.

"I'm sure." Roxy sucked in a hard breath as he plunged into her. One second she was empty and the next she was full. Too full. Too stretched. It hurt. Roxy cried out and tried to move but Blaze crouched over her, holding her down with his body. Everything stayed perfectly still, everything but his hips, those began thrusting. Hard and fast. He'd warned that he'd fuck her that way. Blaze hadn't lied. He didn't give her any time to acclimatize. No time to catch her breath.

The first few strokes hurt. Then there was some pleasure mixed in with the pain. There were no words of endearment and no words of encouragement. Aside from serious heavy breathing and the odd grunt, Blaze said *fuck* every so often. He groaned it like he was in complete awe. Roxy didn't need any encouragement; her skin was tightening again. Her clit was throbbing. His enormous cock may have initially hurt her but right now he was hitting every nerve inside of her, including the ones responsible for vaginal orgasms. She'd only ever had a couple of those in her life. This one was going to be the mother of all vaginal orgasms. It was going to be epic. She might even start writing romance novels just so that she could describe this moment.

Roxy could hardly breathe. It felt too good to do anything other than feel. Oh hell but she was wet. Blaze slid in and out of her easily. He was grunting more and thrusting harder. He pushed down harder as well. Her cheek was pressed up against the desk. Then he was fisting her hair. It stung a little. It turned out that hair pulling and hard fucking might just be her thing.

That, or she must have some serious screws loose because it made her lose it. Her orgasm slammed into her. It was the mother alright. She saw stars but that was probably due to lack of oxygen because she could not breathe. There was too much happening inside her body for it to waste precious energy on breathing.

There was a sting as Blaze bit down on her shoulder. It hurt. Her stupid body's response was to orgasm all the harder. She couldn't be sure, but it was quite possibly an overlap orgasm. From one into the next. She'd read that it was very possible for women to have multiples, she'd never thought it would happen to her. So it turned out that the first orgasm wasn't the mother, the second was. She made a deep groaning noise as it rushed through her.

Blaze grunted loudly and his body jerked. He fucked her a little harder. Thankfully he didn't pull her hair any more than he already was. Roxy couldn't move a muscle. At least she was breathing again. It was ragged and loud.

Blaze jerked some more. She could feel him coming inside her in hot spurts. He finally slumped over her. Shit, he was heavy. His chest heaved against her back. He was sweaty. His beard tickled her ear. Endorphins flooded her system.

His dick twitched inside her. Say what? The guy was

still mostly hard.

Roxy moaned. "Can't breathe," she managed to squeeze out.

He eased his weight off of her, just a smidgen, but stayed inside her. He was still breathing hard. "Are you okay?" he sounded husky.

Roxy swallowed and licked her lips. "Yes, I'm fine."

"Did I hurt you?"

"No . . . I've never had rough sex like that before but I think I liked it." She sounded seriously out of breath.

"You think you like it or you liked it?"

"No, I liked it."

"Good." Blaze pulled out of her and turned her around, moving back between her thighs. He lifted her so that her butt was on the edge of the desk.

His come ran down the sides of her thighs. "We're doing that again." He moved her dress, his gaze moving to her vagina.

"Right now?" she croaked, having to work not to close her legs, which was stupid since he'd just been inside her.

Her girl parts were a little overgrown. It wasn't like she'd had much time to prepare and like an idiot, she'd forgotten to pack a razor. She needed to speak to Julie about getting some supplies.

Blaze licked his lips, a frown marred his forehead and he had that pinched look. He looked really angry, except, it wasn't anger, he was just very horny. She'd come to recognize the look.

His fully erect cock did this little twitch thing. Yup, it

was definitely lust. He didn't seem to mind that she was a little bushy.

"Yeah, right now," he groaned. "I'm going to fuck you again."

"Okay." Her girl parts liked the idea. There was a whole lot of throbbing and puckering going on down there.

There was no further discussion. Blaze bent his legs, going down a bit at the knee and thrust into her. He linked an arm around her to hold her in place. Roxy moaned.

"Hook your legs around my waist," he growled.

Roxy did as he said. She grabbed his biceps and tried to keep her eyes from rolling right back into her scalp as he thrust into her using circular motions. With his free hand, he pulled one of her thighs higher up on his body.

"Oh god!" she moaned as he hit the spot.

"Fuck," Blaze groaned. "You feel good." A sheen of sweat glistened on his forehead. His lids were at half-mast. His features were strained. So incredibly sexy.

He didn't go at it with quite the same ferocity as before but it wasn't far off. The guy knew what he was doing. That much was for sure.

Then he was pushing her back so that she was lying with her back on the desk. He leaned over her and ripped the top of her dress, freeing her breasts. "Perfect. You're perfect." He palmed one of her boobs. Her nipples were already hard. Then he pulled her legs up, as in, straight up and at a right angle to her body. He hugged them to his chest and continued to thrust.

Oh.

Oh.

That was it. Over and out. She cried out as the pleasure train took her for a ride. Blaze followed, with her this time. He hugged her legs tighter and grunted louder. On and on until at long last he slowed his movements and then stopped all together.

They both worked hard to catch their breath. *Wow! Just wow.* That was the best sex she had ever had.

"We're compatible," Blaze announced. "I guess I knew we would be." It was weird but he didn't sound happy about it.

He pulled out of her. Then he carefully put her legs down. "I would love to rut you again but I think you need a break."

"Um . . . yeah. A break would be good." Her girl parts felt a bit tender. From no sex to hard sex with a giant cock. No wonder!

Blaze's lips quirked up and nodded. He reached down and righted his pants. Oh boy, he was still sporting a semi.

"I'll just get something for you to clean up with."

She nodded. Roxy moved to a sitting position. Shit, he'd done a number on her dress and her bra. There was no salvaging either. She tried to close the big gaping tear but her boobs had decided that free was so much more fun. They spilled out in all their glory. This was the reason she could never go braless.

Blaze returned a few minutes later with a damp towel. "Here." His eyes heated as they landed on her chest. Oh good! He was still turned on by her. Even though they had just had wild sex, twice. "I'm sorry I ruined your dress." His stunning green eyes locked with hers.

"Um, it's okay, just don't ruin anymore." She cleaned between her legs and down her thighs.

Blaze rubbed across his mouth. "I can't promise that."

"I thought once we had sex things would calm down," she raised her brows.

"Yeah, but we're so compatible," he groaned the word compatible.

She frowned.

"I enjoyed being inside you so much that I'll want back in very soon and if there are barriers I might destroy them. Don't wear anything important to you over the next few days. Things should calm down after that."

Roxy decided to toy with him a bit. Blaze was so damned serious about everything. "How do you know I even want to have sex with you again? You're just assuming I do, since I said I that I liked sex with you but maybe I didn't like it that much."

Blaze frowned, he narrowed his eyes, then he smiled. The guy was so attractive. Far more than what should be allowed. "You came, three times. You screamed my name the last time."

"I did n . . ." She was about to say 'not' but swallowed instead. Yup, her throat was a tad raw. Now that he mentioned, someone had been screaming something. That something may have been 'Blaze.' Come to think of it, someone was shouting his name and since there were only two of them in this room and Blaze would never have screamed his own name that left . . . her.

Her cheeks heated. "Fine," she huffed. "The sex was really good," she added, her face felt like it was about to self-combust.

He laughed. She shook her head and laughed along with him. Just as quickly, he turned serious and looked about the room. Blaze sighed. "What a mess. No more rutting in here."

Roxy looked around the room. Really taking in all the details for the first time. "We should avoid your desk but we could do it on the couch, or on that rug," she pointed to a Persian in the middle of the big space. "Or maybe your desk chair, I could be on top and . . ."

Blaze made a pained noise. "Enough. You need a break. If you keep talking, I can't promise you'll get one." He walked towards the door, turning to talk to her over her his shoulder. "I'll be back in a few minutes. I'm going to fetch you something to wear."

"Thanks." Roxy watched as he walked out of the room. She grabbed one of the overstuffed pillows off of the wingback and held it in front of her chest. She doubted that anyone would just barge into the king's office but then again, a girl couldn't be too careful.

So they'd established that the sex was good . . . no, make that great. Now they needed to see if there was more there. He was just so closed off and so serious. It felt like he had a wall up around him or something. Something had definitely happened in his past. Something that had emotionally scarred him. Thunder had mentioned a human and so had Julie. It made the most sense.

Roxy had also suffered heartbreak but she was still open to new possibilities. She hoped the same of him. In the meanwhile, she'd enjoy the sex and chip away at getting to know him.

CHAPTER 11

The next day . . .

T he tiny, silver purse landed with a dull thud on the floor at her feet. Roxy grappled with the zipper on her dress. The light blue material was bunched up around her waist. The human had forgone wearing underwear.

Good.

She was learning. Blaze didn't like human coverings. They got in the way.

Her eyes widened as she caught his stare. "Don't tear my dress. It cost . . ." She swallowed her words as he spun her around.

"Fuck," he growled, as he caught sight of her ass. Two rounded globes. Magnificent. "Open." He stuck his knee between her lush thighs.

Roxy moaned, she glanced back over her shoulder. "All I said was that you looked handsome. It's not that I'm averse to a quickie but it doesn't take much to get you going does it?"

"It wasn't what you said." Blaze yanked his pants down,

freeing his cock. He palmed her slit. "Fuck, you're wet." This female was so damned receptive. It was a highly-prized quality.

"You don't sound too shocked about that." The little human stuck her ass out further, she arched her back. She was just as desperate for this as he was.

"I'm not. Your scent of arousal is driving me nuts."

"You look good without all of that facial hair and whoever cut your hair deserves a medal."

"I planned on eating your pussy and thought you might prefer it if I was clean-shaven."

Her breath hitched and her scent grew even sweeter, even more tempting.

"You make it sound like I was an ugly bastard before." Blaze didn't wait for her reply he thrust into her tight confines and began to move. His breath turned ragged in an instant. She had such a snug pussy. He had to squeeze his eyes shut to keep from shooting off.

Sex had never been this good before. Not ever. He knew he was attracted to her and that they would be compatible but this was next level stuff. His gums ached and his scales rubbed. His dragon wanted him to mate her. It wanted him to vocally claim her and demanded that she do the same back. It wanted him to bite and mark her. Blaze had never experienced this before. It made him nervous. Then again, fantastic sex would probably do that to a male.

Her fingers were splayed on his front door. She panted and groaned and moaned and whimpered. Each and every sound drove him more and more crazy with need. What was it about her that made him feel more like an animal than a rational, level-headed person?

Blaze continued to pound into her. He loved how she felt suctioning around him. He fucking loved the noises their bodies made as they came together. The slapping of his balls. The thudding sound as his hips hit her ass. The wet noises as his cock slid in and out of her wet pussy.

Blaze bent his knee, wanting to . . . Roxy cried out. Yeah, right there. Her pussy began to flutter around his dick. He grunted with each thrust, working hard to keep from coming. *Not yet!* Even the noises he was making were odd to him, he normally rutted in silence. Aside from heavy breathing, he normally kept really quiet. On another loud grunt, he palmed her breasts, groaning in frustration when his hands met material and sequins. Her mammary glands were amazing. Soft and full. Her nipples were dark and ripe. They were big and tightened with just a glance. He squeezed her flesh, enjoying how she felt in his hands despite the barrier.

Roxy shouted his name, her pussy clamped down around him. His balls pulled up all the way. His skin tightened. The air froze in his lungs. He groaned as he lost his load in hard spurts. Blaze couldn't help himself, he had to sink his teeth into her. Just a careful nip. Just a . . . he growled as his teeth bit down.

Roxy screamed his name, her whole body seemed to spasm around him. Every muscle tensed for the longest time. He squeezed her breasts and rolled her nipples between his fingers.

Using easy circular thrusts, he wrung out the last of her pleasure, as well as his own, already dreading pulling out of her. This level of need was not normal. He'd returned home, the night before, after she was already in bed and had woken her up so that he could fuck her. After grabbing a few hours' rest, he'd woken her up a second time, leaving straight after because he was worried he was going to hurt her if he kept rutting her like he had been. Twice in his office and then twice during the night and it wasn't like he was gentle with her. Gentle didn't even compute. The moment he saw her he had to have her. The moment his dick entered her, the need to fuck would overtake him. Just a couple more days and he'd get his control back. He was sure of it.

Roxy fell forward against the wall. He put an arm around her waist to hold her up. Her breath came in short pants. "You didn't just do that?"

"I thought you said a quickie would be fun."

"Not the quickie, you ruined my dress." He could hear that she didn't sound very happy.

Blaze carefully pulled out and stepped back. Roxy turned. By all that had claws. "Oh fuck! I'm sorry."

Her dress was ripped across the bodice, her heavy breasts exposed. He couldn't say that he was unhappy at the welcome sight. Blaze groaned. He bent down wanting to suck on one of her plump nipples. He couldn't seem to stop thinking with his dick.

"No, you don't." Roxy put a hand on his forehead.

"We're late. I need to find something else to wear, which means that we're going to be ridiculously late." She turned towards the closet. "I can't believe you ruined my only formal dress."

Hearing her say that made Blaze feel like a colossal jerk. "I'm sorry." She didn't acknowledge him. Roxy yanked open the closet door and began to sort through the limited garments that hung there. "You can buy more stuff. Anything you want. I'll have someone send a catalog tomorrow."

"It doesn't help me now or later tonight. I didn't bring a second pair of pajamas you know." She glanced at him over her shoulder. This time he could see that she was only pretending to be angry.

Blaze winced, he had ripped the one she had been wearing the night before into shreds. He'd warned her not to wear anything that she needed. "Let me rephrase that," he tried hard not to smile. "You can buy whatever you need, barring new pajamas. I think it would be better if you slept naked from now on."

"Is that right?" She removed a black garment from the rack. Roxy sighed. "It'll have to do."

"You'll look amazing in whatever you decide to wear." Blaze meant every word.

Roxy blushed, and gave him a shy smile. "Yeah but it's doubtful the others will feel the same way as you do."

Blaze folded his arms across his chest. "It's not like you're trying to impress any of the other males." He hated the way his voice had dropped a couple of octaves. He hated the strange feeling that had taken up residence inside of him.

She gave a laugh. "Well, you never know." Her smile widened. "Things might not work out between us."

Blaze couldn't suppress the low growl from being torn from him.

"I'm only joking," she laughed. He could see that she was teasing him but the strange feeling wouldn't go away.

Roxy began to shimmy out of her damaged dress. Within the next few seconds, she would be completely naked. If he saw her completely naked then he would have to have her again.

"I'll wait in the hall." He didn't wait for her reply. Once in the hallway, he could breathe again. Jealous. He, king of fire, was jealous. It was pathetic.

It took every ounce of self-control he possessed to keep from going back in and rutting her again. The female was his. All that was left was to discuss the terms of the mating with her. If she agreed, they could go ahead.

His dragon would stop harassing him and things could get back to normal. Although, he suspected, that until she was pregnant, he would probably remain just as rattled as he was right now.

Five minutes later, she stepped from the room, her purse under one arm. Roxy gave him a dirty look.

"What's wrong?"

"This," she pointed to a red welt on her neck.

Blast and damn! "I'm sorry. I guess I got a little carried away." Seeing his mark on her eased something inside him. At least the others would know that she was taken. There would be a couple of single males in attendance this evening. It was rare for a dragon to mark a female before they were mated. This might raise some eyebrows but he didn't give a shit. "It doesn't hurt, does it?"

Roxy shook her head. "No, it's superficial." Then she frowned, looking thoughtful for a moment. "I was told that dragon shifters only bite their mates. Julie mentioned it during our initial briefing. She said that relationships progress pretty quickly with shifters so she didn't want us to be alarmed if it happened."

"Yeah, it's mating behavior, when I hold you down, pull your hair, bite you, the rough sex, it's all mating behavior." Blaze ran a hand through his much shorter hair. He felt so much better with all of it gone. He'd let his appearance deteriorate over the last couple of weeks. Coal's theory was that he had done it because deep down Blaze didn't want a human. He'd gone for a grooming session because he had changed his mind and was now trying to win Roxy. It was absurd. Utter garbage.

"Okay." She didn't sound so sure.

"The hunt must've spurred it on. Don't be alarmed, just because I'm exhibiting the behavior doesn't mean that we are mated or anything. I'll try and be more careful."

"No, don't. I kind of like it." Her eyes widened like she hadn't meant to say that out loud. He liked that she didn't have much of a filter.

Blaze chuckled. "We'd better get going."

Something flared in her eyes. "Shit! We're crazy late at

this point."

Blaze walked slightly ahead of Roxy so that he could direct her through the maze of hallways that worked their way through the vast lair. Within a few minutes they were outside one of the formal dining halls. "Ready?"

Roxy looked pale. Her lips were shiny and her eyelashes looked longer and darker. She was wearing make-up. She really wanted to impress the entourage this evening. Another lash of jealousy hit him. This one had barbed hooks of silver. Fuck! He needed to get these emotions under control and as soon as possible.

Without thinking, he cupped her chin. "You have nothing to worry about." Her gaze softened and she seemed to relax.

Blaze pulled his hand back. "Julie is here as well. I'm sure you will have been seated next to her."

Roxy let out a breath. "Let's do this." It was their first public appearance together since claiming her fully. The human was right to be a little nervous; as his potential mate, she would be judged. Thing was, she had nothing to worry about. Roxy would make a fantastic queen. She wasn't afraid to stand up to him, she had a backbone. The female was also intelligent. She'd shown emotion which meant that she could be compassionate. It was an important quality for a female in power. Roxy would make a good business partner, she would be a good mother and raise strong potential heirs. That made her perfect.

Everyone hushed as they walked into the room. Roxy froze in place as soon as she laid eyes on the busy table.

Blaze put his hand on Roxy's lower back. The gesture served to guide her forward. There were two seats still available.

Inferno rose to his feet. "It's about time." The fucker's beady little eyes drifted up and down his human's body.

The dress she changed into was form-fitting. It hugged her curves lovingly. Inferno's gaze settled on her chest.

Fuck that. He wrapped an arm around her waist. *Mine.* The thought startled him. This level of jealousy was new to him. It was the hunt and the whole claiming thing, it was messing with his mind. It was purely instinctual and had nothing to do with emotions or feelings.

He'd never been this close to mating someone before. That wasn't entirely true. He'd been close to mating someone once before. Too fucking close. It was like a wound opened up inside him. Blaze released Roxy. This was business. He was the fucking king, he could handle this. He could handle all of it.

CHAPTER 12

Roxy had never been more nervous in her whole life. She felt like a bug underneath a microscope, although the guy at the end of the table was making her feel like she was a naked bug. That last bit didn't make sense since bugs were naturally naked. Now she was talking nonsense to herself. Clearly overly nervous.

Then Blaze was stepping in next to her. She caught Julie's eyes, the other woman was smiling at her. It made her feel marginally better. Although, Julie was sitting at the other end of the table. Nowhere near the open seats. *Oh shit!*

Blaze was talking. Damn! She hadn't been paying attention. He was introducing her to people at the table.

The guy sitting next to Julie smiled and gave a small wave. Shit a brick but she needed to pay attention. She forced herself to focus.

"Next to Coal is Pauline and Flame. Flame heads up the Pinnacle warriors and Pauline is his mate; she's also human."

What were Pinnacle warriors? She'd have to ask Blaze

later.

"Hi. Nice to meet you," the tiny blonde smiled at Roxy.

"You too," she managed to get out. It felt like she was grimacing rather than smiling. Her muscles were just too tense for casual hellos.

"That's Lisa and Scorch. Scorch is also a Pinnacle warrior and Lisa, his mate, is a human." The dark-haired Lisa was sitting on the big guy's lap. Neither of them acknowledged that they had heard the introduction and from where she was standing, it looked like his hand was up her skirt.

"A pleasure to meet you both." Roxy quickly averted her eyes as his hand disappeared even higher up her thigh.

She recognized the next lady. "Sue, how are you?"

The other woman's chestnut-colored hair curled about her face. She smiled but it didn't quite meet her eyes. She didn't look happy to see Roxy. That couldn't be right. "Hello." Her voice was flat. The other woman was probably just nervous as well.

"I'm sure you remember Lava." It was more than likely her imagination but Blaze's voice became a little deeper as he locked eyes with the big shifter. The guy had wanted to fight Blaze for her.

The shifter gave a nod.

"Are the two of you together?" Roxy blurted.

Lava smirked, he put his hand around Sue's shoulders and drew her a little closer to him. "I had to take down a couple of others in order to win her, but yes, this beauty is my human."

Sue seemed to tense as he touched her, she even folded her arms and turned away from him with her knees. Roxy found the whole dynamic quite interesting. Lava didn't seem to notice or maybe Roxy was reading too much into things. More than likely the latter.

"Then we have Burn, Heat and Crimson." Blaze looked at each of the huge males in turn. "Aside from Flame and Lava, these males are my best Pinnacle warriors."

Although, Burn and Crimson were ogling the hell out of her, Heat was the one who was all out undressing her. His gaze moved from her boobs to between her thighs and back again. He even made a sniffing noise as he did so.

Blaze growled. "Roxy is my female. Mine." Then his eyes widened in what looked like shock. He was quick to school his expression and then pulled a chair out for her. She couldn't help but notice how he put his body between her and the three men.

"Your female. We can all see that," a younger looking guy said. Although, he was seated at the table, Blaze hadn't introduced her to him. "Let me guess, you tripped and fell and your teeth pierced into her," he laughed, his eyes trained on her neck. She knew exactly what he was looking at, it was the bite mark. The shifter pulled out the chair closest to him, he gestured for her to sit. "I'm Inferno, Blaze's brother. Come on, take a seat. I can't wait to meet the female who has got my brother so rattled." He patted the chair.

"Careful," Blaze warned.

"Apologies, my lord." Inferno gave a semi-bow from his seated position. It was more mocking than respectful.

Roxy glanced at Blaze; his eyes were narrowed, his jaw was tight. She took a seat, Blaze slipping into the chair next to her.

"Good to see you finally got rid of the animal that was growing on your face."

"Beards are in." Blaze reached for a pitcher of red wine.

"So are man buns," Inferno laughed. "Come to think of it, you would look awesome with a man bun."

"Shut it," Blaze snarled at his brother before looking her in the eyes. His demeanor softened . . . just a tad. "Would you like some wine?"

Her nerves were frayed. Alcohol would loosen her up a bit. Roxy nodded. "Yes, please." She had to strain to pick up the golden goblet in front of her. "Sheesh. This thing is heavy."

"If you think that's heavy, try this," Inferno held his own silver-looking goblet out to her. Roxy could feel her eyes practically bug out of her skull as she took the cup from him. She had to use two hands and she made a squeaking noise.

Inferno chuckled. "Yeah, stick to the gold, leave the platinum cups to the shifters."

Gold.

Platinum.

She took another look around the room. There was a golden chandelier with what looked like emeralds, rubies and diamonds. Surely not? The picture frames were gold gilt. *No!!!*

Blaze filled up her gold goblet. *Gold.* Roxy took a big slug of the wine. It was really good. Smooth as silk and just the right temperature. Not that she was an expert. Not even close. It seemed that dragons enjoyed the finer things in life.

"So, Roxy . . ." Inferno leaned forward, drawing her attention. "Tell me a little about yourself. What did you do for a living?"

"I work, worked . . ." She cleared her throat. At this point she didn't know if she was going back or not. She decided to err on the side of caution. "I work in a bakery. I run the sales side of things. All the front of house stuff."

"Oh, so you can bake?" Inferno smiled. "Blaze loves chocolate chip cookies, so that's a good thing."

"Actually," She felt herself blush, "I can't cook, let alone bake, to save my life. I've tried it a few times and nearly burned down the bakery. My best friend owns the place so it would've been terrible if I'd succeeded."

"Don't worry about it," Inferno winked at her. "Blaze might enjoy chocolate chip cookies but I know another type of cookie that he's way more into."

Roxy couldn't help but to choke out a laugh, she tried hard to hold it back but failed. She could practically feel the tension radiate off of Blaze.

Just then a couple of servers walked in carrying large trays. She turned to the male in question, hoping to change the subject and to start a conversation with Blaze. "I'm starving." And then she whispered under her breath. "It's so good to be out. Your brother seems really friendly."

"Hmmmm." he sort of smiled then muttered something under his breath that sounded very much like 'don't confuse horny with friendly.'

The servers began putting plates in front of each of them. The entrées looked amazing. "I love scallops," she announced, brushing her arm against Blaze's.

"Me too," was his short, curt answer.

Everyone talked amongst themselves. Lina stayed sitting on her mate's lap and they fed each other. It was rather bizarre.

Roxy picked up her knife and fork—even the cutlery weighed a ton. She wondered if the knife and fork set were white gold or platinum. It didn't really matter to her, only that she found it a little excessive and a lot bizarre.

"So," Inferno stuck his fork into one of the scallops. "What do you do for fun, Roxy?"

"What is this?" Blaze asked. "Twenty questions?"

"Roxy might just be my future sister-in-law, thank you very much." He raised his brows. "I'd like to get to know a little bit about her, if you don't mind."

"As long as there are no ulterior motives," Blaze's voice had dropped dangerously low. "I know you, brother, better than you know yourself."

If Roxy didn't know better, she'd say that he was jealous. Her heart beat just a little faster and she found herself actually liking the idea. It meant that maybe there were some feelings for her alongside the lust. It was still a bit early to tell, but hopefully there was more there than just really good sex for him.

Inferno chuckled, lifting a scallop to his mouth. He paused just in front of his lips. "I would never move in on your female."

Blaze narrowed his eyes. "Not if you want to continue breathing."

Inferno popped the scallop into his mouth and chewed before swallowing. He licked his lips. "By claw, brother, I think you might be smitten."

"My relationship with Roxy is none of your business."

"I would be interested to know as well," the big shifter sitting next to Blaze said. She couldn't remember his name.

Blaze pursed his lips, a tic developing in his jaw.

"What are your interests?" Red . . . no . . . Flame . . . no, that was the other guy with the human mate. It was another term for red . . . Crimson, his name was Crimson.

She suddenly recalled that he'd asked her a question. The couples talked to one another but all the single guys eyes' were glued on her. It was definitely a tic in Blaze's jaw.

"I bet you enjoy swimming," the guy at the head of the table answered for her. "Do you prefer to wear a one-piece or a two-piece swimsuit?" He pushed his empty plate aside and leaned forward, his eyes narrowed in on hers, they dipped to her boobs for a second before lifting to her eyes once more.

She felt Blaze stiffen next to her. *Oh shit!* "Actually," her voice was high-pitched but she needed to head this off. "I love reading and taking long bubble baths."

"Mmmmm . . ." Long, drawn-out and deep. The guy at the head of the table rubbed his jaw. "Bubble baths are awesome, especially when shared," he winked at her and Blaze growled.

There was a really naughty side to her that loved the attention. Roxy had an okay body, her hips were a tad wide and her bum . . . well let's just say she had some junk in the ol' trunk but she was comfortable in her own skin. Guys did show interest in her from time to time, but never like this. They didn't come on this strong. They weren't this attractive either. At the same time, she felt really uncomfortable as well. Blaze seemed to hate every minute of it.

"I also love baked goods," she gave a nervous giggle. "I have that in common with you, Blaze." She gave his arm a bump with her own.

He nodded once.

"I love cream buns and donuts. My favorites though are the coconut tarts from Sweet Treats." She glanced Inferno's way. "That's my friend's bakery, the place where I work." She turned back to Blaze. "I also love chocolate chip cookies, by the way." She was rattling off but couldn't seem to help herself. Roxy gave her thighs a tap. "I eat way too much of the wrong things, as you can tell."

"You are quite beautiful," Crimson said.

"I would have to agree," Inferno remarked. "Lush and—"

"Do not talk to my female in that way." Hearing Blaze

refer to her as his made her feel warm and fuzzy inside.

Inferno leaned forward. "I was merely stating a fact. Setting the record straight."

"Well don't," Blaze growled.

"They're just trying to be nice," Roxy said under her breath; she could see that this was going in the wrong direction.

"Nice!" Blaze snorted. "They're not trying to be nice. These males don't know the meaning of the word nice. All they can see is a beautiful female. You are a fertile human, highly-prized. You also have a very appealing scent. They're not being nice; they're trying to . . ." he paused. "Don't buy into their bullshit. I'm not." He gave Inferno a long, hard stare and then turned his attention to the other three males.

All three visibly paled and seemed to shrink in their chairs. Roxy wasn't sure if she liked the caveman bullshit or if it irritated her. Maybe a bit of both.

"Um . . ." she put her napkin on the table and pushed her chair back. "I need to go to the little girl's room." Roxy was perfectly fine, she just needed a break. She made her way to the restroom. There were communal facilities. The only toilet was separate from the actual restroom, which had a large vanity with a lounge area complete with an antique-looking couch. It looked like something straight out of the French Renaissance. Marble, gold and intricate motifs made the space warm and inviting. Thankfully the toilet was free.

Roxy put down the toilet lid and sat for a few minutes.

Julie had mentioned that shifters were highly territorial. They could be overbearing, overprotective and even a little caveman-like. If memory served, she'd even used the term barbaric. She wondered if this was more of the mating behavior that Blaze had referred to. It had to be.

It was so peaceful and relaxing in the small stall, but she couldn't hide out here all night. Roxy flushed the toilet and walked out, almost colliding with Sue.

"Oh, hi," she said. It was nice to see a familiar face.

Sue gave a nod. "Hi. If I didn't know better, I would say that you were hiding out in here."

"Busted." She pulled a face. "It's getting a bit hot and heavy in there." She pointed at the door that led to the dining hall.

"Yeah, the shifter males are all pretty desperate. They sniff around any unmated women." She gave a laugh. "They'd have to be seriously hard up to hit on the king's shag."

Roxy didn't really like the way Sue had worded that. It made her feel a little bit worthless and a lot slutty. "I'm sure they're just being nice," she reiterated what she'd said earlier.

Sue pursed her lips and folded her arms. The other woman looked like she was mulling over something. She finally sucked in a deep breath. "The advice we were given was bullshit!" she shook her head, looking pissed.

"What advice are you referring to?"

"The whole, *the further you get the more chance you have of snagging a royal* is a load of bullshit. That Julie chick is some piece of work."

Roxy narrowed her eyes. What was this woman on about? "No one could have predicted how the hunt would go."

"No!" she snapped back. "We were told to get as far as we could. The more distance we put between ourselves and the others would almost guarantee a royal shifter. I got the furthest out of all of us." Sue pointed at herself as she spoke. "How is it that you and that other useless girl pretty much give up on the whole hunt and you both ended up with kings?" So that's why she looked so unhappy. It was because Roxy and Lily had both been won by kings and she'd missed out. What a piece of work.

"Well," Roxy shrugged. "Maybe you shouldn't have left. Lily was exhausted. She was suffering from a bad stitch. The right thing to do was to stay with her until she was ready to go on."

"You said you were tired as well. Don't pretend you did it for her."

What a bitch! Roxy needed to keep her cool. She wasn't about to let someone like this rattle her. "I was tired, but not too tired to keep going. I only told Lily that so she wouldn't feel bad about my staying with her. There was no way I was just going to abandon her out in the middle of nowhere. You chose to keep going." Karma had a hand in how things played out. Roxy kept that line of thinking to herself. "Lava seems like a really nice guy."

Sue rolled her eyes. Roxy couldn't believe that she had found the woman attractive when she had first met her.

What a bitch! She puffed out a breath. "I suppose if I had to get stuck with one of the lessers, then I'm thankful it's with one of the best fire warriors. I didn't come all the way out here for nothing you know. I want to be pampered. I don't want to have to work . . ." she shook her head. "If I have to push out a couple of brats for the privilege, then my life had better be really good."

Roxy didn't know what to say to that. "I need to get back." She didn't plan on getting involved in things that had nothing to do with her. Hopefully Lava would see through Sue. She didn't wait for a reply, she just walked out.

Halfway through the main course, Julie and Coal swapped places with two of the single guys. Roxy mouthed *Thank you* to the other woman. Up until then, things had been awkward and heated. The guys kept asking her all sorts of things and subtly hitting on her. Blaze was like a bear with a sore head. He calmed after the seat swap but remained quiet and withdrawn. He announced that they were leaving straight after they finished dessert. The plates hadn't even been cleared yet.

He proceeded to march her home where he ripped off the last formal dress she owned and made love to her first against the wall, then on the floor halfway to the bed and then, a third time on the actual bed. Making love was not the right description. Blaze called it rutting and that was far more fitting. All three times were from behind. Hard, fast and mind-blowing, were good descriptions as well. They'd finally fallen asleep, totally exhausted. Blaze was gone when she woke up the next morning.

This was the pattern for the days that followed. They attended a few formal functions. Blaze was withdrawn and they left as soon as possible. The one really good thing was that he couldn't keep his hands off of her when they were together. The problem was that their relationship was made up mostly of sex. There wasn't too much room for talking. Roxy felt herself longing for more.

CHAPTER 13

Five days later . . .

"Darcy is mated to one of the earth princes," Coal flipped through the folder. "She and Rock took the plunge yesterday."

"I have no news on Thunder and his human."

"I will be surprised if they are not mated already." Those two had been sickening together.

"The human, Sue, and Lava are still together. He has said that he is still working on winning her but that it won't take long."

Blaze shook his head. "The male suffers from an oversupply of confidence. The female doesn't look all that interested in him. I'm sure that she is biding her time, she won't stick around after the two weeks are up. Mark my words."

"So," Coal put down the folder. "You have been paying attention. Your focus seems to revolve around a certain human lately." His brother smiled.

Blaze didn't feel like having this conversation. He

flipped to the final page in his file. "What about the last human?"

Coal laughed. "Way to change the subject. Emma is mated to one of the water warriors. According to Torrent, the female is in heat and they are trying for a baby. It is another success story."

"That's excellent news," Blaze said. "I will finalize the report and send feedback to the vampire kings. I am sure that they will be satisfied with the results thus far."

He watched as Coal's eyes began to glint with mischief. The male sucked in a deep breath.

Oh no, he didn't want to talk about his relationship with Roxy, it had nothing to do with any of them. "How is Julie? How is the pregnancy coming along?"

Just like that, the glint in Coal's eye went away, it was replaced by a faraway look, filled with tenderness. Blaze almost wished he hadn't asked. "She's doing well. My female craves pickles and peanut butter," his brother pulled a face. "Apparently it is a human thing. Her lower back has begun to ache a little. You saw her yesterday." The male looked excited, his eyes widened and his voice rose by a few octaves. "Julie is definitely showing. By the size of her rounded belly you can tell that she is with child." He narrowed his eyes a smidgen and leaned forward. "She's insatiable at the moment." Then that damned glint was back. "Talking about insatiable . . . what's happening with Roxy?"

"We're good." Blaze left it at that.

"You both scent of each other. You're having a ton of

sex which is really good, but . . ."

Blaze didn't want to hear it. He sucked in a breath and held it in his lungs.

" . . . a word of advice," Coal added.

Oh boy, here we go! Blaze felt like rolling his eyes.

"Females—human females—like for their male to acknowledge them in public."

Blaze made a grunting noise, not sure where this was going.

"It needs to be clear to all that you are together," Coal went on. "Little things like holding hands or putting your arm around her, showing affection, will go a long way."

Hand holding? Cuddling? Kissing? It was all romantic crap. Blaze wasn't a romantic male. He just wasn't. What they had was not a romance, it never would be. They were in a relationship but it was one with definite boundaries. He hadn't actually spoken to Roxy about them yet, however, he had made his stance clear through his actions. "I have made it very clear to all that Roxy is my female."

Coal pulled a face that told Blaze that the male thought he was full of shit. "If you say so. Growling at other males, telling them to back off . . ." he paused, "treating Roxy like she is a possession instead of your potential mate and future partner is not how to go about it. You've been with humans before. I think out of all of us, you have the most experience."

"I don't," Blaze practically snarled. Why did they keep bringing up his past? His only serious experience with a female was a terrible one. It had left a bad taste in his mouth.

Coal gave Blaze a good-natured slap on the shoulder. "It was merely an observation," he shrugged. "I like the female. I think she's good for you and I agree with Inferno," he snorted out a laugh. "I think you're smitten."

"Bull-fucking-shit!" he growled before he could stop himself.

Coal laughed and Blaze had to stop himself from punching his asshole brother. He didn't want to give any more credence to the male's beliefs, which were utter nonsense. If this was what the others believed though, what did Roxy think? Did she believe him to be in love with her? He hoped not. He also hoped that she wasn't falling in love with him. Such emotions would ruin things.

Blaze needed to speak to her right now, before it was too late. The sex was good. It was better than good. Roxy had proven herself as a potential queen. Not just because they were compatible. There was more to it than just that. He liked the idea of her raising his heirs. The last thing he needed or wanted was her misguided love.

"I have to go." Blaze felt the sense of urgency grow.

"I'm sure you do," Coal snickered.

"I have a meeting." Why the fuck had he explained himself to the male?

"Sure you do." More snickering. "If you—"

Blaze ignored Coal. He slammed the door behind him. After a search of her room, he went to Julie's place. There was no sign of either female. Coal rounded the corner, his brother was grinning from ear to fucking ear.

Blaze clenched his jaw.

"I was trying to tell you that Julie and Roxy are visiting with Flame's mate, Pauline."

Blaze nodded once and headed in the direction of Flame's chamber.

"You are most welcome!" Coal shouted after him. "Good luck with Roxy. It looks like you've come to some conclusion, I only pray that it's a not an asshole one."

Blaze kept walking. Just because he didn't plan on having a conventional relationship with Roxy did not mean that he planned on hurting her or mistreating her. On the contrary, they could have an honest, open relationship filled with friendship, a relationship where both parties respected one another. It would be better than the over-emotional other option. One where things got messy, where one party had the ability to harm the other. No fucking thank you. He was sure he could make her see it his way. He had to.

Julie held her belly. It was crazy how quickly it had grown since Roxy had met the other woman. "So, you guys have decided to wait. I'm not sure how you managed to convince Flame of that."

Pauline pulled a face. "He wasn't happy. Going through my first heat was a bit of a challenge but it was also really fun." She blushed. "You have no idea how many condoms we went through."

"I think I can guess," Julie laughed.

"I'm going into town tomorrow to see the vampire

doctor. She's a human, her name is Becky. Anyway, we decided it would be better if I went onto the Pill, that way I won't ovulate. My heat was stressful on Flame. These shifters really do operate on instinct. Their base urges are way more prevalent than any human guy's, that's for sure."

Roxy could certainly attest to that, even though she hadn't been here for very long.

Julie nodded. "Coal wants to do everything for me. I swear that he would carry me around if I let him."

Julie and Pauline laughed. "I can only imagine how bad Flame would be. I want to wait for at least a year. I'm still really young. I want to enjoy my mate and our time together as a couple first before we have kids. We have plenty of time for all that."

Julie nodded enthusiastically. "I would've liked to have waited a bit as well but we don't always have a say in these things." She gave her belly another affectionate rub.

Pauline glanced at Roxy. "The condom broke."

Julie laughed. "I had a serious panic session, I wasn't sure I even wanted to be a mom." She paused. "I've had one or two panic sessions since then, but I'm really excited and truly happy. This baby may not have been planned, but he is definitely loved."

"What's going on with you and Blaze?" Pauline raised her brows.

Roxy picked up her glass of cranberry juice. It was cold and condensation had begun to form on the outside of the glass.

"Yeah," Julie lowered her head and looked at Roxy

through narrowed eyes. "Spit it out. All I can say is that he's certainly possessive of you. I hope he's not as grumpy when you two are alone together."

"Um . . . he's just as intense." As in, the sex was intense. "I wouldn't call him grumpy though."

"So, he still has a stick up his ass?" Julie giggled. "I must say, I'm disappointed. I had hoped that once he got some nookie, that he would calm down, but it hasn't happened. In fact, I would say that he's worse."

She didn't like that Julie was putting Blaze down even though she knew that she didn't mean anything bad by it. "He's a serious guy. It's the way that he is, it's not a bad thing." Having said that, she'd hardly ever heard him laugh. When he did, his guard seemed to slip just that little bit but never for long. "He told me he's experiencing mating behavior and that it's making him a little nuts. It's probably those base instincts you were talking about earlier."

"Mating behavior," Julie gushed. "That's so exciting. Have you discussed mating one another?"

"We haven't really had a chance." Roxy took a big sip of her juice, trying not to blush.

Pauline narrowed her eyes. "You guys have been together for over a week now. You're living with Blaze. Shifters tend to move quickly. Flame and I had already set the date by then. Lisa was already mated by then. I heard that two of the others who were in the hunt with you are mated already as well. One couple is trying for a baby."

"Everyone is different. Coal and I took a little longer."

Julie lifted her eyes in thought. "Has he mentioned it at all? He should've said something by now."

"Um . . ." Roxy chewed on her lower lip. "I guess we haven't talked much about anything."

Pauline laughed. "Flame and I talked very little for those first few days as well."

Julie laughed. "Okay, I totally get it."

"I don't think he can be near me without ripping my clothes off and I mean literally. Thank god the clothes I ordered came yesterday or I swear I would have to wear a towel or a sheet."

Julie picked up her own glass of juice. "Yup, that's mating behavior for sure. Acting all possessive in public and ripping your clothes off in private. Blaze has it bad for you."

"Do you think so?" Roxy hated that she sounded so unsure.

"Definitely," Pauline was grinning wildly. "I would be very surprised if he didn't bring it up soon."

Julie nodded. "Yeah, he's showing all the signs."

Roxy put her glass down and clasped her hands in her lap. "I think it might be a bit soon to start talking about mating. Forever is a long time."

Julie leaned forward. "I've seen the way you look at him. You have feelings for the guy."

Roxy shook her head. "It's too soon to tell." They hadn't spoken much at all. She hardly knew Blaze. The sex was fantastic but that was hardly enough to base a relationship on.

Thankfully they changed the subject. Julie showed them a catalog filled with furniture for the nursery. They looked at all the various options for the layout, as well as the bedding. Julie wasn't sure whether to go with brown and mint green or brown and baby blue.

Julie paged through the catalog. "I think I'd like to go with a teddy bear theme, or—"

There was a knock at the door.

Julie put the catalog down on the coffee table. "Hmmm . . ." she looked confused for a moment. "I wonder who that could be." She eased herself off the couch and headed for the door.

"Hi, I believe Roxy is here."

Shit! It was Blaze. "Yeah, we're kind of in the middle of something. Girls' stuff," Julie answered.

"I need to borrow her for a short while. There is something I have to discuss with her." Julie had yet to invite Blaze in.

Roxy couldn't help but to glance at Pauline, as if the other woman had the answer to her question . . . *Why was Blaze here?* Which was crazy of course. Roxy could feel that she was frowning.

Pauline grinned. She mouthed, "He wants to talk." Her grin widened. "See, I told you," she said without making a sound.

Roxy gave a shake of the head. It couldn't be. She got to her feet and walked to the door. Blaze's features relaxed as soon as he saw her.

"I'll come by later," Roxy said.

"Sure you will," Julie gave her a knowing look.

"Sorry to mess up your plans," Blaze said, after the door closed behind them.

"No problem," Roxy said. She snuck a little peek at Blaze from under her eyelashes. Believe it or not, he looked even more tense than usual. "Is it something serious?"

"Yes."

Okay then. What could this be about? "Should I be worried?" she tried to sound upbeat, like she was joking and failed. Instead she sounded nervous.

Blaze tried the handle on one of the doors in the hallway. It was locked. He grabbed her hand and marched forward to the next door, trying that handle. This one opened. He pulled her inside, closing the door behind them. It was another one of those dining halls, similar to the one they'd been in the other night, only this one was a little more intimate.

"Okay. Out with it. I'm ready." She folded her arms across her chest.

"There is something important I need to discuss with you." Blaze's eyes were fixed firmly on her boobs. He licked his lips.

"Um . . . is it a conversation you plan on having with my breasts? Something important you need to tell them?"

Blaze made a groaning noise, he scrubbed a hand over his face and walked to the other side of the room before turning and coming back. His loose-fitting pants were tented. "I just . . ." He finally looked her in the eyes.

"Let me guess, you're having those mating urges again?" Again she tried to make light of it.

Blaze folded his arms. He was breathing deeply. His chest was as chiseled as they came. His abs were a thing of beauty. His green eyes were filled with lust. "I need to have a serious conversation and all I can think about is getting between your thighs."

"I don't know whether to be upset or flattered."

"Flattered." He took a step towards her, grasping her hips with his big hands. "Definitely flattered. I like this dress." He gave the material a tug and the boob-tube top somehow managed to hold on, his move only exposed the tops of her boobs.

Blaze growled again. He licked his lips. "I don't think I'm going to be able to concentrate on this conversation until I've had you." He leaned down and kissed the tops of her breasts.

"We had sex during the night and twice this morning. You're like an energizer bunny."

"I'm not sure what that is but I don't think I like being called a bunny," his voice had turned husky. So sexy. "I want you again, Roxy."

"Take me then."

He picked her up and put her on the table. "Lie back," he instructed, shoving her dress up her thighs. Blaze growled low in his throat.

"Wait!" she squealed, quickly pushing her thong down and yanking it off before he could rip it. She leaned back on her elbows and watched with fascination as he moved between her thighs.

The thing was that she wanted him just as much. There were times when he woke her up during the night and just like that she was wet. He'd stroke her clit for ten seconds and then he'd be inside her. No foreplay required. It was embarrassing how quickly he could make her come. Fact was, the mating urges—as he called them—seemed to go both ways. It didn't matter that she was human. She couldn't wait for him to be inside her.

This time, instead of freeing his cock, he leaned in. Hot breath hit her straight on the vagina. Her clit throbbed. It was like he was touching her already.

Roxy's ragged breathing filled the small room. Was he going to look at her all day or . . . he tongued her clit. *Holy shit!!*

Roxy whimpered.

"I haven't done this in a while," he rasped before closing his mouth over the little bud of nerves and giving a suck. He may not have done this for a while but he wasn't rusty. Not even a little bit. He gave her clit another lick.

Goodbye eyes, it was nice knowing you. The organs in question rolled so far back into her skull that she wasn't sure she'd get them back again. She made a drawn-out moaning noise. Then his tongue was inside her . . . in and out in a quick rhythm that had her back bowing and her hands flying to his head.

She buried her fingers into his hair. Blaze took back her clit and suckled on it until she was begging. It was incoherent begging. Begging that was thick with moans, cries and whimpers.

When his tongue lapped at her, circling her clit before laving over it, she felt her nerve endings catch alight. Her mouth rounded into a startled *oh* and her hands grabbed his hair.

Her hips jerked. Roxy grit her teeth as an orgasm of epic proportions ripped through her. She was still riding the pleasure train when Blaze derailed it and pulled away.

His face was wet. Using the back of his hand, he wiped most of it away.

His hair stood at strange angles. *Oops!* She may have torn a couple of chunks out. Blaze picked her up like she weighed nothing. He looked angry but she knew better.

Then he was sitting on one of the dining room chairs. A high-backed, intricately-carved, antique looking chair covered with purple velvet.

She ran a hand through his hair. "Did I hurt you?" she sounded breathless.

He gave her a tight smile. "I'm a dragon shifter. You can't hurt me." He yanked his pants down, and lifted her up with one hand while pulling her dress out of the way with the other. Then he was sliding into her. His eyes changed, a look of utter rapture appeared as he joined with her. She was sure her own eyes would reflect the same. Blaze frowned and clenched his jaw. "You feel good," he groaned.

"So do you." Whose voice was that? Surely not hers. So wanton, so needy. She put her hands on his shoulders. Her feet didn't touch the ground so there was no way she could ride him. Her pussy fluttered around his thick girth, still feeling the aftereffects of her orgasm.

Blaze's hands tightened on her hips. He lifted her and let her back down. Her head fell back as she slid up and down his cock. Slow and easy. Up and down. Careful but deliberate.

Blaze was breathing hard through his nose. She let her hands slide down his chest and then back up. All those muscles felt really good. His eyes were a bright, brilliant green. So unnervingly beautiful. She leaned forward, having to reach up to kiss him. A soft brush of the lips.

He didn't reciprocate other than to breathe harder. She tried again, this time licking the seam of his mouth. She could taste herself on him. It turned her on even more. She clenched the walls of her vagina around him, eliciting a growl. Blaze kissed her back. His tongue breached her mouth and his hips thrust up.

She moaned, his strokes had turned more urgent. His cock hit her deeper and quicker. Their kiss turned frenzied. His grip tightened as his hips jerked up. Her boobs jerked up and down and her dress slipped with each hard thrust until they spilled out. Her nipples were hard but they grew even harder as they rubbed against his chest.

Blaze broke the kiss and sucked on one of her nipples. She clawed at his back. He sucked again. The sharp sensation zinged through her, making her pussy clench. It was like her nipples were directly attached to her clit. He moved to her other breast, this time nipping at her flesh.

His biceps bulged from holding her up so that he could thrust into her. He was making loud grunting noises. She could hear sucking sounds as he used his mouth on her. Her boobs bounced around his face and his abs pulled tight with every thrust.

Blaze gave a particularly hard suck and she was done. Her back arched. Her nails dug into him. Her head fell back and she groaned his name. His movements slowed just a smidgen as they turned jerky. He buried his face in her chest, making a loud noise that was a mix between a grunt and a groan. Then he fucked her harder for a few seconds before easing off. His breathing was hard, his lips so close that she was sure she could feel them against her skin.

Then he ran his hand up and down her back, falling backward to rest on the chair back. His eyes were closed. Blaze licked his lips. He pulled the top of her dress up, only opening his eyes when her boobs were covered. "I suppose I should pull out of you now so that we can talk." He didn't look excited at the prospect.

"If it's important then maybe you should. I'm not sure we can conduct a conversation like this." She was breathing hard. Her voice was a little raspy from all the groaning.

He gave a little circular motion with his hips and she whimpered.

Blaze tucked a wayward strand of hair behind her ear. Her ponytail felt like it had loosened. "You are the most receptive female I have ever been with."

"Is that a compliment?"

"Yes, it is."

"Okay, I'll take it, even though you are indirectly referring to sex with other women." He didn't say endearing or flattering things often.

"I have been with other females," he shrugged. "It is what it is." Blaze frowned. He looked pained for a moment as he lifted her off of his still hard shaft.

She put a hand over herself to keep from messing everywhere.

Blaze lifted her off of his lap and disappeared into a side room that had to be the restroom. He returned with a warm towel.

"Thanks," she gave him a smile and cleaned herself up.

"We need to talk about our relationship."

Roxy nodded. She sat on the chair he had just vacated. Blaze sat down next to her. He turned his chair so that he was facing her. "We have something here." He ran a hand through his hair and sat forward so that his elbows rested on his thighs. "The sex has been phenomenal. I can't keep my hands off of you."

She had to smile. "The sex has been amazing but sex isn't the be all and end all." She was glad he had brought this up. Maybe he felt the same as she did, that there needed to be more.

Blaze smiled back. "No, it's not," he paused. "I want to discuss our future. I want to discuss the possibility of us mating."

Her heart beat faster. She gave a quick nod to

encourage him to continue.

"Compatibility is an excellent foundation. I realize that we haven't spent much time with one another or talked very much."

"It's kind of hard to talk during sex, especially the kind of sex we seem to have."

He smiled, looking so handsome. "Yeah, the mind-blowing kind. The kind that leaves no room for anything else."

"Yup, that sounds about right."

"It's my best kind," he gave her a half-smile before turning serious.

Well, she wouldn't mind the slow kind. The more intimate kind. Slow could be just as mind-blowing, maybe even more so. Roxy kept that to herself, for now.

Blaze sucked in a breath. "I think that there may be a future for us."

"It's still too soon to know that," she blurted. Roxy liked the idea of them, but that's all they were right now, an idea. There wasn't anything substantial there. Not really. Why was her heart beating faster though? Why was she leaning forward to hear what he had to say next? Was she falling in love with him already? No way. Not possible. She did long for more though and it looked like she was going to get it. She tried not to smile like an idiot.

Blaze smiled. He looked happy with her answer. "I think we're headed in the right direction. We would make good partners. I think that in time we could become good friends."

He must have seen the look on her face because he quickly added. "Best friends even."

"Friendship is important in a relationship." She meant it too. One part of her liked where he was going with this but another part was convinced there was going to be a *but* somewhere.

"I know that you would make an excellent mother. You are kind and sweet," he smiled. "You try and keep the peace at the dinners and functions we've attended. You don't like it when I growl at the single males. You try so hard to be polite and not to hurt anyone's feelings. If only you knew the disgusting thoughts those males have about you."

Roxy laughed. "Rubbish. I don't believe it for a second. Then again, maybe Heat has rude thoughts but not the others. They are all well-mannered and kind."

"Well-mannered," Blaze snorted.

"How do you know what they are thinking?" she raised her brows.

"Because I have the same dirty thoughts about you myself," his voice deepened. "All the time. Any red-blooded male who lays eyes on you would have them."

She felt her cheeks heat.

"It's true," he cleared his throat. "Let's not talk about that right now though." He adjusted himself in his pants. "Where were we?"

"You said I would make a good mother."

"Family is important to me. I want children. I am sure that you are like-minded or you wouldn't be here."

Roxy nodded. "Yes, I definitely want children. I always thought I would've had them by now but it hasn't worked out . . . yet," she quickly added the last.

"I wouldn't want to wait too long. Would you be willing to start trying soon after we were mated?" This was starting to sound a little too planned, like a business takeover or something.

"I'm on the Pill right now. We were urged to start taking a contraceptive during the final interview stage."

His eyes darkened and his shoulders tightened up.

"I could go off the Pill though . . . although . . ." It was her turn to pause and to choose her words carefully. This conversation was pretty hectic. It was so soon. She knew that things progressed quickly with non-humans but they had yet to hold hands or to have a romantic dinner together. They had yet to do any of the things that couples did. The few dinners they had attended had been formal and uncomfortable. "I still feel that it's too soon to be having this conversation."

"No . . ." Blaze looked her deep in the eyes. "It's the perfect time for this conversation."

Roxy felt herself frown.

"I want a partner, a queen, and, yes a friend and mother to my children. I, in return, will take good care of you. I will treat you with kindness and respect. I would want an honest relationship. I would promise to be a good male. You would want for nothing." It was like he was reading out lines from a résumé. "It is important that you know that my people and the four kingdoms will always come first. Everything I do will first be for the good of them. It is why you are here."

She wasn't sure how to take that. What did he mean? She got an uneasy feeling.

"I can see that I have upset you. I do not want to be in a relationship based on dishonesty. I respect you, Roxy. I am fond of you."

Fond.

What?

"If it were up to me, I would remain alone but for the good of my kingdom, I need to have heirs."

"So the only reason I'm here is to make babies and that's it?" It was difficult to keep the anger out of her voice.

"No. I told you that we would be friends, partners."

"Best friends," she struggled to keep the sarcasm out of her voice.

"A solid friendship and a good sex life between two people who respect one another, it is more than most people have."

"It sounds like settling to me," she blurted.

Blaze rose to his feet. "I can't do love. I tried it once and it didn't work for me."

"Okay." She also rose to her feet. She spotted her underwear on the floor and picked them up. "You are interested in possibly mating me but you just needed me to know that it will be a loveless relationship. Do I have that right?"

"You make it sound terrible. We would be in a

partnership and have an understanding."

"Yeah, friends with benefits who just happen to have kids." She had to work not to roll her eyes.

"I want you to give it some thought before we move forward with this, or not. You might decide that my terms are not for you. I can't do love. I can't do long walks on the beach. I can't do candlelit dinners or any of that other romantic crap. It doesn't mean that we can't have fun together though. We don't need love to be happy."

"Yeah and by fun I'm sure you're referring to sex." She struggled to keep the emotion and disappointment out of her voice. How in the hell had she managed to snag the one non-human who wasn't going to love her with all of his heart? That's what shifters did. Sure, they hooked up a hell of a lot but when they mated, it was for life. When they loved, it was deeply. Probably even more so than vampires. Not Blaze though. At least she hadn't fallen for him yet. Why the hell was she so upset about this then?

Blaze shook his head. "Not just sex. We could . . ." He let the sentence die like he couldn't think of one thing other than sex. That's all she was good for, sex and popping out babies. There was a huge lump in her throat. If she tried to talk right now, she was afraid that she might cry. She didn't want to give him that satisfaction.

"Just tell me one thing. It's important that you are honest." He stepped towards her. "Are you in love with me?"

What an asshole! The nerve! His question made anger course through her, which helped dry up any potential tears in an instant. "No!" she practically shouted at him. "I told you it's too soon and I meant it. How damned arrogant are you anyway?"

Blaze smiled. The asshole smiled. She could see the tension drain out of him. "I can see that you are angry. This isn't what you were expecting. All I ask is that you think on it." He took another step towards her and cupped her cheek, allowing his thumb to trail over her jawline. The move contrasted sharply with what he saying. It confused her, making her feel upset all over again. It was just disappointment. "Take some time to let it sink in. I really do think we could be good together. I think you would make a fantastic queen. If you can agree to the terms, then we can continue."

In other words, he thought she was a good lay and that they would make pretty children. It wasn't enough for her. Not even close.

Unfortunately, she was on the verge of crying. If she opened her mouth the floodgates would open. There was no way she was going to cry in front of him. He'd probably think she was weak.

"Will you think about it?" Blaze frowned. He looked worried about her answer. The guy didn't care either way. She was misreading this.

Roxy needed to get away. She needed time to pull herself together. She stepped into her panties and pulled them up.

"Come on . . ." Blaze went on, "give it some thought. We'd be so good together. We are good together." Shit!

He actually looked like he cared.

She could see that he would argue with her if she shot him down. She couldn't deal with it. Not right now. Roxy decided to take the cowardly route. "Okay," she said. "I'll think about it." Then she added, "I need to go back to Julie." She was already walking to the door. She couldn't look at him.

She did hear him sigh in what sounded like relief. "Good. I'll see you later."

"Sure." She turned left, back towards Julie's. She heard him move in the opposite direction. Roxy forced herself to keep walking. All she wanted right now was to be alone. To get herself together and to pack her bags, but she couldn't risk running into Blaze.

She found herself knocking on Julie's door. Roxy burst into tears as soon the door opened. She was the biggest baby alive, but it couldn't be helped.

CHAPTER 14

Julie's expression morphed into one of concern. "Come in!" She threw an arm around Roxy, which only made her cry more.

"What happened? What's wrong?"

Roxy covered her face with her hands. She felt like an idiot but she still couldn't stop her bawling.

"Sit," Julie instructed.

Roxy was relieved that Pauline had left. At least Julie would be the only witness to her embarrassing meltdown.

"Here," Julie put a bottle into her hand.

"Water," Roxy sniffed.

"And here." She handed Roxy a couple of tissues. "Now," she sat down next to Roxy, "have a good hard cry and then replenish your lost fluids with the water. It's important to rehydrate. Then you need to dry your eyes with the tissues and we can have a good talk."

"Rehydrate!" Roxy choked out a laugh. Tears still rolled down her cheeks. Damn these waterworks.

"Yup, whatever it is, it can't be so bad."

Roxy blew her nose. "I'm not even sure why I'm so

upset. I shouldn't be. I'm disappointed but it shouldn't have affected me this badly." Another tear slipped out and she wiped it away.

"Have some water," Julie pointed at the bottle.

Roxy forced a smile and did as Julie said. She did feel a bit better after a couple of good glugs.

"Now. What did he say to you? I'm going to assume that Blaze is the cause of all this."

"You were right about the mate talk. He wanted to talk to me about us and our future."

"Let me guess. He came on too strong?" Julie pulled a face. "Shifters can be so overbearing. I'm sure he wanted to hit you over the head and drag you to his bed. I'm sure he mentioned that he wants kids right away . . . that you're starting right now. They are so emotional, so—"

"Please stop," her lip wobbled. "I wish that's what had happened. It was the total opposite."

Julie frowned. "He wants to send you home? That can't be right. He's definitely showing mating behavior both in public and behind closed doors. I don't think that Coal was even as hectic as Blaze." Her frown deepened. "I can't believe he would send you away."

"He's not sending me away. It's worse actually."

"Worse?" Even her voice was laced with confusion. "What could be worse?"

"He wants us to be friends."

"That can't be right," Julie shook her head. "The guy can't keep his hands off of you. That's not friend-on-friend behavior."

Roxy blew her nose again. "No, it's not. Blaze told me that he could see a future for us."

"Well that's great."

"You would think. He said that I would make a great queen and mother," she sniffed.

Julie pulled her legs underneath herself on the couch. "Yeah, I'm not understanding what friendship has to do with this."

"It was like he was reading a contract or something. Like he was trying to convince me of a business deal. He said that he would be a good mate to me, that he wanted respect and honesty between us . . ."

"That's important."

"He also said that . . ." She felt her lip tremble. Roxy took a deep breath and paused for a few seconds. "He said . . ." she tried again, sounding better this time, "that he put his kingdom and his people first. The only reason he was taking a mate was for heirs."

Julie leaned forward as much as her growing belly would allow. "He. Did. Not."

"Yes, he did. He said that we could be friends . . . best friends . . ." Roxy mock laughed. "Can you believe that? He told me that he didn't do love or romance. That if I wanted those things then this relationship wouldn't work."

"Oh shit!" Julie whispered, almost to herself. "The idiot. Why am I not surprised?"

"He asked me to think things through. He said that I needed to agree to his terms if we were to continue."

"The no love or romance terms?"

Roxy nodded. "He asked me to think about it."

"Please tell me you agreed." Her whole expression was animated.

"I shouldn't have." She felt angry all over again. What a jerk. "I did by default. I was too upset to talk," Roxy swallowed hard. "I didn't want to cry in front of him so I agreed to think it over and ran."

"Good," Julie rubbed her neck. Roxy could see that she was deep in thought. "You do know that he's full of shit?"

"I think the situation is full of shit. I think his proposal is full of shit. I don't really know what to make of him or this situation." She pulled in another deep breath, trying not to cry. "I guess I'm just really disappointed. I really thought . . . it doesn't matter. I'm thankful he told me this now before I had a chance to . . . invest more of myself. I'm going to go and pack. I'm sure he won't make me stay the two weeks in light of everything that's happened."

Julie shook her head. "You're not packing anything. That whole thing about you not being invested yet is bullshit. Back to my earlier comment, I've seen the way you look at him. You may not know Blaze all that well but you're plenty invested. That's why you're so upset."

"No, I . . ." Was she invested? Was she already falling for Blaze? It was crazy but possible. She sighed. "I guess I'm also sad. I do have feelings for him but what good will that do me? I want a real relationship. I want to hold hands and have candlelit dinners. I want to make love and to be loved. I want it all, that's why I'm here. I was in a relationship with a guy who didn't really love me and it sucked."

Julie gave a deep nod; she was smiling broadly.

"Why do you look so happy? I'm falling in love with a guy who wants to be friends. It's awful and can only lead to heartache. I need to pack." Roxy stood up.

"Sit," Julie commanded. When Roxy didn't obey, she tapped the chair. "Hear me out."

Roxy sat back down.

"I think . . . no, I'm sure that Blaze has feelings for you. Feelings that go beyond friendship," she rolled her eyes. "He's such an idiot." Julie locked eyes with Roxy. "I've seen the way he looks at you and let me just tell you, friends don't look at each other like that."

"It's lust. Don't mistake it for love."

"I think there's more there. The guy is so possessive. His brothers are mocking him about being smitten. There is no way in hell it's just lust and friendship. No freaking way. Blaze is fooling himself."

"He seemed upset with the idea of me leaving, but I still don't buy it."

"We need to make him fall properly in love with you if he isn't already." Julie rubbed her belly.

"How do you suggest I make that happen? You can't make someone fall in love with another person."

"No, but you can make feelings that are already there deeper. Why don't you propose a few things as well? Tell him you want to give it a try but that there are conditions."

Roxy narrowed her eyes. "What conditions?"

"Tell him he needs to spend time with you. Quality time. Tell him that you need to get to know each other as friends. Don't get me wrong, you need to still have plenty of hot sex but that can't be all you do. He's already halfway in love with you, I'm sure of it. If he gets to know you, he'll fall properly in love with you."

"I don't know," Roxy shook her head.

"You need to get him to open up, to relax and have a bit of fun."

"If I spend time with him and get to know him, I might fall properly in love with him myself. If I leave now it'll be hard but I'll be okay. If I fall all the way in love with him, I'll end up leaving with a broken heart. This might not work out." Roxy felt adrenaline churn through her veins. "I might be worse off."

Julie gave Roxy a sad smile. "It's a chance you'll have to take. Sometimes it takes risking it all to come out victorious. No one ever got anywhere by playing it safe. You need to decide if it's worth it. I'm sure that Blaze has feelings for you. You need to make it so that it's impossible for him to let you go and then you need to tell him how you feel. I'm sure it'll scare the shit out of him but he'll come around. I can only hope that it shifts that stick up his ass," Julie grinned.

Roxy laughed. "I don't know." She covered her face with her hands and made a pained noise. The thought of leaving was horrible. It felt too much like giving up. The thought of staying was terrifying. Blaze could really hurt her. There was a good chance he *would* hurt her.

"I know it's scary; before meeting Coal, no one had ever loved me. I didn't even know what love was." By the look in Julie's eyes, Roxy could see that she was deep in thought. "Not even my own parents loved me. I don't think I ever met my father. My mother was an addict, too involved with finding her next fix to care about me. I lived in orphanages and foster homes, often one of many children. Always a number."

"I'm so sorry," Roxy said.

Julie folded her arms. "I'm not telling you this for sympathy. When I came here, I didn't trust anyone, least of all Coal. I couldn't believe he didn't have an ulterior motive. I didn't believe him when he said he loved me. I was afraid, so very afraid. I had to face those fears and take a chance. I was scared to death. I still am," she whispered the last as she rubbed her belly. "I'm glad I did though. I haven't looked back. It was the most difficult yet, the best decision of my life. Take a chance on Blaze. I think he needs you more than he knows and I think you need him right back."

Roxy swallowed hard. She nodded. "You're right."

"You'll give it a chance?"

"Yes, I will. I don't want regrets," Roxy smiled. She was terrified but she was also excited. This was nuts. It was crazy but she could do it.

"I'm here for you," Julie squeezed her hand. "Let's talk about the finer details."

CHAPTER 15

Blaze breathed out the pent-up air from his lungs as he caught sight of Roxy. He sucked in a lungful of air and wrinkled his nose. His chamber scented of a fire pit. He looked about the space, expecting to see burn or smoke damage. The smell was that bad.

There was none to see. Everything was in its place.

He frowned when he took a closer look at Roxy, she was fully-clothed and half upright in the chair. She'd fallen asleep waiting up for him. He felt like a jerk for staying away.

Blaze huffed out a breath. At least she was still there. He had half expected Roxy to have left. He'd stayed away to give her plenty of time to think things through. Maybe that hadn't been the best idea after all. He'd dropped a bomb on her . . . but she was a rational female, surely she would understand.

Leaning in, he carefully lifted her into his arms. Roxy stirred, making a soft snoring sound. He paused for a few seconds while she settled, and then headed for the bed. Using one arm to cradle her, he pulled the bedsheets down.

Just as he was lowering her to the mattress, her eyes opened. She blinked a couple of times as he placed her on the bed. "Blaze," Her voice was croaky.

"Shhhh." He pulled the covers over her. "Sleep."

Roxy pulled herself up to a semi-reclined position. "We need to talk." Her eyes were glazed over with sleep.

"We can talk in the morning. It's late," he added when it didn't look like she was going to listen.

She shook her head. "Let's talk now," her voice was much clearer.

"Okay," he sighed, flicking the light switch on the wall. He didn't like the determination in her voice, the resolve in her eyes.

A partnership based on the terms he had put forward was not going to work for a female like Roxy. She was about to turn him down and then he would have to let her go. Truth was, he enjoyed her company. No, not her company . . . it was the sex. Blaze would struggle to find another female who put fire into his loins like she did.

It didn't matter. He would deal. If she couldn't agree, then she was gone. An uneasy feeling stirred inside him. He would make her see it his way. He would make her understand.

"Would you like something to drink? I can make you a hot chocolate or something."

"Sounds good," she replied as she gave her eyes a rub.

"What happened in here?" The smell of burning grew worse as he entered the kitchen and lit the gas.

Roxy walked back to the couch. "I had a bit of a cooking accident. Sorry!"

"I can't even smell what it was you were making." He had to smile. "You weren't lying when you said you're a bad cook." He put chocolate powder into a cup and added milk.

She shrugged. "I'm terrible." Roxy sat down. "Is it a problem? You're not going to add cooking requirements to your terms are you?"

He wasn't sure if she was playing with him or being sarcastic, which hinted at anger. Maybe it was a bit of both. "The no cooking thing is not a big deal." He tried to sound relaxed but failed. There was definite tension in his voice.

Blaze busied himself with making the hot chocolate and walked over to the living room area. He placed the steaming mug on the table in front of Roxy. "Did you give it some thought?"

Roxy nodded.

"What did you decide?" Either way, he needed to know.

Roxy picked up the mug and folded both hands around it. "Actually, I thought there was more to discuss. I haven't quite made my mind up yet."

So it wasn't an outright no. Good! This he could work with. He didn't relish the thought of starting over with another female. "Okay. What would you like to talk about?" He sat down on the opposite side of the coffee table.

She blew on the contents of the cup. Her blue eyes were

clouded in thought. She wore a pair of leggings and an oversized sweater. This was not a good time for his dick to wake up but damned if he could help it.

Roxy locked eyes with him. "You said that you'd like for us to be friends but we've barely spent any time together outside of the bedroom."

Blaze nodded.

"We don't even know if we could get along long-term. Hold a conversation."

Blaze felt himself frown. "We've talked. I know we could be friends."

"*Deeper, faster* and *fuck me harder* should not be misconstrued as a conversation."

His cock gave a lurch as it went from semi to fully erect in zero point three seconds. Blaze picked up one of the couch cushions and casually held it over his lap, leaning on it like it was for comfort instead of a cover-up.

"We've talked at the various functions. We've talked after sex."

Roxy shook her head. "We either fall asleep right away or we have to leave to go somewhere or you run off. I'm *sorry I ripped your panties* or *let me get you a towel to clean yourself up,* does not constitute a conversation either. We don't talk at functions. Other people talk to me and you growl at them."

His blood churned as he thought of all those single males who buzzed around Roxy. He didn't really blame them though because she was the most beautiful female in the room. Her scent was the most intoxicating thing he had ever scented. His blood boiled none the less. "They're a bunch of assholes with one-track minds. They're hoping I mess up so that they can get a crack at you."

Roxy laughed. "It's mainly Inferno and he's just being sweet because he knows I might end up being family."

Blaze snorted. "Sweet, my ass. He'll move in quicker than the blink of an eye if he thinks he can have a shot at you."

"Be careful, I might start to think that you're jealous and friends shouldn't have those kinds of feelings for each other," she raised her brows. It seemed that Roxy was telling him off for being jealous. It gave him hope that this could work out.

"I'm not. I have mating urges. They are instinctual not emotional."

Roxy nodded. Her expression gave nothing away. If she was upset by his comments, she didn't show it. She seemed indifferent. Good! This was moving in the right direction.

"Bottom line. I don't want to have kids with someone I might not get along with. Like I said earlier, sex isn't the be all and end all. I'm willing to stay on two conditions. The first being that we spend some quality time together."

Something tightened inside him. "I told you, I don't do long walks and candlelit dinners."

Roxy rolled her eyes. "I didn't say that I wanted to do lovey dovey, make a person vomit stuff, let's do friend stuff."

"What do friends do?" He'd never had a female friend

before. He wasn't sure what she meant.

"What do you do with your friends?" Roxy took a sip of her drink.

"We fight." He saw her frown. "It is to hone our one-on-one skills. We go flying together. We swim in the ocean. The guys go on the stag run twice a year, they drink and rut."

"Um, I think we'll give that a miss."

"I wasn't suggesting . . . I was merely answering your question. I don't think I know how to have a female friend. I don't have many male friends for that matter. Subordinates . . . yes . . . friends . . . not so much. We can't do any of the things I mentioned," he smiled. "Vomit-inducing stuff is out so what do you suggest?"

"Let's start with something simple. Why don't you stay for breakfast tomorrow morning?" Roxy took another sip of the hot chocolate. "I could get up early if you need to leave early."

"Okay, we can try that."

She pulled a face. "I can make toast but that's it. I can't do pancakes or waffles. I could try boiling an egg or two, but . . ." She widened her eyes looking nervous . . . about boiling some eggs. It was adorable.

"I'll fix the eggs and you can get the toast."

She smiled. "See, this isn't so hard is it?"

He shook his head. "I guess not. As long as you keep the terms in the back of your mind. We can't let emotions get in the way. I think I like the idea of us becoming friends. That way, if one of us feels we are falling for the other, we can put a stop to the relationship before we are mated. Once we are sure that it's working we can take the next step."

She clasped and unclasped her hands like the thought of mating him worried her. Roxy eventually nodded. He liked her reluctance. He fucking loved that she brought her own terms to the table. She would make an excellent queen.

Then he had a bad thought, an unacceptable thought. "We do still get to have sex though, right?" The thought of not rutting Roxy made his hands feel clammy.

"After breakfast, if you have time." She stared at him from under her lashes. He could scent that she was aroused.

That made two of them. "I'll make time," he growled.

"There was something else." She put the mug down.

"Name it."

"There has to be some sort of show of affection in public . . ." she paused. "For all intents and purposes, we are dating. It would be even more important if we ever mated. I've watched how couples interact with one another. Shifters are affectionate, always touching, kissing, holding one another's hands."

"It would be purely for show?" Blaze didn't like it. Females were wired to fall in love with such contact.

"Yes, of course." She looked like she meant it. "I don't want people to talk. It would be seen as unnatural otherwise."

Blaze thought back to the conversation he and Coal

had, had. His brother had called him out on his lack of affection shown in public and if Coal had noticed then others would have as well. He planned on having an unconventional relationship but it would still be a partnership. He wanted others to see them as a close-knit unit. As a proper mated couple because they would be a proper mated couple just without all the nonsense. Blaze finally nodded. "You're right. We should be affectionate in public. Just the basics."

Roxy nodded. "We're already intimate with one another so what's a little hand holding or the odd kiss?" She shrugged like it wasn't an issue.

Blaze nodded as well. "No kissing during sex though. No making out. We keep the rutting as purely for pleasure."

"I like kissing during sex. It makes me come harder," she quickly added.

"You come just fine without it. It's an unnecessary risk." He knew he was being a bit of a dick but he couldn't help it. The last thing he wanted was for Roxy to fall for him. The more time he invested in this, the more he wanted it to work. It would be a shame to have to start over.

Roxy snorted. "Whatever," she shook her head.

"Was there anything else we needed to talk about?"

She shook her head again. "I think we're good."

"I think so too," he grinned at her. "In fact, I think we're more than good. You had me worried. For a moment I thought you had fallen in love with me. You looked like you wanted to cry earlier."

"I was a little shocked. I was pissed off that you thought I would fall in love with you so easily. You really are full of it. I thought about it and . . ." she paused, "I think it could work."

"I'm really glad. I meant what I said, I think we have something good. I know we can be great together. Best buddies."

Roxy smiled, she looked a little sad for a moment and then it was gone. "Best buddies." There wasn't a hint of sadness or emotion present in her voice. He must've imagined it.

"You'll let me know if you start to fall for me and I'll do the same."

Roxy nodded. "Definitely."

"Good!" This was fantastic. "I think we should celebrate." Blaze rose to his feet.

"How do you propose we do that?" Her stunning eyes drifted to his fully erect cock.

"I can think of a couple of things. They all involve you screaming my name."

"In true fuck buddy style," her voice was laced with sarcasm. Maybe she wasn't as okay with this as he thought. Then she pulled her sweater over her head and his mouth went dry. Her breasts were full, her nipples so damned plump. "Let's celebrate," she bobbed her eyebrows and gave him a naughty grin. Nah, she was okay with this. More than okay.

Blaze almost tripped trying to get out of his pants while

walking to her. His blood burned in his veins. All he could think of was being inside her, of marking her and branding her, of mating her. *Soon.* If he had his way, it would happen very fucking soon. Roxy was his, he would never love her but she would still be his female. It was for the best. Not just for him but for the both of them.

CHAPTER 16

Three days later . . .

"I'd rather be unzipping you," Blaze said as has he pulled up the zipper on the back of her dress. Up, not down. "There should be a rule against this."

The garment was red for Claw's sake. It clung to every curve. He stepped in behind her, pushing his erection into her lower back. Her ass was a thing of utter beauty. "I can make it very quick," he whispered into her ear, eliciting a shiver.

"We're late. Besides, you came home for lunch."

He had come home for lunch. Roxy had made them ham sandwiches. They talked. He found that he enjoyed their time together . . . as friends. They hadn't done much else other than share a meal or two per day. Quality time as Roxy put it. He'd never had a female friend but if there ever was a candidate for such a thing it would be Roxy. He'd fucked her on the dining room table after lunch. A fitting way to end a meal. According to Roxy, it was what fuck buddies did. Blaze found that he didn't like the term.

He didn't know why, he just didn't.

"Lunch time was hours ago." He nuzzled her neck and nibbled her earlobe. She gave a small whimper.

"We're leaving right now," her voice was breathless.

"Five minutes."

"Right now!" She gave him a shove with her elbow and he took a step back. "Poor baby." She turned and a beautiful smile graced her face as she gave his hair a light ruffle. "You'll live."

"Hmmm, I'm not so sure. Males can die from having blue balls."

She raised her brows. "There is no way in hell your balls are blue."

"Are you sure about that?" he had to laugh. "Maybe you should check just to be sure."

She gave him a light slap on the arm. "We need to leave. Thanks again for my earrings." She moved to the side so that she could look in the mirror. Roxy touched the dangling jewelry on one ear. "They're so sparkly, you would swear they were real."

Blaze chuckled. "They are real." This female was a breath of fresh air.

Roxy's eyes bugged from her skull. "Oh my god!" She shook her head and started to take them out.

"What are you doing?"

"I can't possibly accept these. How many diamonds are on each of these things?" Her hands were shaking but she managed to get the first one off. She held it up. "Oh my . . . there are at least a dozen. They're not tiny stones either. How many carats are in my hand right now?" She was talking more to herself.

Blaze walked over to her. He took the earring from her. "I bought them for you. I want you to have them."

"Fuck buddies don't give each other gifts like this."

Blaze frowned. He really hated that she kept calling them that. "Take the jewelry. I'm enjoying our friendship. I want you to have them."

"I'm enjoying the friendship as well, but this is too much."

"No," he shook his head. "It's not. I want you to have them." He tried to put the earring back but she turned her head.

"Keep them, if we end up mating then I'll wear them but I don't feel comfortable taking them now."

"Look," he hadn't planned on having this conversation just yet. "I want you as my mate. This is working. The friendship thing is going really well."

"I'm not ready to take that step." Her eyes widened even further. "It's too soon."

"Wear the earrings. Take them as a loan. If you decide to mate me then you can keep them and if not, you can give them back."

She visibly relaxed. "What if I lose them?"

"Roxy, wear the damned earrings. I don't give a fuck if you lose them. It's not important to me. It's only money." He didn't know why it meant so much to him that she wear the earrings, but it did.

She held his gaze for a long while. "Are you sure?"

"Yes." He moved forward. "Now, tilt your head to the side and stand still."

"Bossy boots," Roxy murmured.

He couldn't help but smile. "I'm not wearing any boots." He closed the clasp. "There."

"Well, I'm not wearing any underwear so I guess that makes us even." Roxy winked at him and walked out of the chamber.

Blaze groaned. The human killed him. How the hell was he going to get through this evening knowing that her pussy was bare under that sexy red dress?

Blaze's arm was around her waist. It felt as weird as it did right. He pulled her closer as Thunder approached.

"Hello, human. How are you?" The huge shifter boomed over the noise in the crowded room.

"I'm good." She smiled at him.

Thunder and Blaze said their hellos while Roxy looked about the room. "Where's Lily?"

The air king's face clouded. "She's gone back home."

"Why? What happened?" Roxy couldn't believe it.

"She was only interested in the prestige and material things."

"Really?" Roxy could hear the shock in her voice. "She seemed really sweet. She looked like she was seriously into you."

"The rutting was good. It was nice to have a female in my bed every night. Someone to talk to and spend time with," Thunder sighed. "Some things about her didn't sit right with me from the start though. She asked me strange questions. It started out in the wild. Remember how she wanted to know how big the air castle was? She was very excited that I was a king. Then she started asking things like, where did dragon shifters get their money? She wanted to know if she would get a crown if she became queen and seemed disappointed when I told her that we don't wear crowns," he frowned.

"Maybe Lily was just excited about becoming your queen."

"Nah, that wasn't it! She wanted things. Lots of things. Dresses, jewelry, more jewelry. The diamonds weren't big enough. The pearl strings weren't long enough. She asked for bags that cost more than the jewelry and shoes that cost more than the bags." He made a growling noise that clearly expressed his annoyance. "We're talking leather here. I couldn't bring myself to buy some of that stuff. I just couldn't. So Lily refused to talk to me, she withheld sex and threw a tantrum." He looked sad. "I was tempted just to buy them for her to keep the peace."

"So, what happened?" Roxy couldn't believe Lily had behaved like that. She seemed sweet. Then again, she thought about Sue who was also clearly here for more than just finding love and a future. That woman also had some serious ulterior motives. She was still hanging off of Lava's arm so he hadn't wised up to her yet.

"The vampire kings warned of such females. They have had a few try their luck in the program as well," Blaze said.

Thunder raised his brows. "We should brief our males.

Tell them what to look for. I went back later to talk it out with her and she was digging through my things." He shook his head. "She had found some of my family heirlooms. My mother's rings and a pair of earrings that belonged to my grandmother. Lily was wearing them."

Blaze stiffened. "I am sure that something like that must have made you angry."

Thunder grit his teeth. "It was the last straw for me. She didn't realize how angry I was. She went on and on about our mating ceremony. How lavish it was going to be. She told me that she wanted me to buy her a car . . . I can't remember which one. One of those fancy convertibles, low profile with doors that open sideways."

"A car?" Roxy asked. "Why?" She had to laugh. "Sorry, I don't mean to make light of it."

Thunder grinned. "Don't worry about it. I laughed my ass off when she asked me for the thing as well," Thunder went on, "She wasn't too thrilled at my reaction. The female was crazy. When I told her it was over she lost it. She busted my lip and gave me a black eye. She broke every plate and every glass in my chamber. I eventually had to restrain her. Crazy is too nice a description."

"I can't believe it. You guys seemed perfect. She seemed so nice."

"Well, looks can be deceiving. People can be deceiving." He continued, "I'm glad she's gone. I'm wary about meeting any more humans."

"We're not all bad." Roxy felt guilty. She was technically being a bit dishonest with Blaze. She was trying to get him to fall in love with her against his will. It was probably worse than gold-digging. She didn't like misleading him. Hopefully he would understand when she came clean.

"I would love a female like you," Thunder smiled.

Blaze growled. "Roxy is taken."

"I can see that," Thunder laughed. "You are one lucky male. I'm surprised you guys haven't mated already."

"We will be soon." He kissed her temple. "I'm working on convincing Roxy that mating me is the right thing to do."

"Good luck, although, I don't think you'll need to convince her for much longer." He lowered his voice, "I can see that your female is crazy about you." Thunder laughed, then he stared somewhere over their shoulder. "The snacks have arrived. I'll talk to you later."

Oh shit! It must be obvious that she was falling for Blaze – and boy, she *was* falling for him. The more time they spent together, the worse it became. This whole plan could backfire on her big time.

"Did you hear that?" Blaze whispered in her ear.

"Hmmm," she made a bit of a squeaky noise. Was he going to call her out on it? She tried to stay calm.

"We're doing a good job convincing them," he whispered. "We look great together. We are great together. Think about mating me, will you?" He pulled away so that he could look her in the eyes.

Roxy nodded. "Okay." She got away with it, this time.

Blaze smiled. He cupped her chin and gave her a kiss

on the lips. Blaze held his mouth against hers for a moment or two, their breaths intermingling. It wasn't a friendly kiss. It wasn't a fuck buddy kiss either. It was confusing because it felt like more of a lover's kiss. It was just for show though, she reminded herself. *Just for show.* Blaze didn't mean anything by it.

CHAPTER 17

Two and a half weeks later . . .

"Just say yes already," Blaze nuzzled her neck. Then he planted kisses all the way along her collarbone before kissing the side of her mouth. He probably didn't realize it but he was touching her more and more in private and not just to initiate sex.

He stepped away. "What can I do to convince you?"

Love me.

It was the one thing he said he couldn't give her and the one thing that she needed the most. "Soon," Roxy finally answered.

"I like spending time with you. We're friends . . . really good friends. That was your one concern wasn't it? That we wouldn't get along, and we do. So why should we wait any longer?"

"I'm not quite ready."

"Okay." He looked disappointed. There was a part of her that wanted to throw the plan out the window. She would love Blaze whether he wanted her to or not. In time, he might reciprocate and he might not. They did have a good relationship. He would look after her and respect her and they would have fun, but – it was a big but – there would always be something missing. They would always have this whole 'terms and conditions' thing hanging over their heads. What if she accidentally told him that she loved him? What if she didn't need to tell him? Her actions, her eyes, the way she held him, surely these things would give her feelings away? What then? Would he leave her? Turn his back on her? What if they had kids together?

She couldn't live in a state of limbo. She'd done it for eight years with someone else. A man she didn't have half the feelings for that she did for Blaze. A half-assed relationship wasn't for her back then, and it certainly wasn't for her now. She was an all-in kind of girl and she needed an all-in guy.

"Soon though?" He squeezed her hand to draw her attention.

"Yes, soon," she nodded. Roxy would need to have a serious conversation with Blaze and very soon. There was no doubt in her mind that she was in love with him. She only prayed that he had fallen at least a little bit in love with her as well.

He smiled broadly. "Now, are you going to let me taste one of those cookies?"

Roxy shook her head. "I was just about to throw them out. They're no good."

Blaze gave a big sniff. "I recognize that smell." He

grinned, looking so handsome. His green eyes glinted. His long lashes lowered as he narrowed his eyes. "That night I came home to a burnt smell. Did you try and bake chocolate chip cookies then too?"

"I planned on giving you my own terms and then celebrating with your favorite baked goods when you agreed to them."

"You were that sure I would agree?"

She nodded. "I was hopeful. Besides, it's rude to table a whole list of terms and not be willing to accept a couple in return."

"Agreed," he smiled. "You trying to bake for me is very sweet." He looked at her with such affection such . . . love. His gaze heated up. Then he put his hands on either side of her and caged her in against the counter, grabbing behind her.

"Don't," she warned. "You'll be sorry."

Blaze took a really big bite. The cookies were partially burnt but that wasn't the worst of it. He chewed twice and stopped, trying hard not to grimace.

"I tried to warn you," Roxy said.

Blaze swallowed. What a sweetheart. He actually swallowed. Roxy had spat out her bite and it wasn't nearly as big as the one he had taken. "Um . . ." She had to laugh. "I think I put in too much bicarbonate of soda and not enough sugar. The chocolate chips are dark instead of milk, that's what the bitter taste is . . . Oh, and they're burnt . . . not as badly as last time though."

"Chocolate chip cookies aren't my favorite anymore

anyway." He pushed his hips against hers and leaned in close, his mouth was against her ear.

"They're not?"

She felt him shake his head. "Your cookie is my favorite. My little brother was right on the money on that count."

"Oh yeah," she sounded breathless.

"Yeah." Just hearing him talk in her ear, feeling his body pressed against hers, smelling his manly scent, it was enough to have her panting, enough to soak her underwear.

Then he was pulling her dress up and ripping her soaking panties right off. Roxy pulled at his pants and wrapped her arms around his neck. Blaze lifted her and entered her in one stroke. Roxy wrapped her legs around his hips. He pressed his forehead against hers. "This is where I belong. You need to say yes." He didn't wait for a reply; he began to thrust. Roxy lost herself to the sensation. Lost herself to Blaze.

The next day . . .

"I can tell that you're backpedaling." Julie sat down across from her. One hand on her back and the other on her distended belly. She lowered herself carefully, falling heavily into the back of the chair.

"I'm surprised you haven't popped yet!" Roxy's eyes were trained on the other woman's stomach.

Julie laughed. "Any day now."

"How are you holding up? You seem really relaxed considering . . ."

"I feel at peace." Julie's legs were a little apart to accommodate her belly. She looked about six months pregnant in human terms with a neat, tight belly. Her friend wrapped both hands around her stomach. "I'm not looking forward to pushing this egg out but at the same time, I can't wait. It will be nice to get my body back. I don't know how women do this for nine months." She sighed. "He'll come when he's ready though." Then she raised her brows. "Don't try and change the subject. Blaze has started to get suspicious. You guys are getting along so well yet you keep refusing to mate with him."

"He spoke to me about it this morning," Coal said from the kitchen. Julie had asked if she could confide in Coal and Roxy couldn't say no. It just felt even more wrong where Blaze was concerned. It felt like she was going behind his back. It didn't feel right. It made her feel like a horrible person. Julie kept reminding her that it was for his own good, it was the only thing that helped with the guilt.

"What did he say?" Roxy asked.

Coal put a plate of biscuits on the tray and came through to the living room. "He can't understand why you won't mate him. He asked my advice on what to do. The asshole didn't tell me about his agreement with you. I had to bite my tongue to stop myself from saying anything." He poured what looked like homemade lemonade into three glasses and handed one to her.

"You can't put this off any longer. The guy is crazy about you, anyone with working eyeballs can see it. Thanks, baby," Julie took the lemonade from Coal and took a sip.

Roxy pulled in a deep breath. "Are you sure? Maybe I should wait a little bit longer just to be on the safe side." Her gut churned at the thought of coming clean. At the same time, she couldn't wait to get it off her chest.

"I agree with Julie. Blaze is an extremely private person. He doesn't confide in others easily yet he opened up to me this morning. That means that it's weighing on him. He might suspect that something is up. I think that he really wants to mate you because he's in love with you. He's been out of sorts since the hunt."

Roxy nodded. She wasn't convinced that Coal was right. "I will talk to him today." She had to speak up though. She couldn't wait any longer.

"He probably won't take it very well," Coal warned. "We'll be here for you. Come to us, night or day. Don't let him bully you."

"Okay. I'll let you know how it goes." Her stomach churned. Roxy forced herself to take a sip of her drink. Her hand shook so she clutched the glass harder.

"Don't look so petrified." Julie gave her a smile that was full of concern. "I'm sure it will go better than you think. Blaze loves you whether he likes it or not. It is what it is."

Roxy prayed that Julie was right. Even if he did love her, he might not admit it, not even to himself. What then?

She couldn't think too far into the future. One step at a time.

A warm body came up flush behind her. Roxy woke up from the contact, her mind still fuzzy with sleep. It took a moment or two to orientate herself. The room was dark. The bed warm. Blaze was warmer. "Hi," he whispered, wrapping his arms around her.

She felt something press to the side of her head. It felt like a kiss but she couldn't be sure. "I'm sorry I'm so late," he murmured.

"You missed dinner." They ate together most nights.

"I know." Another soft brush against her hairline. Definitely a kiss. "I'll make it up to you."

"How do you propose to do that?" She felt him hard against her back.

"Oh, I don't know." She could hear that he was smiling. Roxy couldn't help but to smile as well.

She turned to face him, putting her arms around him. The full moon caused light to spill in, making it easy for her to see him. She should talk to him first but she needed this. It might be their last time. A lump formed in her throat, she swallowed it down. She had to stay positive.

Blaze licked his lips and she watched his tongue roll over his full bottom lip. "I'm sure you'll think of something." She hooked her leg over his thigh. She needed to talk to him but the conversation could wait. Right now, she needed to show him what she felt about him. What she needed most was for him to show her back.

Roxy kissed him. Just a soft caress of the lips at first. Then she sucked on that full lower lip, eliciting a low growl.

Screw the no kissing rule!

Blaze pushed her onto her back and pulled her legs up higher on his body. He rubbed his cock against her seam. Her clit fired up on all cylinders.

Rub, rub quickly turned to slip and slide as she grew wet and needy.

Blaze kept his mouth about a half inch above hers. Their eyes were locked onto one another. Roxy moaned softly as he ground his cock against her sensitive clit.

Screw it!

She leaned up and kissed him again. It was a dangerous thing to do. A no go zone. Up until now, she'd let him do the kissing. Although he touched her and kissed her all the time it was never fully on the mouth. At least, not behind closed doors. Mouth kissing was against their agreement. Blaze found it too emotional. Too romantic.

Well screw it.

Roxy covered his mouth with hers and shoved her tongue inside. She hooked her ankles behind him and arched her back. She held him tighter, her fingers digging into his back.

Blaze growled. Using a careful thrust, he pushed into her, simultaneously sucking on her tongue. Sweet lord up above. Her toes curled and she groaned. He moved slowly, making love to her mouth. Kissing her like no one else had ever done before. His thrusts were just as slow yet they were also powerful.

Blaze grunted as he cupped her jaw, changing the angle of their kiss so that he could deepen it. He continued to thrust. She grabbed his ass, feeling his glutes contract beneath her fingers. Roxy moaned. Their joining went on and on. They both became slick with perspiration. Their breaths ragged from the exertion and from the sheer pleasure.

Blaze pulled back as her pussy began to flutter around him. He looked so serious, so angry, so intense.

Her orgasm hit, rolling through her. This time, it seemed to affect every part of her. Every cell, every nerve ending, every inch of skin.

Blaze's face took on a strained look as he began to jerk against her. He grunted once, twice, then he called her name too. A choked growl. He buried his face in her neck and bit down. Another orgasm exploded through her, making her call his name. Making her back bow and her pussy clamp down. Blaze roared as he released her neck, his thrusts way more urgent than before.

He finally fell against her. Both of them were breathing hard. Blaze's lashes fanned his cheeks. He moved to the side to give her breathing room. His own chest rose and fell more slowly, more deeply. They normally fell asleep or had more sex and then fell asleep. They didn't normally talk this late at night.

Maybe she should wait till morning?

No.

This couldn't wait.

"Blaze."

"Mmmm?" He sounded sleepy.

"Are you asleep?"

He chuckled, his chest vibrated against her side. "No, but I was getting there."

"I'm sorry I kissed you."

"What?" He lifted his head, his eyes were glazed over from sleep or maybe still from coming or possibly both. "Don't worry about it. Go to sleep." He pulled her closer to him and kissed her forehead.

They had just made love. That wasn't just sex. Quite frankly, their coming together had been morphing over the last period. Sometimes urgent but other times, something different, something more intense. Way more emotional. He did have feelings for her. He had to. Either way, she would soon know.

"I liked it," she blurted. "The kissing that is."

"You said it makes you come harder." He was smiling. Trust Blaze to try to bring it back to sex.

"I was with someone for eight years. He broke up with me about a year and a half ago."

She could feel Blaze stiffen next to her. He pulled away, using an elbow to prop himself up. "I'm sorry it happened to you but I'm glad at the same time, otherwise you wouldn't be here. Now, get some rest." He tried to pull the comforter over her but she grabbed his hand and shook her head.

"Essentially I forced him to break up with me. I knew that Ben didn't love me, not really. I was fooling myself into thinking that he did. It was a comfortable set-up for him, for both of us. We lived in a beautiful home, we had many mutual friends, we even had two dogs together. We had a good life, a comfortable life. We got along great, had plenty of good times. Even went on a vacation once a year."

Blaze clenched his jaw so hard that she heard his teeth grind. "Why are you telling me this?" He moved to a sitting position.

"I broached the marriage subject with him every so often. Especially once we hit two years of living together. I wanted the white dress and more than anything, I wanted kids. I loved Ben."

Blaze growled. "I'm sorry it didn't work out for you." His back was ramrod straight, his jaw tight. His eyes blazed.

Roxy also moved to a sitting position. "I eventually told him that he either needed to commit to me or it was over. I moved out two days later. He kept the house and the dogs."

"That's not fair," Blaze growled.

"He bought me out of the house, and the dogs were more his than mine."

"I'm glad you told me. I understand now why you're onboard with our arrangement. You were badly hurt." He paused for a moment. "We're like-minded. Let's get some sleep."

"I want to know what happened to you, Blaze. Who hurt you?"

His eyes narrowed and he pursed his lips. "It's not important. Why do you need to know?"

"It is important. You want to mate me. You want a future with me. We need to understand one another. I want to know things about you. What makes you tick. Why you do certain things. I want to know you, Blaze."

"Some things that happened in my past are not relevant. That part of my past is *not* relevant."

"Ben still lives in that house. He's with someone else. He replaced me within a month or two of my leaving. I sometimes miss those dogs . . . I used to get really lonely living in my small apartment . . . all alone. I used to wonder sometimes if I'd made the right decision when I forced Ben's hand. I loved Ben, so I would wonder if I should have settled."

Blaze ground his teeth, he shifted on the mattress.

"I'm not telling you this to hurt you."

He pulled a face of indifference. "You're not hurting me."

"I'm making you uncomfortable and I think it's because I keep saying that I loved Ben."

Blaze shook his head. "We're fucking." Again with that face of indifference. "I don't like hearing about this male because you fucked him too. That's it."

"It has nothing to do with fucking."

"Of course it does. It's those mating urges. That's where my jealousy is stemming from." He gave a one-shouldered shrug.

She wasn't about to argue with him. "I left Ben because

I wanted more."

Blaze shrugged. "You're going to get more. I want to mate you. I want children with you."

"It's not enough for me. There were moments where I tried to convince myself that it would be, but it's not good enough. It wasn't before and it isn't now. I feel even more strongly than ever."

"What the fuck are you talking about?" He shoved a hand through his hair. "We have an agreement."

"I said I would give it a try."

"Fuck!" He leaped off the bed, reminding her more of a cat – one of the big ferocious kinds – than a dragon shifter. "Fucking hell!" he muttered, more to himself than to her, as he walked away. "That's why you keep refusing to mate me." He shook his head. "You fucking didn't." He turned to face her. "Please tell me you didn't fall in love with me. I hope you didn't fuck up a good thing."

Roxy swallowed hard. She turned on the side lamp and pulled the comforter over herself. "You can't tell me that you haven't fallen in love with me either? You can't." She whispered the last as she watched his eyes darken.

"Fuck! I can't believe this." He yanked open the closet and pulled out a pair of pants.

"I wouldn't believe you if—"

"You would be wrong. I don't fucking love you." He shook his head. "It's all this touching shit isn't it? I knew I shouldn't have agreed to that term. You females can't separate the hand holding shit from the emotional shit can you?"

"I've seen the way you look at me. We made love just now. You can't deny that."

"I've never denied our compatibility. You're a good fuck."

Ouch! Hearing him reduce what they had to just sex hurt. It hurt like mad.

"It's part of the reason I wanted you as a mate." He yanked the pants on. "Compatibility."

"I was already halfway in love with you when we agreed to those pathetic terms!" she yelled.

"What?" His eyes blazed. "Why did you accept then? What the fuck is this?" He took a step towards the bed. Every muscle was taut. "Why did you tell me you weren't in love with me if you were?" He looked so angry, even his hands were fisted. "You accused me of being arrogant to even suggest it."

"I was angry. I didn't even realize that I had feelings for you. Not at that moment." Roxy tucked the comforter a little more firmly around herself. "I wouldn't say that I was in love with you but I knew that it wouldn't take much for me to get there."

"Why did you agree to my terms if you knew you could never keep them?" His voice was soft. Everything else was hard, intense and ready.

"I took a chance."

"What kind of a chance? Fuck, Roxy!" He took a small step back.

"A chance on us. It was a risk. Stupid, I guess."

"Seriously fucking stupid," he growled.

"No!" she yelled. "I disagree. I think you love me right back."

"No fucking way." He shook his head. "You're delusional. I warned you. I thought I was clear about my feelings."

"You're too scared to admit it. Too afraid to take a chance in case you get hurt again. I won't hurt you, Blaze. I'm all in."

He shook his head, looking disappointed. Like she'd failed a test or something. "What we had was a mistake, nothing more and nothing less. A big fucking mistake. Pack your bags. Someone will be here to take you back in the morning. We're done, your scheme didn't work." He turned and headed towards the door. "This whole thing just confirms my suspicions; humans are not to be trusted. I will replace you with a less emotional human. One who can agree to simple terms. Good-bye." He didn't turn back. It was the first time he had ever said goodbye to her. Up until now, he'd always said 'later.' Goodbye had such a definite ring to it. It hurt. It hurt so damn bad. Blaze wanted her gone. He was so convincing that she was inclined to believe that he didn't love her. What if she was wrong? She watched him walk away. She wanted to shout a whole lot of things at his retreating back.

You can't be serious!

You don't mean it.

Wait!

Stop!

I love you.

Don't go.

No! Please!

They all went through her mind. More than once. It was almost like he was moving in slow motion.

"Blaze," she finally managed to squeeze out.

He paused for half a second. His back stiffened. Then he was gone. The door clicked softly behind him.

Roxy just sat there. She continued to clutch the comforter to her chest. Her heart beat wildly. Her eyes stung so she blinked a couple of hundred times.

She should pack. She really should. Unfortunately, she was a sucker for punishment because she wasn't ready to give up yet. Not by a long shot. There had to be something she could do.

After a shower, she quickly dressed. It was a little after midnight. Coal had said to come at any time. Hopefully he meant it.

CHAPTER 18

Roxy knocked on the door a second time. She was just considering leaving when Coal opened it.

She expected to see his hair mussed and his eyes heavy with sleep. Instead, he was frowning heavily. There was an air of nervous tension surrounding him. The guy was wide awake. He blinked twice like he was shocked to see her. Had he been expecting someone else at this time of night?

"Oh, Roxy," he huffed, leaving out the *it's you* part of the sentence. Leaving no doubt in her mind that he had been expecting someone else. He ran a hand through his hair, reminding her of Blaze.

Then he looked over her shoulder and his eyes widened. He sighed heavily. "Thank god you're here."

Roxy heard footfalls from down the passageway. What the hell was going on? She turned towards the sound. It was an older-looking woman, a dragon lady, judging by her size.

Just then, Roxy heard Julie moan. It was a noise that was heavily laced with pain.

"Oh my god!" Roxy said. "Is Julie about to . . . have the

egg?"

Coal nodded.

"Oh shit!" What bad timing. What a selfish thing to think. What was wrong with her? "Oh wow! Okay."

"Come on in." Coal was looking at the dragon lady.

"Oh!" Roxy realized that she was hogging the doorway. "Sorry. I'll just be on my way. Wish Julie all the best . . ."

"Roxy!" Julie yelled from somewhere inside the room. "Get in here."

She glanced at Coal who looked more stressed than anyone she had ever seen before. His eyes had this wild look and he kept scrubbing a hand over his face and through his hair.

"You'd better do as she says." He stepped to the side and frowned even harder. Once she was inside, Coal raced past her and grabbed Julie's hand. The other woman was standing. She wore leggings and a t-shirt.

"This is Smoke. She is one of our best healers."

The older lady smiled broadly. "I am honored to be able to deliver a royal egg. It has been many years since I've had the privilege of delivering an egg but fear not, the birthing process is not one a healer forgets." She put down her brown leather bag. It was worn and ancient-looking. "Are you sure you would not prefer to go outside? Fresh air encourages the pains which in turn speeds up the process."

Julie shook her head. She clutched her belly and grimaced. "Here comes another one." She began breathing in pants.

The healer went to Julie, saying words of encouragement.

"I take it you had your talk with Blaze?" Coal asked. He kept glancing at Julie, his concern for his mate evident.

She nodded. "You were right, it didn't go well. He wants me packed and gone by morning."

Julie moaned, but continued to pant.

"You've got your hands full. I'm going to go. We can talk about this tomorrow."

"No," Julie half moaned, half yelled. "Wait, it's nearly over."

"If Blaze said he's sending you away, then chances are good he will do just that. He's so damned stubborn."

"Look who's talking." Julie gave a laugh filled with tension. "Okay so he's being an idiot. I hope you haven't given up."

Roxy pulled a face. "I'm tempted. He said a couple of things . . ." The lump came back, clogging her throat and making her eyes sting. No crying.

"I'm not sure that there's much we can . . ." Coal glanced from Julie to Roxy and back.

"Call Inferno," Julie said.

"What?" Coal frowned. "I don't know . . ."

"Maybe he can talk some sense into Blaze." Julie's eyes were wide.

"No!" Both Coal and Roxy said, in unison.

"He won't even listen to me," Coal went on, "He sure as hell won't listen to his fledgling baby brother."

"We have to do something." Julie grit her teeth and

clutched her stomach. "Not now."

"I can't think of anything other than this birth." Coal pinched the bridge of his nose. "I'm sorry," he turned to face Roxy. "Maybe Inferno can think of something – although his harebrained schemes often get him into huge shit."

Julie began to pant.

"What choice do we have?" Coal locked eyes with Roxy. "What do you want to do? Is there someone else you would rather call on for help or do you want to go home?"

Her eyes began to well with tears.

Julie moaned. "Of course she wants to stay." She ground out between pants.

Roxy nodded, she had to work hard not to cry. Her nose burned, eyes stung, her throat was starting to hurt. She sucked in a few deep breaths. Who else could she ask for help? She kept coming up with blanks. Inferno had always been so sweet. He would help her. She was sure of it. Roxy looked Coal in the eyes. "I think Inferno would be the best person."

Coal nodded. He walked to Julie and took her into his arms. "I'll be back in a few minutes." He kissed her on the brow and looked at her with such tenderness that Roxy felt her own pain so much more acutely. "Come on." He walked towards Roxy, he gave her a tight, sympathetic smile.

"Thank you," she said. "Good luck!" she glanced Julie's way.

Julie gave a smile that spoke of nervousness and excitement in equal measures.

"Your female will be fine," the healer said. "You can help this human. I will take care of the birthing."

Julie got a panicked look. Her eyes widened and she gave a small shake of the head.

"I'll be back in a few minutes," he growled. "I'll see you in a few," he spoke to Julie, using a much softer tone. "My female is a human," he added, looking at the healer, before walking to the door.

Roxy had to move fast to keep up with Coal. "What was that all about?"

"Dragon shifter females prefer to give birth outdoors. They prefer to be alone or with a healer. It is unusual, if not unheard of for a male to be present." He rolled his shoulders. "Julie is nervous about the birth. She asked me to stay with her and I will be there every step of the way."

Roxy smiled. "You're a good guy."

Coal slowed down a smidgen. "Blaze will come around." He glanced at Roxy. "I've been watching the two of you. Don't give up on him. If you really do love him then fight for him. I know he feels something for you . . . I know it. The way he looks at you. The way he treats you. Inferno will help you, although I'm a little worried about it. He's a loose cannon. Be careful what you let him talk you into."

"I'm sure we'll think of something that doesn't involve us getting into deep shit. I'll stay away from loose cannon behavior."

Coal stopped abruptly and rapped on a door. He knocked again almost immediately, this time harder.

"Okay, Okay." Inferno yawned as he opened the door, he was rubbing the back of his neck. His hair stood up in all directions. He was also completely naked.

Roxy looked away.

"I need you to help Roxy," Coal said, sounding gruff. "Do not fuck her around or get her into trouble."

"What's going on?" Inferno's voice was still a bit croaky but at least he sounded more awake.

"I need to go." Roxy could hear the urgency in Coal's voice.

"Thanks so much. I'll speak to you guys tomorrow." Roxy touched the side of Coal's arm. "It's going to be okay; Julie I mean, it'll all be fine." She sounded stupid saying it. How the hell did she know?

Coal nodded. "I know." He looked even tenser and panicked than before. "I need to get back."

Roxy had to say her goodbyes to his retreating back.

"Um . . ." Inferno scratched his head. "care to enlighten me as to what the hell's going on?"

"Can I come in first?"

He gave his head a small shake. "Sorry! Sure." He stepped to the side and Roxy walked inside, trying to keep her eyes averted.

Inferno switched on the light.

"How can I be of service?" She could hear that he was smiling.

She turned, then quickly turned back around. He wasn't

quite as buff as Blaze but he was still huge compared to most guys she knew. Okay, all the guys she knew. "Would you mind putting on some pants?" Of course, his *you know what* was semi-erect and they pretty much matched up in that department. Not that she wanted to know, or stare. Roxy just needed him dressed. This was awkward.

"Oh yeah! Sorry!" She heard Inferno walk to the other side of the room. Roxy turned a bit more so as to keep him out of her line of sight. She heard him put on some clothes.

"It's safe." He sounded amused.

"I'm sorry to barge in on you." Roxy turned to face him.

Inferno folded his arms and leaned against the closet. "No problem. What's up?" Then his eyes widened and he stood up straight. "Is Julie in labor? She is, isn't she?"

Roxy nodded.

"Why didn't I think of it sooner?" He gave his head a rub, mussing his hair even more. "I guess I was half asleep."

"I just came from there. The healer had just arrived. Julie seemed okay but what do I know?"

Inferno gave a small shrug and visibly relaxed. "She'll be just fine. There's nothing anyone can do." He looked so calm about it. Then Inferno chuckled. "Coal looked terrified."

"He's worried about his mate and his unborn . . . child . . . egg." It was still a weird concept to her.

"Yeah." Inferno nodded. "That makes sense." Then his

eyes narrowed in thought. "That doesn't explain what you're doing in my chamber at this time of night. Fuck!" he growled. "If Blaze finds you here he'll remove my head."

Roxy swallowed hard. She pressed her lips together and tried not to cry. She'd barely cried during the whole Ben break-up. Not once when she'd given him the ultimatum, not once when he'd turned her down, not once when she'd moved out. Only that one time once she was out. Just once. Lauren had given her the spare bedroom. It was the first night and she'd had a little cry and that was the end of it.

This time around, it seemed that she couldn't help it. Her body just reacted. Her eyes filled and her throat constricted and it all happened against her will.

"Oh no!" Inferno huffed out a breath. "What did he do?" He gestured towards the living room area. "Sit. Can I get you something, warm milk? A juice? A bat to hit the asshole over the head with?"

Roxy choked out a laugh. She shook her head. A tear or two escaped so she quickly wiped them away. She took a seat, feeling a tiny bit better.

Inferno sat next to her but gave her some space. "Tell me all about it."

Roxy told Inferno everything from beginning to end. He nodded. It was only when she got to the part where Blaze basically kicked her out that he reacted.

"What a dickhead! Doesn't he know what he has in a female like you?" Inferno looked pissed. He shook his head. "Any unmated male in the four kingdoms would give their left testicle to be with a female like you and he just casually throws you away. I don't get it."

"He's afraid of getting hurt again. At least I think that's the problem. Maybe he genuinely doesn't feel anything for me. That could be it too." She sniffed, fighting those damned tears all over again. "I should never have tried to trick him into falling in love with me. It was wrong and—"

"You can't trick someone into falling in love with you," Inferno smiled. "It's not possible. You felt something between the two of you right from the start . . . I still can't believe you kicked Thunder in the balls." He laughed. "I so wish I could've seen that."

Roxy couldn't help but smile back.

"Now we have to decide what the fuck we're going to do about this. I take it you don't want to leave if you're here?" he raised his brows. "You love my idiot older brother . . . I swear sometimes you would think that he was the younger male . . . when it comes to females that is," Inferno winked at Roxy and she had to laugh. Somehow Inferno made her feel more relaxed about this whole thing.

"I want to at least give it one more shot. I'm not sure how, but I can't just leave things like this. I'm sure Blaze has feelings for me. I just wish he would admit it already."

"A male doesn't act the way he does unless he has feelings for a female."

"He said that it's instinctual mating behavior and that it

has nothing to do with emotions." Roxy could only hope that Blaze had it wrong.

Inferno shook his head. "He's working damn hard to convince himself. Idiot!" Then Inferno leaned forward just a tad. "This is what we're going to do, let's go back to Blaze's chamber to collect your things. You can stay here with me. I'll become your protector for a time."

Roxy looked about the room. As was standard, there was only one bed.

"I'll take the couch," Inferno rolled his eyes. "Don't look so nervous."

Roxy nodded.

"Now, the whole protector thing won't last for very long. Once our males become aware of the situation, they'll start to become restless, this is especially true of the higher-ranking males. They will start to demand a chance to win you. They will start challenging one another. Testosterone levels will go through the roof and sporadic fights will start to break out throughout the lair. This can be dangerous for our human inhabitants. Hell, it's dangerous for everyone."

"How long will we have?"

"A day or two tops."

Roxy pushed out a breath through her nose. "I don't think a day or two will be enough." She pictured the look on Blaze's face, the resolve in his eyes.

"It'll buy us some time to come up with another plan."

Roxy nodded.

"Good!" Inferno rose to his feet. "Let's do this." He

held out a hand and helped her up. She felt really tired all of a sudden. "Besides," Inferno gave her hand a quick squeeze and grinned. "you might decide after living with me that it's me you want instead of him."

Roxy could see that he was only joking. "You might fall in love with me instead. Shit . . ." he laughed, "that would serve that asshole right. Blaze would go fucking insane. He might kill me but it would be worth it." Then he became serious. "Wait just a minute, something like that might actually work."

"What do you mean?" Roxy could hear the caution in her voice.

"You and me." Inferno looked deep in thought.

"Um . . ." She didn't want to hurt the guy's feelings. "I'm sorry but . . ."

"No," Inferno growled. "I'm not actually suggesting that you and I get together. Not for real anyway." He frowned. "I know you love my brother and besides, I would never move in on his female despite how sexy you are." He gave her another wink. "I'm suggesting that I fake win you to make him jealous."

Roxy laughed, sounding nervous. "I'm not sure that whatever it is you have in mind is a good idea."

"It's a brilliant idea. Blaze needs a kick in the ass and me winning you would do that."

"I don't know," she shook her head. "Isn't it risky? Blaze might end up hating me."

"If he does love you, he will go into meltdown. He won't be able to help himself. You can come clean immediately at that point and get him to admit his feelings in the heat of the moment." Inferno looked excited. "It'll work."

"How would you win me exactly?"

"I would need to go head-to-head with the highest-ranking unmated male." Inferno didn't look worried.

"I'm sorry, but I have to ask. Are you sure you can win?" Coal had referred to Inferno as a fledgling and it was clear to her that he looked younger than his two older brothers. He looked younger than many of the guys she had seen.

"I'm a prince," Inferno grinned. "I'm getting stronger by the day." He flexed his biceps and he did look really strong. "Besides, all of the top warriors have females. The only three I would normally have to worry about are Flame, Scorch and Lava. I can beat the others easily. Nothing will go wrong . . . trust me. I'll beat Crimson, who's the next highest ranking," he quickly added. "Blaze will go nuclear, then you'll know for sure that he's in love with you. You can both declare your undying love for one another . . . the end."

"You make it sound so easy." It sounded harebrained and loose cannon.

"It will be easy. Worst case scenario, Blaze pretends to be indifferent — in which case we'll have two weeks to drive him crazy. I'll sleep on the couch. I promise not to try anything." He touched a hand to his chest. "What do you say?"

"Can I think about it?"

"Yeah, but you don't have much time." He looked her square in the eyes. "I know this will work. I want Blaze happy . . . I like you, Roxy. This will work, I know it will. I know dragon shifters, moreover, I know Blaze. Let me win you, nothing will go wrong."

CHAPTER 19

The next day . . .

Roxy felt sick with nervous tension. Her stomach churned so badly that she hadn't been able to eat breakfast that morning.

"Congratulations!" Roxy looked down at the most perfect egg she had ever seen. It was golden. So bright and shiny that it looked like it was made out of the actual metal. It was big considering Julie had to push the thing out of her body yet small considering it housed a baby. Julie had explained that the egg shell was soft during the birth, to make it easier to push out. That it hardened up within minutes of being expelled.

"We are very proud." Coal pulled Julie closer to his side.

Julie was beaming; her smile was a mile wide but she also looked really tired and had yawned behind her hand numerous times since she and Inferno had arrived fifteen minutes earlier.

"I'm sure you're relieved to see that it's golden."

Inferno gave his brother a slap on the back.

"I'm just glad that my mate is well and that the egg is healthy. I don't care about the rest," Coal's voice was rough and deep.

"Okay, okay." Inferno held up his hand. "No need to be so touchy."

Coal growled.

"We won't keep you," Roxy said. "We need to be somewhere."

Coal narrowed his eyes. He looked from Roxy to Inferno and back again. "What's going on here?"

"Nothing," Roxy's voice was a little high-pitched.

Coal's eyes narrowed further. "You haven't let him talk you into anything, have you? Because if you have, it would be a mistake."

"Ye of such little faith." Inferno grinned.

"Don't agree to anything," Coal shook his head. "Let's hope Blaze comes to his senses before chaos ensues. Maybe you should go and have another talk with him today. He's coming by this evening. I'll talk to him if things aren't resolved. We don't have long before things get hairy."

Roxy knew that Coal was referring to the fights that would break out. She felt her stomach clench. "I appreciate it. I will talk to him. You guys get some rest. Don't worry about it." She tried to sound light-hearted and upbeat.

"Good luck. Don't let Blaze bully you. Stand up to him."

She nodded.

"Thanks for coming by." Coal gave them a tight smile. "My female needs to get some rest now."

Julie nodded. "Six hours of labor . . . I only managed two hours of sleep." She yawned. "I'm pooped."

"Your egg is really . . . oval and beautiful and . . . congrats!" What the hell! She'd never had to congratulate someone on an egg before.

"Don't worry," Inferno said. "I've made it clear that no one is to visit today. You can rest up. I'm sure you'll have a ton of guests tomorrow though." He grinned. It was a plan Inferno had devised to make sure that Coal didn't find out what was about to go down. Roxy swallowed hard, trying to calm her nerves. Everything would go as planned, it would all work out. It had to.

Both Julie and Coal smiled. They said their goodbyes and left.

"Are you sure about this?" Roxy asked.

"I can't think of a better plan, can you?"

Just then, Heat rounded the corner, he was one of the higher-ranking warriors she had met at a couple of functions. His eyes roamed her body and heated as they did. The big shifter approached them. He sniffed at her.

Julie grabbed Inferno's arm and stepped in closer to him.

Heat sniffed at her again and Inferno growled. "That's fucking rude," he said.

"Sorry!" He had the good grace to look sheepish. "I can't help it, you have a delectable scent. I heard that you were available since Blaze renounced you."

A sharp pain sliced through her somewhere in the vicinity of her heart.

Inferno stepped forward. "We are headed to the great hall. Move out of the way."

Heat grinned. "I am on my way there as well. I think that all of the Pinnacle warriors will attend." He glanced back at Roxy. "I am hoping that Crimson doesn't pitch. I am next in line and would love a chance to fight for you." His eyes narrowed in on hers.

"I wouldn't hold my breath." Inferno pushed past him and they continued to walk. Roxy kept her arm looped through Inferno's. As they continued on, more and more big shifter types seemed to enter the hallway, moving in the same direction. They all smiled at her and winked. Some of them openly ogled her. The sniffing noises were ridiculous.

Oh god! This was a mistake.

"I'm not so sure about this anymore," she whispered.

"It will be fine. The highest ranking male will challenge me – that's Crimson. If not Crimson, then Heat. I'm not worried." He did look completely relaxed.

"If you say so." Roxy prayed for the hundredth time that Blaze would be there, that he would swoop in and put a stop to the whole thing. In her mind's eye he would take her into his arms and that would be that. No fighting. No chaos. No heartbreak.

There was a fat chance of that happening though, this was real life. A girl could live in hope though.

Inferno had set it up so that Coal wouldn't find out – hopefully – because he would try to put a stop to what he would consider a harebrained scheme. He also made sure that Blaze would hear all about it. This all hinged on how he would react though. *Please come and save me.*

"You need to stay far away from the fighting. Stand on the dais." They entered the hall. Roxy gasped at how many big, burly shifters were in attendance. They all turned to look at her. In that moment, she wanted to run far away.

Inferno pointed to the raised dais. "Go up there. It shouldn't take more than five minutes for me to whip Crimson's ass." He gave her a cocky grin.

"Inferno," someone growled. "It looks like you and I are going head-to-head." The deep voice sounded from somewhere in the crowd of shifter dragons.

Inferno stiffened. He clenched his fists, his eyes going to her. She registered shock and something else, something that looked very much like panic. "Oh shit!" Inferno whispered.

"Oh shit indeed." A huge shifter shoved his way between all the warriors. "Let's get to it. Every second we stand here and chit chat is a second wasted. I can't wait to get to know my female."

"Fuck you, asshole!" Inferno growled. "Roxy will never be yours."

The shifter, who she recognized, threw his head back and laughed. "I beg to differ." Despite having just laughed, he looked angry, he also looked really upset. She could guess what, or who, had put him in this mood.

"Go wait on the dais," Inferno instructed. "I've got this." She could see the doubt in his eyes. He gave her a casual wink but he wasn't fooling anyone. Inferno was afraid. What the hell had she just agreed to?

Blaze crumpled up the piece of paper. A note from Roxy. Pretty words that meant nothing. He snarled as he threw the paper in the garbage. Fuck it!

Inferno was going to fight for his female. He was going to try and win and claim her. There was only one way this was possible, Roxy had to have agreed. Screw it though! Screw her! He didn't give a fuck.

The female would've been perfect as a queen. Fucking perfect, but she couldn't agree to some simple terms. No! She'd agreed knowing full well that she couldn't keep them. Roxy had no honor. She was just as dishonest as the rest of them. Not to be trusted.

Next, he picked up the diamond earrings. She'd probably thought that he bought them as a symbol of his feelings or maybe as a warning to others that she was his. Well, it couldn't be further from the truth. He'd wanted to show her off. She needed to look decent as the future queen. Needed to look the part. That was all.

He tossed the earrings into the bin along with her stupid fucking note. Good riddance. Good fucking riddance. He wished his little brother luck! Blaze punched the wall. A chunk of rock came loose and clattered at his feet.

His fledgling, piece of shit excuse for a brother could

have her. He punched again and another piece of rock crashed down, smaller bits went flying.

Fuck them both. They deserved each other. Conniving and scheming behind his back. In fact, he was going to exile them. They could live in the far corner of the fire kingdom. That way he wouldn't have to see them ever again.

The thought of seeing Inferno with Roxy had bile rising in his throat. Of course it did, they were traitors. The thought of Roxy ripe with Inferno's egg had adrenaline coursing through his veins. Blaze hit down with both fists on a nearby table. It splintered into several pieces. He forced himself to calm down by breathing deeply. He would exile them. Out of sight, out of fucking mind.

There was a stag run coming up. He would go and slake his needs with another female. Hell, he might even find himself a couple of females. The only reason sex had been so good with Roxy was because he hadn't been with a female for so long. It was a mistake and one he wouldn't make again.

In a couple of weeks, there was another hunt. He'd take a female then. He'd be sure to select the right kind of female. In hindsight, Lily would have been perfect. So what if she wanted prestige and material things. Those were items he could easily give. No emotional crap. His future female would keep his dick warm and give him heirs. That's all he fucking needed.

Blaze growled as he pictured Inferno fighting with Crimson, he almost hoped that the other male would win.

That would foil their plans. Fuck! He lashed out at the wall, the hole growing bigger as rubble fell to the floor.

A knock sounded at the door. His heart rate sped up. Maybe it was Roxy. Maybe she was here to . . . it didn't matter, he would send her away. Fuck her!

Blaze yanked the door open and one of the hinges ripped out of the wall. "If you—" he stopped short. It was a human female, but it wasn't Roxy. What did she want?

Roxy gasped as Lava hit Inferno in the face. Even from where she was standing, she heard a crack as his nose broke. Blood gushed down his face and chest. He punched back but Lava deflected the blow. They'd been fighting for a couple of minutes. It was amazing how slowly time could go.

Lava feigned a right hook and as Inferno stepped to the left, to avoid the punch, he gave a left jab into Inferno's ribs. Roxy couldn't be sure but she thought she heard another crack. Inferno staggered back a step or two before regaining his balance. The next few blows were superficial. Both shifters looked evenly matched.

"Thank you."

Roxy nearly jumped out of her skin. She clasped her chest for a second before realizing that it was Sue who had spoken.

"Don't sneak up on a person like that." Roxy felt irritated. She was watching Inferno fight for what looked like his life and all because of this woman. Okay, that wasn't entirely true. She'd known deep down that there were risks going into this but still, Sue was a piece of work. She couldn't help but dislike the woman even more. Then she realized what the woman had said and that she had a shit-eating grin on her face. "Thank you for what?"

"For whatever you did to cause Blaze to kick your ass to the curb."

Roxy decided to ignore Sue's bitchy comments. She was clearly here to wipe Roxy's nose in it. She was probably one of those women who enjoyed watching others suffer. Well, she wouldn't give her the satisfaction. She turned her attention back to the fight.

Inferno snarled, he pulled Lava into a chokehold and kneed the male in the stomach, one, two, three times before Lava managed to break free. *Go Inferno!* She couldn't help notice that Inferno was more bloodied up. One of his eyes was swollen shut and his nose looked horrible.

Lava had a split lip. Other than that, he was in good shape.

"I went to go and speak with Blaze." Sue sounded like she was on top of the world.

Roxy continued to watch the fight, trying hard to ignore the other woman. It didn't matter that her blood felt like it had iced up in her veins. That the air in her lungs had frozen.

"Yup." From the corner of Roxy's vision, she could see how Sue rocked back on her heels. "I asked him to give us a chance. I really think I would look damn fine on his arm. We are perfect for one another."

Do not cry! Hold it together. This woman is full of bullshit. She was probably lying. No, she was definitely lying.

Lava punched Inferno and he went flying backwards. Roxy gasped and stepped forward. He sprang to his feet but staggered badly before shaking his head. His stance was weaker.

"He gave me this list of terms," Sue gave a laugh.

No! Please let this not be happening. Her whole body went cold. Her heart seemed to stop beating for a second or two. It hurt so much that she struggled to breathe.

"No romance, no love, just fucking and I have to produce heirs for him." She laughed again, sounding so full of it. "I told him that it was the perfect set-up. It's what I want too . . . so . . ." She paused. "It looks like I'm staying. It looks like I'm getting not just a royal but *the* royal. The king of all the dragon shifters. It doesn't hurt that he's ridiculously hot. That he can kiss like nobody's business." Sue gave Roxy a shoulder bump. "You would know though wouldn't you?" Then she made a groaning noise. Roxy tried to block out Sue's voice but it didn't work. "He can fuck like a mad man possessed. You know that as well, I guess." This time she didn't even feel the shoulder bump.

The other woman continued to talk but Roxy couldn't hear her anymore. She didn't want to. She felt numb, yet at the same time, her heart beat out of her chest. Roxy stepped forward. "Stop!" she shouted. She couldn't stand to see Inferno being beaten any longer because at this point, he was being beaten. The tables had turned, Lava had taken over the fight and seemed to be toying with the young prince.

It was a lost cause. This whole thing was a lost cause. Inferno was getting hurt for nothing. "Stop it!" she screamed louder as Lava punched Inferno in the mouth.

Streaks of blood and saliva went flying. *No! God!* Some teeth went flying as well. Roxy jumped off the platform and ran towards the fighting shifters. She screamed for them to stop but no one listened. Lava pummeled Inferno until he fell to his knees. Then he gripped Inferno around the throat. His face and chest were covered in blood.

"Stop!" She clouted Lava on the back. "Let him go, you big bully. What the hell is wrong with you?" She clouted him a second time.

"Do you concede?" Lava snarled. Roxy watched in horror as his hand gripped Inferno's neck tighter. Inferno made choking noises. One eye was swollen shut but the other widened.

"Leave him alone." She tried to pull him away from Inferno but Lava wouldn't budge. "He gives up, you asshole dickhead."

"Do you concede?" Lava asked again, his eyes on Inferno.

"Yes, he does!" Roxy screamed. "Just do it, Inferno. Concede. It's over. Please just do as I say." It felt like forever but eventually, Inferno gave a small nod of the head.

Lava released him and Inferno slumped forward. Roxy dropped down on her knees next to Inferno. The shifter was lying on his side, he was badly messed up. She should never have agreed to this. Blaze was the biggest asshole alive. He deserved someone like Sue. "I'm so sorry." Shit, she was crying again. Roxy wiped away the tears. "We need to call someone. A paramedic . . . a healer . . ."

"I would've had him," Inferno croaked. He tried to smile but his cracked lip started to bleed. She noticed that a couple of his teeth were missing.

"Oh god!" she whispered. "You need help." She glanced at Lava. "Get him help!" She was starting to sound a bit panicked but who could blame her? Everyone just stood around like nothing had happened. "He's hurt."

She turned to Lava who grinned. "He will be fine, female. Inferno is a shifter; in a few hours you won't even be able to tell that he's been injured."

"I don't care about how he will be in a few hours, I care about how he is now and he's not great. He's even got teeth missing."

"I'm fine." Inferno's voice was already much stronger. He moved to a sitting position and wiped his mouth with the back of his hand. "My teeth will grow back and my bones will knit. I'm sorry I let you down."

"Thank you for trying." She sucked in a deep breath, waiting for her eyes to fill with tears. Thankfully, it didn't happen. She glanced at the dais. Sue was smiling broadly, she looked so smug.

"Come, female. I want to show you my chamber . . . our chamber." Lava gripped her by the upper arm and drew her into a standing position. He tried to put his arm around her but she stepped away.

"Yeah, about that, thanks but no thanks."

She looked back down at Inferno. "I'm going to get my stuff and go back home." There was nothing left for her there. Sue's words kept running through her head. The nerve of Blaze. He couldn't even wait for her to leave before replacing her. He couldn't even put two and two together and realize that what she had done was a ploy to get his attention, to snap him out of whatever it was that was holding him back.

Of course, he'd chosen to believe the worst about her.

"I won you, female. You are coming with me." Lava gripped her by the arm again and yanked her against him.

These shifters needed to learn some manners. "Let go of me." Roxy was in no damn mood. Sue was still watching them, that smile still firmly in place. She seemed to be enjoying the show. Roxy felt her blood boil inside of her. She clenched her teeth and tried to pull free.

"I'm really sorry you had to fight for nothing but I'm not staying." She tried to pull free, but he held on tight.

"You need to give me two weeks to convince you." He slid his other arm around her.

"No, I can't. I'm sorry."

"I too am sorry," Lava growled, "because you are staying, female, best you make peace with that. I'm going to claim you now. I think I've earned a kiss."

"Let her go, Lava," Inferno groaned as he pulled himself into a standing position. He was nursing an arm, although she suspected that it was his ribs on that side that were the problem.

Lava laughed, his eyes looked haunted. "What? Are *you* going to make me?" His jaw tensed. He looked Inferno up and down.

"Don't be a dick," Inferno said. "The female doesn't want you."

"I suppose she wants you and I should just hand her over."

Inferno shook his head. "She wants to go home." He looked at Roxy quizzically. "Are you sure that's really what you want?"

Roxy tried to get out of Lava's hold. "Yes, I need to go and say a few parting words to a certain someone and then I'm out of here." She'd been wrong about Blaze. She needed to give him a piece of her mind. Get some closure in this messed up situation and then she would go home and lick her wounds. It was funny, she'd been with Ben for eight years and only with Blaze for a couple of weeks, yet, she had a feeling it was going to be way more difficult to get over the shifter king. The thought angered the hell out of her. Blaze should not have that level of control over her emotions.

"You are coming with me." Not only did Lava hold on tight, but he picked her up and held her against his chest so that they were face to face. "Kiss me, female."

Roxy pulled back, arching her back away from him. Her legs dangled. "No!" she yelled. "Let go of me!" She kicked and squirmed. It was Thunder all over again. The guy was going to plant one on her whether she liked it or not. "Let go." She tried one last time. "Don't you dare."

Lava wasn't listening. His eyes blazed. His hold tightened. His eyes were on her lips.

Roxy sighed. Then she kicked Lava square between the legs. He groaned, his eyes rolled back and he dropped her. Roxy tried to stay on her feet but ended up landing on her ass. She scrambled to her feet and headed towards Blaze's office.

Inferno laughed somewhere behind her, the sound quickly morphing into a groan. "Go get him, Roxy. Kick Blaze's ass!"

Get him. Hardly. She'd give him a piece of her mind and move on. She wouldn't cry. She would definitely not shout or rant. She was going to be Miss Cool, Calm and Collected.

Then she was out of there. She didn't care about the two-week rule or any of that other stuff. If she protested loud enough, they would have to send her home. She picked up her pace. The thought of seeing Blaze and Sue together was too horrendous to comprehend. She couldn't deal with it. Wouldn't. Bile rose in her throat just thinking of how smug Sue would look on Blaze's arm. She'd love every minute of Roxy's misery, she was just that kind of person.

Blaze wasn't in his office. She went to his chamber. He'd better be there. Thankfully no one tried to stop her or talk to her, or sniff at her. They could probably sense how angry she was. Roxy had never been this mad before.

The door was at an odd angle. She had to put her back

into it to get it open.

"What do you want?" Blaze growled. His eyes blazed and his muscles bunched. In short, he looked just as pissed as she was feeling.

"So, you've already replaced me?" Roxy put her hands on her hips. "I've hardly even moved out and you have another woman all lined up." She shook her head. "It seems I was very wrong about you. You really didn't feel a thing for me, did you?"

"You have no room to talk." He took a step towards her. "We have one fight and you move in with my brother. My flesh and blood. You couldn't have the king so what, you'd settle for a prince? I didn't peg you for one of those gold-digging females. You said you weren't the type to settle, it seems you lied about that too."

"Screw you," she growled. "A fight . . . a fight? You make it sound like we had a little spat. You kicked me out. You told me that you felt nothing for me and that I was easily replaceable. You called what we had a mistake."

He folded his arms. "The biggest fucking mistake of my life and that's saying something. I hope that you and Inferno will be very happy together." He clenched his jaw, the muscles on either side of his neck roped.

"You are such an asshole and so blind its crazy. The only reason I stayed and agreed to Inferno's harebrained scheme was for you . . . you!" She screamed and pointed her finger at him. Damn, she was ranting. Roxy took a couple of deep breaths. "I was an idiot. The plan was to make you jealous, to force you into admitting that you . . .

never mind, it doesn't matter. I hope that you and Sue are very happy together. She's not a very nice person so she'll be perfect for you. There is no way a woman like her can ever love someone other than herself so she's absolutely perfect when it comes to your rubbish terms."

"She is perfect for me." Blaze seemed to relax. "More than perfect. She was exactly what I had in mind from the start. She's the type of female I reminded myself I needed when you left last night. When I said I would replace you, it was with a female like her that I had in mind."

Stop wobbling lip. Eyes, don't you dare cry. Don't you dare! Roxy swallowed thickly and nodded. "I'm going now. I can't believe I was so wrong about you."

"You weren't wrong," Blaze said, his eyes were focused on her, they were so intense that she couldn't look away. "I was the one that was wrong. Sue came here. I let her in. I was so fucking angry with you."

Roxy wasn't sure she wanted to hear this. She looked away, focusing on a broken table instead. It was in about eight pieces with wood chips lying all around it. There was also a massive hole in the wall, chunks of rock and a pile of sand on the floor below.

"Sue left Lava as soon as she found out I had renounced you. She came to proposition me."

Roxy snorted. "I believe that." Roxy kept on hearing the other woman's words running through her mind.

Blaze didn't react to her outburst. "She wanted her and I to make a go of it with me."

"I get the picture." No way, she couldn't hear this all

over again. Sue's bragging had been bad enough.

"Hear me out," he paused. "I gave her the terms, only, I was way blunter than I had been with you. The terms were harsher. She agreed to everything. I could see that she was perfect . . . way more interested in being a queen than in the other bullshit."

"By bullshit, you're referring to love. Not just love between the two people in the relationship but between a family. I'm done with this whole thing . . ." she began to walk to the door. "I can't believe that you want a person like that anywhere near your kids . . . even worse, she would be a contributor to their DNA. I'm not saying this to try and change your mind about us. I—"

"You're right." Blaze clutched her hand as she tried to walk past. "You were right about everything. I do have feelings for you . . . strong feelings. I thought I could push them aside. I thought I could continue with my plan and bring a female like Sue onboard . . . it had been my plan from the start. Having her here in my chamber . . . hearing her talk . . ." He ran a hand through his hair. "I realized that it's not what I want. I realized what an idiot I had been. It was only once I gave her the terms and she accepted so wholeheartedly . . . unlike you did . . . It took me a while to figure out but I finally realized how much I fucking love you."

Roxy pulled her hand away. "Why did you agree to her staying on then? Why did you fuck her if you love me so much? Let me guess, it took screwing her to realize that you actually want me."

Blaze folded his arms, he clamped his mouth shut and gave a shake of the head, like he was pissed at her for being upset that he had slept with another woman.

"If you really did love me, if you knew my feelings for you, then you must have realized why Inferno was fighting. I would never mess you around like that. I was trying to buy us time, trying to get you to stop with the denial. I couldn't think of anything else at the time. Coal and Julie were a bit busy having a baby. I didn't want fights to start breaking out but I couldn't just leave . . . and do you know why I couldn't just leave?" She paused. "Because I was crazy enough to believe in us . . . but I can see that you don't feel the same." She laughed, sounding a tad hysterical. "I know you don't feel the same because you would never have jumped into bed with Sue if you felt anything for me, even the tiniest little thing. You didn't believe in us." She said the last more for herself than for him. Her stupid sixth sense was still telling her that they belonged together. She was crazy. So gullible and stupid.

Blaze shook his head. "I didn't believe in us. I'm sorry, I should have."

"I don't see how we can be together." It hurt her so badly to say it, but it was true. It felt like he had cheated on her even though they had technically broken up at the time. Blaze wasn't capable of love. He couldn't be. She couldn't be with someone like that.

"I met a female a few years ago on one of the stag runs." Blaze's throat worked. "We clicked. I spent every minute with her that weekend. I did something we're not supposed to do, I made arrangements to meet with her on the next run . . . and the next . . . and the next . . ." He rubbed a hand over his chin, the stubble catching.

Why was he telling her all this? Now that it was too late. Roxy folded her arms across her chest and listened anyway. It wouldn't make any difference.

"I started going into town just to see her. I'd sneak away. It was completely against every rule in the book. I fell in love with her."

Roxy chewed on her lower lip. Was he trying to torture her?

"I began to make elaborate plans. I was willing to do anything and everything to have her." He paused. "I was even willing to give up the throne. Mating with a human was forbidden back then. My people began to talk amongst themselves. The other kings caught wind and called me out on it." He licked his lips. "I wanted to try and keep my throne with her at my side but I needed time to convince the others, I needed time to find a way to make it happen. I went to see Terry-Ann. That was her name."

Roxy nodded, despite her rampant emotions, she found herself wanting to know what happened. Maybe knowing this about him would give her closure and help her forgive him and move on in the long run.

"We agreed that I would be gone until the next stag run which was almost five months away. In that time, I would come up with a plan to ensure that we could be together. Failing that, I would leave my people, give everything up in order to be with her. It was difficult parting with her. Five months is a long time for lovers. I missed her every day. I already considered her to be my mate. There was no way for us to communicate during that time. I struggled through each day without her." He paused. "About three months into our separation, two warriors from one of the other kingdoms took human females. It seemed that the time was right to introduce Terry-Ann as my female. It would be difficult for the others to stand against me. I was so excited. I couldn't wait a second longer. I left for Walton Heights immediately to give her the good news. If they had done it, then so could I. It was the break that we had been looking for."

Blaze's jaw tightened. He grabbed a handful of hair and tugged.

"What happened?" Roxy asked.

"She scented of another male. My Terry-Ann, my female had rutted with another male in my absence. She was shocked to see me. She swore that it had been a mistake, that it had only ever happened once but I could see that she was lying. Even if she wasn't, she was mine and I was hers. I couldn't come to terms with it. I had been willing to give up everything for her. My whole life, my family, my kingdom, everything . . . and she couldn't stay faithful for a few months."

"I'm sorry that happened to you." Her heart ached for him. "It doesn't change things though. You gave up on us too easily. I feel like you betrayed me. I can't be with you, Blaze."

"I didn't give up on us." He stepped forward and took her hands. Roxy wanted to pull away but she couldn't. "As soon as I realized what a fool I was and how much I loved you, I told Sue that it wasn't going to work. She spent the next few minutes trying to change my mind. All I could think of was you. I thought it was too late though. I thought you'd moved on."

Roxy tried to pull away but Blaze held on. "Why did you have sex with her? That's the part I'm struggling with. Especially after you were betrayed. You wouldn't kiss me yet you kissed her. You gave up on us so easily." She took a deep breath as the realization dawned. "Oh god . . . you didn't kiss her, did you? She lied about everything. You didn't have sex with her either." Roxy paused, her mind racing. "She's such a bitch."

Blaze smiled. He shook his head. "I never kissed her. I wouldn't rut that human if she was the last female on earth. She's crazy. She tried to kiss me. Tried being the operative word. I was so busy devising a plan on how to get you back that I wasn't paying much attention to her. I pushed her away and asked her to leave. She went on about us and how well we would work together . . . I just kicked her out." He squeezed her hands a little tighter.

"Here I was telling you that you had such little faith in us and I'm guilty of the same thing." She put a hand over her mouth for a second. "I believed everything Sue said. I should never have done that. I'm an idiot. I—"

"Stop." Blaze looked her deep in the eyes. "I'm an idiot too. We're both idiots. It's what emotions do to a person, but I wouldn't have it any other way because I love you, Roxy. I'm sorry it took me so long to realize it. I'm sorry I made you go through all this. You were right, I was scared shitless of getting my heart broken again." He sucked in a deep breath. "Especially considering that my feelings for you way surpassed anything I ever felt for Terry-Ann. I'm sorry I was so quick to believe the worst but given my history, I hope you'll understand where that stemmed from."

Roxy was too stunned to say anything.

Blaze must have taken that the wrong way because he gave a small anguished growl and put his hands on her hips. "Please say something."

Roxy swallowed hard, trying not to cry. This time from happiness. "Um . . ." She licked her lips. Her eyes were filling with tears so she blinked.

"About the note you left . . . shit Roxy, I hope you keep baking for me. I really hope so."

"No, you don't." She gave a half laugh. She'd left a note and the diamond earrings. The note had said that she wished he'd given her a chance to keep practicing making those chocolate chip cookies because she would've made the perfect batch one day. Even if it took ten years, twenty, she'd keep trying. She'd persevere. She wished that he had felt the same.

"I don't need a perfect batch of damn cookies, what I need is you. Although, I sure as hell hope you keep trying because that will mean that you are here, at my side. I promise to eat them all. Every last crumb, just tell me you'll stay." He looked so anguished. "I will never give up on us. We are meant to be, Roxy."

"You'll eat every single cookie?"

He smiled. "Every last fucking crumb. I swear."

"Now you're talking like a crazy person."

"I believe in you, Roxy. I believe in us. I'm sorry I—"

"Shhh." she put her finger to his lips to shut him up. "I should never have believed that bitch, Sue. I'll keep baking for you, even though I wouldn't recommend you eat any of it. I love you, Blaze."

He smiled so broadly. His eyes lit up. Blaze put his arms around her. "Can we kiss and make up now?"

"I thought you'd never offer. I—"

"That was really touching," a booming voice came from behind them.

Roxy gasped and turned. It was Lava, his dark brown eyes looked black. "With all due respect, my lord, get your hands off my female."

"Fuck!" Blaze growled. "Inferno lost?"

Roxy nodded and Blaze laughed. "Serves him right. Roxy wishes to be with me—"

"I don't give a fuck." Lava clenched and unclenched his fists. "You renounced her, I won her fair and square."

"I love Blaze. We had a misunderstanding."

Inferno shook his head. "I won you, female, you must come with me."

Blaze huffed out a breath. "Don't do this."

"I want my two weeks. I want my chance to change her mind."

"You heard us talking. You won't change my mind," Roxy spoke softly and carefully. Lava's chest rose and fell in quick succession. Sue had done a number on the poor guy. His eyes had a wounded look. "I love Blaze." As she spoke, he pulled her back against his chest. His warmth seeped into her. She couldn't believe that he'd admitted to loving her, that Sue was lying . . . okay, that part was more than believable. "I love Blaze. It'll be two wasted weeks."

"There is a stag run next week," Blaze said. "Do you want to give up a chance to go on the run, for a female who wishes to mate another male because, make no mistake, I plan on mating this female as soon as possible . . . either today or one minute after the two weeks with you expire. She is mine." He growled so hard his chest vibrated.

"It's not fair. I want another female in return."

"I can set you up with someone," Roxy said.

Blaze shifted behind her. "Don't make promises you can't keep."

"Lauren, she's my best friend, she would love you. You're exactly her type."

Lava narrowed his eyes. "Is she curvy and lush like you?" He glanced at her boobs.

Blaze growled.

Roxy nodded. "Lauren has more curves. She's very pretty."

"I'm interested," Lava said as he looked over her shoulder at Blaze. "I wish to meet this female. If I like her, I want her to take part in the next hunt."

"I can't promise—"

"Why not?" Roxy knew she was being a bit bad asking but she had a feeling that Lauren and Lava would be great together. It wasn't great that Lava was a bit on the rebound but it might just work.

"I can't just pull strings. Lava can't have special privileges."

"You're the king, that must come with some perks. Help Lava out. He had to deal with Sue. He just won me and lost me in a matter of a half an hour and I may or may not have kicked him in the balls."

Blaze choked out a laugh. "You didn't!"

"He wouldn't listen. He was going to kiss me. Shifters need to learn the meaning of the word no."

"If you had kissed my female I would've taken your balls."

"I won her." Lava averted his gaze as he spoke. "I'm sorry. I should never have done that. I appreciate you wanting to introduce me to your friend despite me being an asshole earlier."

"We've been to quite a few of those functions and I could see how hard you tried with Sue. You're a good guy, Lava, but no is no. Remember that for the future."

"I would've fed you your dick if you had put so much as half a lip on my female."

"So you would've bent the rules to cut off his privates but you won't bend them to help him out?" Roxy said.

Blaze sighed. "Fine. You can meet this female on the next stag run. If you get along with her, I will ensure that she goes through the process and is accepted for the next round. She will need to meet the basic requirements though."

Roxy gave a little squeal. "Lauren will be thrilled."

"But," Blaze added, putting extra emphasis on the word. "You will need to win her during the hunt. I can't do anything about that."

"That's fair," Lava nodded. "I look forward to meeting this female. If she is anything like you, I will be a happy male." He narrowed his eyes. "I don't think I will be able to trust humans very easily anymore, so a recommendation from you goes a long way."

"I'm glad I could help," Roxy said. "Not all women are like Sue. Some of us are decent. Lauren is so sweet and kind. She's also really hot."

"Mmmm," it came out as a deep rumble. Lava rubbed his hands together. "I can hardly wait."

"Now, get the fuck out," Blaze growled. "I need to make love to my soon-to-be mate."

Roxy couldn't help the shiver of anticipation that ran through her.

CHAPTER 20

As soon as the door closed, Blaze picked her up. He kept his eyes on hers. Then he threw her on the bed. Roxie squealed as she bounced twice. Blaze went after her, caging her with his big body.

His green eyes as intense as ever. "I'm afraid I have new terms for this relationship. Very important terms if we are to mate." He looked serious.

"Um . . . okay . . . I'm not sure I like the idea of any more terms, I thought—"

"Let's get more comfortable before we negotiate." He ripped off her blouse, as in ripped the garment clean off her body.

"Wait!" Roxie yelled. "I like theses jeans." She undid the clasp and shoved them down her thighs, together with her underwear. She kicked to try and get them off of herself without nailing him in the balls.

There was a tugging on her chest and then a ripping sound. Her boobs sprang free and Blaze growled.

"I liked that bra too!" she tried to sound angry but failed.

"I like your naked breasts way more. In fact . . ." He licked his lower lip and her eyes couldn't help but to track the movement. "one of the terms is no underwear."

"Ever again?"

"Ever again." He bent down and sucked on one of her nipples.

Roxy moaned. "Okay . . . um . . . sure . . ." She was struggling to concentrate, especially when he nipped at her pebbled flesh. She groaned. "What if I wear a white shirt? My boobs would bounce without support."

Blaze growled, it was husky and low. "And the problem is?"

"The other shifter guys would get an eyeful whenever we went out."

Blaze growled again, this time it was deep and menacing.

Roxy had to laugh. "How about no undies when we're home?"

"Mmmmm. . . ." A rumble. "That's acceptable." He sucked on her other nipple and her back bowed. She dug her hands into his soft hair.

Then he moved down, kissing her tummy.

"What else did you have in mind for these terms of yours?" Roxy couldn't help parting her legs even more as he gripped her thighs, his eyes focused on her sex.

Blaze leaned forward, his gaze locking with hers as he sucked on her clit. Roxy bit down on her lower lip to keep herself from crying out. Blaze licked and sucked on her intermittently until her breath was ragged and her throat dry from moaning. Blaze pulled away.

Roxy groaned in frustration, her groan quickly turned into a whimper as he impaled her with two fingers. He thrust deep, curling his fingers so that they rubbed against the inside wall of her channel. *Holy hell! Holy!* "You need to stop taking your pill . . . I want to see you ripe with my egg. This is a deal breaker . . ."

Roxy gripped the sheets in her fists. "You . . . are . . ." she yelped and moaned. She couldn't help but to jerk her hips forward. "So . . . bossy!" she managed to pant out, so close to coming that her mind was hazy was with need.

"I want to start trying for a whelp." Lick, suck, thrust.

Whelp.

Egg.

"Oh god!" she cried, as he sucked on her clit. She groaned. It was too much, his thrusting fingers and hot mouth tipped her over the edge. She made obscene noises as her orgasm rushed through her. Her hips rocked against his face but she couldn't make herself stop. Too good.

"God, yes!" She tried to make herself let go of his hair but that was just as impossible. It was only once he'd wrung the last bit of pleasure from her that he let up. Roxy fell back in a satisfied heap. She struggled to catch her breath.

When she looked up, Blaze was on his knees between her legs. He pulled down his pants and palmed his cock. Maybe she'd been a tad hasty when she had said she was satisfied. She wasn't. Not at all. She licked her lips as she watched him stroke himself.

"So receptive," Blaze grinned. "All mine. You're all mine, Roxy." His eyes held that wild look she'd seen before.

She nodded, swallowing hard as he palmed his cock again. A drop of pre-cum accumulated on the tip of his thick cock.

Roxy leaned forward and gripped him. Blaze made an anguished sound.

"I want to give you a blow job." Roxy licked her lips, she looked up at Blaze who shook his head.

"Why not?" she asked. "It's about time I returned the favor." She had yet to go down on him which was weird since most guys would jump at the opportunity.

"Maybe sometime in the future." Blaze's eyes were bright. "It must be the mating behavior but I need to be inside you. I have to mark that sweet pussy." He gripped her around the waist and turned her onto her knees. Blaze crouched over her, completely caging her in with his big body. His cock was hard and thick between her legs. "These mating instincts are riding me hard. I almost lost you." His voice was husky with emotion.

"Yeah, but you didn't."

Blaze kissed her neck, her cheek and her temple. "It was too close." He made a growling noise that was more animal than man. His whole body quivered. It reminded her of the first time they had gone at it.

"Let me guess . . ." She was breathing heavily. By the way his chest moved against her, so was he. "You need me to stay still."

She felt Blaze nod. "Yeah . . . very still. I need you to brace yourself on your elbows."

"You're going to bite me?" She could hear the excitement in her voice. Shit but she was a serious pervert. *Oh well!*

"Oh, yes. I'm also going to fuck you hard. Don't fight me." He spoke so softly she had to strain to hear him. It was so sexy, he was so sexy, this was so sexy.

Roxy whimpered as he lined his cock up with her opening.

"You never answered me . . . no more pills."

"Yes, I'll stop taking them."

"Good." He thrust into her. Oh god but he was big. It was still funny to her that after having sex so many times with Blaze, her eyes still widened and her breath sucked back in whenever he entered her for the first time.

Blaze stopped moving. "We'll make love . . . lots of slow, beautiful love." He circled his hips, his cock barely moving but hitting all the right spots anyway. "Just not right now." His voice was thick with need. Blaze pushed her down on the bed using his body. "I need you too badly."

"Me too," she choked out as his thrusts became more insistent.

"I want to mate you, Roxy. I want to spend forever with you." Harder and deeper. Blaze grunted. "So fucking good," he growled, pulling her hands above her head, holding them in place with one of his. "What do you say? Will you mate me?"

Roxy tried to laugh but couldn't. She was too damned close to orgasming. Blaze was asking her to marry him now. His cock deep inside her, his body crushing hers. His mouth millimeters from her ear.

It was perfect.

"Yes," she mewled.

"Yes," he groaned. "Yes, more sex or yes . . ." he grunted, "you'll mate me?"

"Mate." Her mouth opened in a gape as she struggled to talk. Her pussy fluttered with the start of her orgasm. "Yes, I'll mate you," she groaned.

She was well and truly pinned down, unable to move an inch. She was panting and moaning.

"Thank fuck." Using his free hand, he gripped her hair and pulled her head back ever so slightly. Yup, she had screws loose. To her, it was the most romantic proposal she had ever heard. Okay, it was the only proposal she had ever heard but . . . semantics.

The proposal together with being pinned down and fucked so thoroughly had her screaming as she orgasmed.

Blaze moaned her name and bit down on her neck. It was hard enough to sting yet not so hard as to break the skin. At least she didn't think so. Her body was strung so tight, her sex spasming so hard that it was difficult to tell. Blaze's swift strokes turned to hard jerks. He buried his head in her neck and groaned.

Blaze hadn't planned on officially asking Roxy to mate with him until after they were done rutting but he couldn't help himself. He needed her. He fucking loved her. To think he'd almost lost her.

Mine.

Mine.

It was all he could think as he kept plowing into her snug heat. She felt perfect. She smelled perfect. She was perfect in every fucking way.

Mine.

His teeth erupted. His jaw elongated. Smoke curled from his nostrils. He was sure that if he looked down, that he would see scales showing through his skin. His dragon was that close to the surface. His dick swelled. His female moaned, the sound laced with pleasure. Her pussy fluttered with the start of her orgasm. Thank fuck, on both counts.

"Yes, I'll mate you," she groaned. He watched her side profile, her eyes fluttered closed. Her mouth open. Her breath was ragged.

Something eased inside him. Roxy was conceding. His balls pulled tight. Not yet!

"Thank fuck!" he managed to grind out. He gripped her hair. Easy! He didn't want to hurt her but he needed access to her neck. Her soft body was beneath his. Her greedy pussy held onto him with a grip that guaranteed pleasure. He would never tire of being inside this female, of having her by his side. Roxy was his.

He could scent how her arousal ricocheted up by a few notches. How her pussy began to pulsate around him. He could smell the endorphins as they began to release in her bloodstream.

Roxy cried out triggering, an instinctual reaction from Blaze. He bit down on her neck trying hard not to hurt her. It needed to be hard enough to mark but not so hard as to damage. Then his own orgasm was tearing through him. *Fucking hell!* He'd never come so hard in his whole life. It was like someone had attached him to a live wire. His dick pulsated and his balls landed somewhere in his throat they clenched so damn tight.

Mine!

His heart squeezed in his chest. Blaze called her name. His female. His. He belonged to her. Forever and always. He wrapped his arms around her.

"That was so good." She was breathless.

He made a sound of acknowledgment. Blaze moved onto his side, enjoying how she snuggled against him, how she buried her face in his chest.

"I love you, mate," he growled.

"Wait . . . what?" She lifted her head, her eyes locking with his. They were a tad panicked. She frowned. "What do you mean?"

He smiled. "We're mated." *Oh fuck!* "You said you wanted to mate me, that you loved me . . . I thought . . ."

She reached up and kissed him. "I'm thrilled, but I expected . . ." She lifted her eyes in thought, "I don't know . . . a wedding ceremony . . . a declaration of love. Guests to attend."

Blaze kissed the tip of her nose. "There will be a ceremony but it is more of a celebration." He felt himself frown. "As to having others present during the actual mating . . ." He shook his head, "Inferno would've loved to have been here, but not a fuck." He palmed her ass. "Are you okay with it? I should've been clearer that—"

"Stop! I'm happy . . . I'm ecstatic. I love you, Blaze."

"We never got to finish discussing the terms."

Roxy laughed. "We're already mated. There's nothing left to discuss. It's too late to back out now." Her cheeks were flushed and her eyes glinted with mischief. "No more terms."

"Oh really?" He rolled her so that she was on her back, pinned under him. Just where he wanted her. "I'm thinking you might like my new terms."

"You think so, huh?" She raised her brows.

He nodded. "About the whole kissing thing."

She frowned. "What about it?"

"I want lots of kisses from you." He kissed her nose.

"Oh, really?" She licked her lips.

"Yep and I plan on kissing you a ton. Especially during sex."

"I like the sound of that." She smiled.

"I want to kiss you everywhere." He kissed her neck and then her jawline.

Roxy giggled softly.

"I want to kiss . . . these lips," he said the last against her mouth. "All the fucking time."

"You're right, I like these terms." She sounded breathless.

"Good because that's not all." He pulled back slightly

so that he could look her deep in the eyes. "I want long walks on the beach." He took her hand and kissed her palm. "Hand in hand."

Her eyes filled with tears.

"I want romantic dinners . . . I'm going to buy candles. Lots of them because every meal with you will be romantic."

"Not if I cook." She swallowed thickly.

Blaze couldn't help but to laugh. "Point is, I want forever with you, with no half measures, I'm all in."

"Me too," she whispered. A single tear fell and he wiped it away. "I'm so happy right now," Roxy sniffed.

"One last very important term."

She laughed. "Oh no!"

"I'm going to give you plenty of orgasms . . . lots and lots of them."

"I love the sound of that, but what about you?" She smiled.

"You can guarantee that if you're coming, I'm not far behind." He brushed a kiss against her soft lips.

"Oh well in that case, I guess you have yourself a deal."

Blaze kissed her again, deepening the kiss.

CHAPTER 21

Six weeks later...

Blaze pulled his mate close to his side as they walked. Their bond had grown more and more with each passing day.

"I just got word that Torrent's mate is pregnant."

Roxy smiled, her cheeks were flushed. She'd never looked more beautiful. "That's wonderful news."

"Torrent is very happy." They reached Coal's chamber and Blaze knocked. His brother opened the door almost immediately. Except, instead of letting them in, he walked out into the hall and closed the door behind him.

"What's up?" Blaze asked.

Coal looked worried. "Don't say anything. Just keep your mouth shut."

"What do you mean?"

"Not a word," Coal warned as he opened the door. "Come on in," he said, sounding unnaturally jovial.

"Thanks." Blaze frowned at his brother who gave him a small shake of the head.

"Congratulations," Roxy gushed. "I can't wait to hold the little one. Please tell me he's awake."

"Yes, you came at just the right time."

Roxy gave a squeal and clapped her hands together. Julie held the little one. She gave them a big smile. "Hi. Let me introduce our son. We decided to call him Flare."

"After our Grandfather." Pride rose up in Blaze. "Congratulations."

"Please, can I hold the little guy?" Roxy sat down next to Julie and held out her hands. Julie put the little one in his mate's arms and Blaze swallowed hard. She looked so good with a baby cradled in her arms. So amazing. Roxy turned to him and grinned. He couldn't help but grin back. His chest tightened.

"So, did little Flare destroy his nursery?" Blaze asked.

Coal gave a shake of the head. "Nah, just the egg." When fire dragons were born, they used fire to crack themselves out of their eggs, often destroying more than just the egg in the process.

"So, he's not as bad as little Tinder who still continues to wreak havoc on the vampire castle?"

"Not as bad, no," Julie laughed. Her eyes were firmly on her son, pride shone in their depths.

"Please can I hold him?" Blaze winked at his mate, who held the baby close to her chest.

"I only just got him." Roxy pretended to look annoyed.

"One quick hold . . . you can get him back in a minute."

Coal tensed. Maybe it was his imagination. Nope, he even leaned forward as Blaze took a seat next to Roxy. His jaw clenched as he took the little one, placing the baby on his thighs.

Julie also began to fidget.

"He has your eyes." Blaze smiled at Coal's mate. Julie sort of smiled back. She also looked tense. What the fuck was going on? Why did they look so worried?

"Can I see his marking?" Blaze asked.

Coal gave a small shake of the head and his eyes widened. The male was trying to tell him to drop it.

Not a fuck.

He was the king. They needed royal heirs. Blaze would not be doing his duty as the king if he let it go. "Is that okay?" He locked eyes with Julie.

She swallowed hard but nodded. "Flare is . . . well he's . . ."

Blaze pulled open the top two snaps. "What the . . . ?"

"Don't fucking say it," Coal snarled. "Don't say anything. He is my son . . . a royal, regardless."

Blaze could feel himself frown. He could feel his heart rate speed up.

"He has markings," his female remarked. "That's different. Wow! Very unique. I think he's absolutely beautiful and perfect in every way. It doesn't matter does it?" Fuck, his female looked worried. Julie was pale and on the edge of her seat. A thin tendril of smoke drifted from Coal's nostril.

Fuck!

Blaze suddenly realized that his mouth hung open.

Roxy gave him a nudge. "Don't you think so, honey?"

His female had taken to calling him after foodstuffs. He found he liked it.

Blaze cleared his throat and nodded. "He is perfect."

Roxy held out her arms. "I'll take him back now. I want more cuddle time." He closed the snaps and handed the baby to her.

Roxy smiled at the little one. "Who's a gorgeous boy?" She held him against her chest, just above her growing bump. His child. His son. His heir.

Fuck!

Blaze forced himself to breathe. "It's fine." He looked his brother in the eyes. "I'm sure it doesn't mean anything."

Coal gave him a tight smile. "I'm sure the gold will come."

"It will come," Blaze nodded. The marking on Flare's chest was just an outline. It was neither golden, nor was it silver.

Just an outline. This could spell disaster for the dragon shifters. What did it mean? Was it a new species of dragon altogether or were human females incapable of producing royal offspring?

Coal was trying to act normal, trying to look relaxed but he could see that his brother was just as worried as he was. The females seemed oblivious. Blissfully unaware. Roxy put a hand on her belly and smiled at him. He forced himself to smile back.

AUTHOR'S NOTE

Thank-you for reading the third book in my new series. It is a spin off from my bestselling series The Chosen and The Program.

This book would not have been possible without the assistance of my editor and beta readers. Thank you KR, Aisha and Enid. I need to say a special thank you to my new proofreader, Brigitte Billings, who has been an editor for many years. She also happens to be my favorite champagne chick. Welcome to the team, you did an amazing job.

Also, a big thank you to my ARC readers for your invaluable input and support. Especially those of you that review my books every time without fail. I'm talking about you Judy, Bridgette, Gretchen, AJ, Brenda, Stephanee, Mrs Duff and Ana . . . there are more of you. Thank you all!!

A big and heartfelt thank you to you . . . my readers. For reading my work and for all your messages and emails. Also, to those of you that take the time to review my books. It means the world to me. You are what keeps me writing on days that I might not feel like it so much.

If you want to be kept updated on new releases please sign up to my Latest Release Newsletter to ensure that you don't miss out www.mad.ly/signups/96708/join. I promise not to spam you or divulge your email address to a third party. I send my mailing list an exclusive sneak peek prior to release. I would love to hear from you so please feel free to drop me a line charlene.hartnady@gmail.com.

Find me on Facebook — www.facebook.com/authorhartnady

I live on an acre in the country with my gorgeous husband and three sons and an array of pets.

You can usually find me on the computer completely lost in worlds of my making. I believe that it is the small things that truly matter like that feeling you get when you start a new book or a particularly beautiful sunset.

BOOKS BY THIS AUTHOR

The Chosen Series:
Book 1 ~ Chosen by the Vampire Kings
Book 2 ~ Stolen by the Alpha Wolf
Book 3 ~ Unlikely Mates
Book 4 ~ Awakened by the Vampire Prince
Book 5 ~ Mated to the Vampire Kings (Short Novel)
Book 6 ~ Wolf Whisperer (Novella)

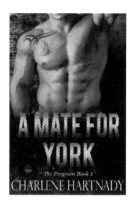

The Program Series (Vampire Novels):

Demon Chaser Series (No cliffhangers):

Chosen BY THE VAMPIRE KINGS

The Chosen Series ~ Book 1

Chapter 1

IT HAD BEEN MANY years since he had been in such close proximity of his birth enemy. Zane looked as arrogant and as full of shit as ever. Barking orders at his royal guard like they were his servants instead of trusted subjects. In some cases, those receiving the harsh treatment were probably his best buddies. Then again, the bastard probably didn't have any friends. Shaking his head, Brant turned and surveyed the crowd. He felt sorry for the female that would soon be chosen to become queen to the likes of that ruthless king.

It wasn't his concern though. His own queen was out there. Brant shuddered, praying that the events of one hundred years ago would not repeat themselves. A bloody war between their fathers had been the result of the last choosing. It couldn't happen again, the vampire species would not survive another war at this point.

As his mind returned to thoughts of his own female, he knew that he would not be able to remain sensible where she was concerned. His focus was on protecting his coven, and he would dispatch the other male without hesitation if he so much as looked at what was his. No matter the odds, and the knowledge of Zane's ruthlessness, Brant would allow nothing to harm her. She was too valuable, too precious of a gift to him.

Turning, he surveyed the crowd again. Feeling the electric pulse of her closeness. According to the lores, he would be able to sense her and to tell of their compatibility almost instantly even in a crowd full of females. From the noise projecting from outside, he could tell there were many females present. He hoped his chosen would be willing from the start. The last thing he wanted was to force her, to have to go caveman on her and throw her over his shoulder. The thought did not appeal to him, but the choosing was not something that could be ignored. She would feel it as well, whether she wanted to or not.

"Ready?" his head guard Xavier asked as he moved in next to him. His brother's eyes never faltered as they stared straight into his. Brant knew the reason for the intenseness. Xavier harbored similar feelings of distaste and distrust for their neighboring king. In order to maintain their strenuous hold on the truce between them, it had always been necessary to keep interactions between the two covens to a minimum. This event was no exception.

"Yeah, as ready as I'll ever be," Brant replied while taking a moment to scan the room.

"Your eyes are glowing my lord, maybe you should stop looking in that direction."

Brant looked into Xavier's clear grey eyes. *Always the cool one in a situation.* "My eyes have nothing to do with that bastard at the moment, and everything to do with my female. I can sense her, and the urge to mate is strong. I just hope that she'll be agreeable to a speedy union."

"I told you to take a female, ease your need. Humans are . . . easily broken. We don't want any accidents." Xavier spoke softly, ensuring that no one else would be privy to their conversation.

"I have a plan."

"Please, tell me you at least drank recently," Xavier's eyes narrowed. When Brant didn't reply, his brother's eyes narrowed even more. He made a sound of disbelief and continued, "Brother, should you harm our future—"

"Enough," Brant growled.

Xavier lowered his eyes.

"I said I have a plan. My future queen will come to no harm."

Xavier nodded. "Yes, my lord. It is time."

Brant took a deep breath. He had been raised for this moment. His decision and the events of the next few minutes would determine the future of his coven.

No pressure.

Tanya had seen tabloid pictures of the vampire kings and they really weren't all that attractive, unless you were into the ultra-big, ultra-built and ridiculously bad non-human types.

She so wasn't.

The whole choosing ceremony was so outdated to the point of being down right sexist. Yet, every hundred years, all of the eligible women would assemble to be chosen. A queen for each of the kings. The worst part was that vampires and humans never mixed so there was very little known about them. Their traditions, their ways, their expectations, she shuddered.

For at least the twentieth time, she wished that her best

friend Becky was there with her. The whole thing was a real circus. Tanya hadn't realized how many women there were in Sweetwater between the ages of twenty one and thirty. Aside from age, there had been a long list of requirements. Everything from weight and height to a clean medical exam.

Tanya sighed as a group of giggling women squeezed past her trying to find a spot closer to the podium. Becky was divorced, a complete no-no. It had automatically disqualified her from being allowed to attend the choosing ceremony. Attend, hah, not hardly, the right term would be forced. If all aspects of the criteria were met, it was mandatory to be here. For whatever reason, the human justice system went along with this whole farce once a century. Only those wanting a fast track to jail failed to show up. What scared her the most though was the thought of how many of these women were actually hoping to be chosen today.

Vampire queen.

Tanya cringed at the thought. For once she was thankful for being a little curvy. Most men were into wafer thin model types, so she would be safe.

The whole courtyard vibrated with an excited hum.

The two kings were royalty but they were also vampires. They drank blood for heaven's sake. Had these women lost their freaking minds?

It was early afternoon yet you wouldn't guess it by how some of them were dressed. Little back numbers, low cut tops, sequins and jewelry were the order of the day. The amount of skin on display was obscene. Tanya did a double take as one of the ladies walked by, she was wearing a sheer dress without underwear. Her lady bits on display for all and sundry. With all that exposed skin, she hoped that the woman had used sunblock. The highest possible factor.

Tanya looked down at her jeans and t-shirt. Maybe she should've tried a little harder but then again, she wasn't planning on getting noticed. She had a life to get back to. It wasn't much but she had her little book store. Some might consider it to be boring, but she liked it just fine.

She'd owned The Book Corner for two years now. Reading had always been a major passion, that and coffee. It had been her ultimate dream to own a little coffee shop on the side. That way potential customers could browse through purchases while enjoying a cappuccino and maybe a little pastry. So far she was way behind on those goals. She was supposed to have had half the money she needed already saved in order to do the required renovations. As it stood though, she may not even have a store soon, let alone an additional coffee shop. She couldn't afford to hire someone to fill in for her today. Just the thought of the closed sign on the door, of losing potential customers, had her looking at her watch. Hopefully this would be over soon. The last thing she needed in her life was a man . . . let alone a vampire who would not only uproot her from her goals but from her friends and family as well. She only had one BFF and her aunt, but she loved them both a ton.

It had been a while since she'd dated and her last relationship had ended . . . badly. Sex was overrated anyway. She could just imagine how much worse it would be with a blood sucking vamp. Wishing she was back at the store, she glanced at her watch a second time.

It wasn't like one of the kings would ever think of choosing a plain Jane like her anyways. What a waste of her precious time.

There was silence followed by gasps as two of the biggest, meanest looking men she'd ever seen walked onto the platform. Tanya had expected fanfare. A trumpet call. An announcement at the very least. What she hadn't expected was to be shocked stupid. Pictures she'd seen of the men didn't do them justice.

Tall, *check.*

Built, *check.*

Mean, *check.*

Ridiculously hunkalious, *double check.*

Several women swooned. One woman, closer to the front, fainted. Medics pushed their way through the thick crowd and placed the young women on stretchers.

The king on the left was slightly shorter, from tabloid pictures she'd seen, he had to be Zane. Although short was the wrong description, the big vampire must be at least around six and a half feet. He was meaner looking, with close cropped hair. From this distance she could tell that he had dark, hard eyes. A nervous chill radiated through her body.

King Brant was taller and even though he had a massive chest and bulging arms, he wasn't quite as broad as the scary one. Neither was classically good-looking. Though both radiated raw energy and sex appeal like nothing she'd ever seen before.

"Pick me!" One of the women closer to the platform shouted waving her arms.

The kings ignored her.

A group to the side hoisted a '*Look over here*' sign. *What was it with these freaking women?* For some reason it bothered her that they were so desperate to become one of the next vampire queens that they would do anything to get noticed? And the question of the hour was, *why?*

Turning back to the platform, she noticed that the taller one, Brant, had medium length dark hair, his eyes were dark and his mouth generous. Tanya was certain he would be even more attractive if he smiled.

Both men were tense. They just stood there, hands fisted at their sides. The crowd grew restless. Some women tried to push to the front while others tried to catch the attention of one or both of the men on the elevated platform.

Eventually, Zane stepped forward, his hard eyes were fixed on her. *What the hell?* Adrenaline surged through her blood, but her mind immediately rejected the idea that he was actually looking at her. It had to be some sort of mistake. His eyes seemed to stay on her for a few more seconds. Just as she began to feel the need to look around her for the true object of his fascination, his gaze moved to the back of the crowd. She breathed out in a gush.

"You," his gruff, smoky voice was a low vibration. He pointed somewhere behind Tanya.

An equally big, equally mean looking man came onto the platform from the side. King Zane didn't take his eyes off the female he had set his sights on the entire time he spoke to what had to be his head guard. All of the surrounding men were dressed in full leather. Though, this one wore a silver family crest on his chest.

Tanya shivered, thankful she hadn't been chosen by the likes of him.

Zane continued to shout orders. The head guard, flanked by two vampires, stepped off the platform and stalked through the crowd. Tanya shifted to the side as they approached. They were big bastards. The women surged forward. One dared to touch. The king's head guard paused, without turning to face the culprit, he growled. His top lip curled revealing sharp fangs. The air caught in her lungs. Her pulse quickened.

They were so close, Tanya could smell a musky male scent, could almost feel heat radiate off their huge bodies as they passed.

"You," a deep growl sounded through the crowd.

"No," a feminine wail responded. "Let go of me!"

Tanya was too afraid to turn. So close to the action, she was fearful of being noticed.

Another wail, louder this time.

"Put me down!" the woman shrieked. It seemed Tanya was not the only one there that didn't want to be chosen.

Tanya moved with the crowd as the guards passed, the woman was slung over the shoulder of the head guard. She kicked and screamed. The big vampire didn't seem to notice though. Tanya caught the look of sheer terror on the young woman's face.

This wasn't right.

How could this be allowed to happen? Tanya looked around her at the multitude of willing ladies. Women that were practically throwing themselves at the vampire kings. *Why did the SOB have to go and pick one of the few that wasn't interested?*

Tanya took a few steps in the direction of the platform. *Not happening.* She stopped. She didn't want to get involved. Couldn't afford to. She didn't even know the girl. It wasn't like she could change the situation even if she tried. This ritual had been going on for hundreds, possibly thousands, of years.

A large group of women at the front screamed to Zane that he pick them instead. One of the young ladies even lifted her top.

The king didn't take his eyes off his chosen woman the entire time that his guard maneuvered through the crowd. They narrowed though as they got closer. The girl screamed louder.

"Please don't do this. Please, I beg you." The screams had turned to sobs at this point.

Tanya couldn't bear to hear them. Each word struck a nerve.

Zane nodded in the direction of the waiting SUVs.

"Oh God, please no," she was sobbing in earnest.

The nerve quickly rubbed raw until Tanya couldn't take it anymore. "Stop!" She marched in the direction of the vampire king. "Stop that at once. Let her go."

Neither king took any notice. Maybe some of the others in the crowd were feeling the same way as she did because the women parted to let her through. "What you are doing is nothing short of barbaric."

The crowd hushed.

"She doesn't want to go with you. Let her go right now." Tanya projected, sounding more confident than she felt.

Zane glanced her way before turning in the direction of the waiting vehicles.

"This is a sexist, disgusting tradition that needs to be put to an end. Why can't you choose someone that's actually interested in going with you? Why does it have to be her?"

He turned back, his dark eyes zoning in on her. Her breathing hitched. Her heart rate increased, a whole damn lot. *I just had to get involved. Couldn't leave it alone.*

"This woman has been chosen as my mate. What is done cannot be undone." He turned and made for the waiting vehicles. Like that was a reasonable explanation. *So not.*

"Bastard! Leave her alone!" She must have completely lost her mind because she walked after him and straight into the massive chest of one of the guards. There was only one thing to do in a situation like this, she beat against the chest in her way while screaming obscenities at the retreating back of the bastard king.

"Easy," a low rumble that had her insides vibrating.

Tanya looked up into a set of dark, penetrating eyes. She froze. It was Brant. The second vampire king.

"What would you like me to do with her?" asked a voice to the right of the king.

His eyes stayed on hers. His nostrils flared and his body tightened. It was then that she realized that her hands were flattened on his chest. She snatched them away.

"Lord Brant?" the voice enquired.

"She's coming with me." He took her hand and strode towards the remaining vehicles. She wanted to pull away, to dig her heels in the ground, but her traitorous feet kept on moving in time with his. It was only when they reached the waiting SUV and Brant opened the door and gestured for her to enter, that she finally snapped out of it. Part of her didn't want to believe this was happening. As ridiculous as it seemed, King Brant had chosen her.

No. Surely not.

"Wait."

His eyes snapped to hers. Dark, fathomless, deadly.

Chosen by the Vampire Kings (Ménage)—available now

19269415R00179

Printed in Poland
by Amazon Fulfillment
Poland Sp. z o.o., Wrocław